"To be prepared for war is one of the most effective means of preserving peace."

George Washington

View the author's website at www.arsenex.com

Visit the author's Facebook page at www.facebook.com/stephenarseneault10

Follow on Twitter @SteveArseneault

Ask a question or leave a comment at comments@arsenex.com

Image on cover from www.RolfMohr.com

Copyright 2015-2017 Stephen Arseneault. All Rights Reserved.

All rights reserved. No part of this book may be used, reproduced or transmitted in any form or by any means, electronic or mechanical, including photocopying, recording, or by any information storage or retrieval system, without the written permission of the publisher, except where permitted by law, or in the case of brief quotations embodied in critical articles and reviews.

This book is a work of fiction. Names, characters, businesses, organizations, places, events, and incidents either are the product of the author's imagination or are used fictitiously. Any resemblance to actual persons, living or dead, events, or locales is entirely coincidental.

Novels written by Stephen Arseneault

SODIUM Series (six novels)

A six-book series that takes Man from his first encounter with aliens all the way to a fight for our all-out survival. Do we have what it takes to rule the galaxy?

AMP Series (eight novels)

Cast a thousand years into the future beyond SODIUM. This eight-book series chronicles the struggles of Don Grange, a simple package deliveryman, who is thrust into an unimaginable role in the fight against our enemies. Can we win peace and freedom after a thousand years of war?

OMEGA Series (eight novels)

Cast two thousand years into the future beyond AMP. The Alliance is crumbling. When corruption and politics threaten to throw the allied galaxies into chaos, Knog Beutcher gets caught in the middle. Follow along as our hero is thrust into roles that he never expected nor sought. Espionage, intrigue, political assassinations, rebellions and full-on revolutions, they are all coming to Knog Beutcher's world!

HADRON Series (eight novels)

HADRON is a modern day story unrelated to the SODIUM-AMP-OMEGA trilogy series. After scientists using the Large Hadron Collider discover dark matter, the world is plunged into chaos. Massive waves of electromagnetic interference take out all grid power and forms of communication the world over. Cities go dark, food and water supplies are quickly used up, and marauders rule the highways. Months after the mayhem begins, and after mass starvation has taken its toll, a benevolent alien species arrives from the stars. Only, are they really so benevolent? Find out in HADRON as Man faces his first real challenge to his dominance of Earth!

ARMS Series (eight novels)

ARMS is cast in one possible future for humanity. After being hurried into the stars for survival reasons, Humans had settled on two colony planets. Differences in philosophies and technical advances soon led to war, a war that had run for a thousand years. The ARMS series begins after the Great War has ended in a truce.

Two Biomarines, Tawn Freely and Harris Gruberg, genetically engineered and trained for war, suddenly find themselves out of work. Thrust into a society that doesn't trust or like them, and lacking the skills to interact well with others, they find themselves caught up in the illegal arms trade.

After a run of wild success, they find the weapons they sold are being used in a way that may restart the Great War. They will do everything in their power to stop it. Can it be stopped? And will a restart of the war be their biggest problem? Can Humans survive what's coming? Only one way to find out... read the exciting and adventure filled series!

Find them all at www.arsenex.com

HADRON
(Vol. 1)
Dark Matter

Forward: *The HADRON series begins as a survivalist story. The science fiction aspect of this first book is thin, but it rapidly gears up in book two and then runs full out through the rest of the series. The story begins as Earth falls to a civilization-crushing calamity. A willing group of friends pushes to stay alive, only being able to speculate as to the cause of man's demise.*

In Dark Matter, humanity is faced with all grid power shutting down and all forms of communication ceasing to function. If trouble comes your way, there will be no calling for help. There will be no police, no firefighters, no emergency workers coming to your aid. It's only you, your family, and your neighbors. All security, and all survivability, becomes local.

In our modern world, we are virtually dependent on civilization providing us with the means to survive. Trucks and trains keep the stores stocked and ready to serve our ultra-convenient lives. What would happen if those trains no longer ran and those trucks no longer delivered? How ready are you to fully take on the survival of yourself and your family?

For most, within a few days, the water coming from the faucets in your residence would begin to run dry. The dry goods in your pantry might last you a week. Food stores would quickly be looted with no new supplies, or relief, coming from neighboring areas. Everyone would rush home to protect their own, not knowing anything more than what they could see and hear in front of themselves. Remember, there are NO communications... only face to face conversation.

In the Dark Matter scenario, a worldwide event, without communications governments have no chain of command. There is no delegation of authority to coordinate survival or relief efforts. Also in this scenario, the military has been told to hunker down, to shelter in place, as the final direction from leadership fears an invasion. Complicating the civilian problem, the supplies the military holds are not shared with the populace. If war is possibly coming, those supplies will be needed. Without the normal order of government, our otherwise civil societies would quickly descend into chaos the world over.

How long could you survive in your home? How long before you would have to go out searching for food? And how many previously good people would turn to violence if their loved ones were starving? If you held out your hand to those who had stockpiled food, and nothing was placed in it, would you return with a club or a gun in order to feed yourself and your family? For a densely populated area, the lack of food would rapidly become a horrifying situation.

With large catastrophes as we currently know them, floods, earthquakes, and hurricanes, even in the best prepared of places, relief efforts can take a day or a week to get moving. For the less fortunate, that relief's arrival can stretch as long as several weeks. In HADRON Dark Matter, the catastrophe is worldwide. There is no one the next city or town over who can or will come to your aid. Relief is not coming. You are completely on your own!

One final set of questions: In this most dire of situations, how long before you would begin to struggle to live? And how far would you be willing to go in that struggle? Asking? Begging? Threatening? Stealing? Attacking? What is your threshold for survival?

Chapter 1

The engines lost thrust as the fuel ran dry. The passenger jet slowed and began to nose over. It spiraled as it plummeted the thirty thousand feet to the ground below, digging a crater and fracturing into thousands of pieces upon impact. The resting place of the disaster being a remote forest in rural New Jersey.

Nineteen hours later...

Power had returned to Barton's Bar after a short outage earlier in the day. A patron rose from his bar stool with a scowl, tossing back a whiskey shot before pitching a dollar into the tip jar. "Keep your feet on the ground, mate. Too easy to lose your head out there."

The bartender, Mace Hardy, smiled and nodded thanks. As the man walked away, his smile turned to wide-eyed look and a head shake. The exchange was odd, as were an increasing number of the world's inhabitants.

Picking up a rag as he listened to the TV mounted behind him on the wall, Mace wiped what he thought was probably the millionth water ring from the top of the bar.

"In a new development, we're hearing from unconfirmed sources this evening, that 'no fatalities' are being reported from the jetliner that crashed in Wharton State Forest of Central New Jersey last night. The military has the entire area cordoned off. This is the first information they have released. The plane was unoccupied. No passengers... or crew members. Daniel."

The news anchor replied, *"Rachel? Unoccupied? Is that even possible?"*

The perky blonde reporter shrugged. *"We'll have to wait to see, Daniel. This accident has been shrouded in secrecy since first being reported. Back to you."*

Attention waned as the smiling anchor began to blather-on about talk of an upcoming commission vote.

"What has it been... six years?" Mace thought to himself. *"I gotta get a life."*

His head shook as he polished the bar top and mulled over his situation. One of the regulars strolled through the front door.

"Johnnnnny..." Mace said slowly. "Let me guess, a cold mug and a Mangrove Special Dark?"

Johnny Tretcher sat on the stool the man had just abandoned. "Wow, it's as if you know me or something. How's biz today?"

Mace looked over at the mostly empty glass jar sitting on the counter. "Slow afternoon. We lost power again for about twenty minutes. Only had a half dozen people in since four."

Johnny pulled out a five. Reaching over he stuffed it in the jar. "There you go. Now you're up a fiver."

Mace smirked. "So you'll be here until what... eleven? That's five hours. Buck an hour? I'd say that about sums you up."

Johnny shook his head. "Hey now! That was rude. I'd like to talk to the management! The workers here are a bunch of ingrates and the customer service is abysmal!"

Mace laughed. "OK, but just so you know, I'll be representing the management today."

"How's your mother doing?"

Mace took a deep breath as he poured the thirty-nine-degree Mangrove into the chilled mug. "She struggles. Her doctor only wants to treat the symptoms with more meds. She's trying out a new doc next week. From what she was told by others, he might be able to help. Just wish she wasn't on the other side of the country. And thanks for caring, by the way. I'll let her know you asked about her."

Johnny replied, "Your mom is a class act. Should be more in the world like her."

Johnny looked up at the TV on the wall as a talking head babbled on about local politics. "Anything new on that plane crash?"

Mace turned to look at the tag lines scrolling by as he propped his elbow on the bar. "They're now speculating it may have been empty. What was it, eleven o'clock last night when it went down? Military has that place cordoned off for a few miles in every direction and they aren't talking."

Johnny took a swig and chuckled.

Mace asked. "What's so funny?"

A finger pointed up at the TV. "Of all the places to go down—Jersey. They'd have been lucky to make it out of there alive anyway."

Mace frowned. "Hey, take it easy on my Jersey people. Half my family comes from there."

Johnny nodded. "And look at what happened. You spend all your free hours working this dive pouring beers for jerks like me. Construction still slow?"

The bartender nodded. "Yeah. Only managed two full days last week and nothing so far this week. This economy... and this job... they're killing me. Almost makes me long for my Army days. Had I stuck it out I'd be at sixteen years now."

Johnny took another swig. "Yeah, but you'd have missed all this."

A second news flash about the crash came up on the TV screen.

Johnny said, "Click up the volume."

The anchor on the screen looked as though he was going to burst with excitement.

"*This just in. We have exclusive word from credible sources about where this flight originated. Through the investigations of our parent network, we have word of a passenger plane gone missing. Flight 7220, traveling from Caracas, Venezuela, to Managua, Nicaragua, with seventy-three passengers and four crew aboard, went off radar early yesterday afternoon. We also have confirmed reports that an unidentified passenger jet briefly entered Dominican airspace last evening, on a northward heading. We may have found our plane. We're working on confirmation from both the Venezuelan and Nicaraguan governments at this time. We'll be bringing you updates live as new information comes in. Daniel Vasquez, Channel 9 News.*"

Johnny leaned back on his barstool. "That has hijacking written all over it. Curious though. All those trees and no fire?"

Mace replied, "Wharton State Forest is Central Jersey. Could have been Philly or New York it was heading for. Had they kept going straight north, it'd be Trenton."

"Trenton? Who'd hijack a plane to Trenton? Even if you were gonna crash it, why there? Headlines would read 'Plane goes down in Trenton, causes fifty million dollars of improvements'."

Mace slowly shook his head as he stared at the screen. "Trenton is loaded with industrials and chemicals. Would have left a mess."

A second customer came through the door. He looked around at the empty tables before walking up to sit at the bar.

"What can I get you?" Mace greeted him with a smile.

The man was short in stature and thin, unlike Johnny, tall, and weighing in at close to three hundred pounds.

"I'll just have a soda."

"Diet?"

An irritated response was returned. "I weigh one forty-five. Do I look like I'm on a diet? Give me the hard stuff."

Mace took no offense to the answer. In bar-land, half the visitors on any given day would be coming in wearing their problems on their sleeves.

A glass with ice was set on the bar before a button was pressed on the soda tap. "Two dollars or a tab, whichever you like."

"A tab is fine. I'll probably be here all week."

"Gotta name?"

"It's Tres. As in uno, dos... I'm the third kid. My parents are comedians."

Mace returned an easy laugh. "Please tell me you don't have brothers named Uno and Dos."

"Nope. Robert and Nathaniel. Bobby and Nate. Normal names. You know what short for Tres is? Tres."

Mace looked him over and asked, "Indian? Tres doesn't quite fit."

"Quarter," Tres sighed. "Mom is half. Father's British. Not a lick of Spanish anywhere in me."

Johnny leaned over with an outstretched hand. "Welcome to our little corner of the world, Tres. Johnny Tretcher. And our attendant this fine evening is Mace Hardy."

Tres took Johnny's hand. "Mace? As in the weapon or the spray?"

Johnny chuckled. "He wishes. His mom likes to cook and mace is her favorite spice. Tres doesn't sound quite so bad now, does it?"

"I'd take Mace in a heartbeat."

"What brings you to our neck of the woods today, Tres? If you don't mind my asking." Johnny gave an interested look.

"Family business." Tres took a sip of his soda. "My father has a patent on a brewing apparatus that speeds up the fermenting process. I'm at the brewery down the street, putting together a demonstration line. And what's with the electric around here? These outages have been killing my progress."

Johnny grinned. "The beer business? Now we're talking my language. I like this guy."

A second news flash came on the TV screen.

"This is Don Vasquez with Channel 9 News. We're going live to a spokesman from the National Transportation Safety Board for new information about the crash of flight 7220 out of Caracas."

The TV changed to an image of a woman standing at a podium. Papers were shuffled in front of her as she listened to an earpiece.

Johnny said, "You been watching this today?"

Tres shook his head. "Don't know anything about it."

Mace leaned back on the bar with his arms crossed as they waited for the report. "They've sure stayed quiet on this one."

"Yeah," Johnny replied. "Well, while we're waiting, how about a fresh brew?" Johnny leaned toward Tres. "The service around here is kinda slow."

As Mace poured a new bottle into a frosty cold mug. "A slow patron calls for slow service."

Johnny held up his hand. "Hold up... they're talking."

"As the investigation into this tragedy continues, we will make every effort to inform the public of the facts. There has been

much speculation in the media focusing on hijacking. At this early point in the investigation, we believe that to not be the case. However, we won't know more until we have recovered and analyzed the data from the flight recorder."

A journalist up front cut in with a question. "*Any survivors? The airline said that plane left with seventy-three passengers and four crew.*"

The spokeswoman continued. "*The plane has been positively identified as flight 7220 out of Caracas, Venezuela. Our early work at the crash site has revealed there were no passengers or crew aboard at the time it came down.*"

The journalists standing in front of the podium erupted in questions.

The spokeswoman again held up her hand. "*Please. I'm sorry. At this time I have no further information other than to confirm there were no known fatalities at the crash site. We're working with the governments of Venezuela and Nicaragua, as well as the airline operating this aircraft. We'll let you know more as new information becomes available. That's all I have for now. Thank you.*"

The spokeswoman turned from the cameras and was hustled away from the podium.

Johnny raised his eyebrows. "Empty plane? You buying that? Somebody had to have been flying that thing."

Tres said, "It *was* coming out of Venezuela. Who knows if the passenger manifest is real. We aren't on the best of terms with that government. Maybe *they* sent the plane our way."

Mace half laughed, "Let the conspiracy theories begin."

Johnny swigged his beer. "OK, how about this... crazy pilot, lowers altitude, forces crew into the back, opens the door and makes everyone jump out. He, or she, then follows."

Tres added. "Or... aliens took 'em. They're all on a ship just outside the atmosphere, probably getting probed about now."

Mace grimaced at the mental image before replying to Johnny. "You know, if the pilot made them jump, and then he jumped with a parachute, enough time has gone by that he could be sitting right here in this bar."

Johnny turned and looked around. "I see Marlene and Tracy. Other than that it's just us."

Johnny stared hard at Tres. "You?"

Tres huffed. "Oh, sure, blame it on the new kid. Do I look like I'd be from Venezuela?"

Johnny joked, "Hey, you come in here ordering a soda when you say you work in the brewing industry. Nothing at all suspicious about that."

Tres took a final gulp and pushed his empty glass across the counter. "Hit me again, Mr. Hardy. Looks like it's gonna be a long night."

The power in the bar flickered off and then back on.

Mace sighed. "Here we go again. Been doing that almost every day for a week."

Johnny said, "They've been trying to pin it on solar activity or something like that. Power going out to our house has always had service problems. Had a generator put in a couple months ago because of it."

"Propane?" Tres asked. "My dad wanted to put in a propane generator."

"Yep."

Several seconds of awkward silence passed before Johnny continued, "You just drinking soda, Tres? Why you hanging out here? Don't tell me you're staying down at the Dortmer. That place is a health hazard all on it's own."

Tres lifted his fresh, carbonated glass of soda. "To the Dortmer. The only hotel in the northern hemisphere without cable and Internet. I was tempted just to sleep in the rental car."

Johnny laughed as he lightly slapped Tres on the shoulder. "The only activities they got going on there don't need cable or Internet. Didn't know the brewing business paid so poorly."

Tres frowned. "My brothers handle sales and stay in nice hotels while they wine and dine the brew-masters. We aren't that well off, and we're trying to expand, so we cut corners where we can. Which means me."

Johnny said, "Look, don't take this the wrong way, but I have a big house, with a guest house, you're welcome to stay there for the week. It's about a mile and a half away, down on the inlet."

Mace pointed at Tres, "If you're staying at the Dortmer, I'd take him up on that offer. The guest house is nicer than most hotels."

Tres turned toward Johnny. "A guest house? And what is it you do for a living?"

"I live. I just sit on my ass and live. I inherited the house and a small but comfortable fortune from my mother's side of the family. In the morning I sit on my boat in the inlet fishing. And at night I come here to pick up stray skinny men who work in the brewing industry."

After a moment of hesitation, Johnny let out a howling laugh.

Tres asked, "He always this creepy?"

Mace nodded. "Yes. But he's seriously one of the most generous people I know. If you stay there, expect his wife to make him offer you breakfast before you leave in the morning. Great people, the two of them."

Tres lifted his chin in curiosity. "You have a wife? What are you doing here?"

Johnny laughed. "As I said, I fish in the mornings. Then I sit around the house bugging her all afternoon. By five o'clock she's begging me to leave."

Mace said, "You'll be begging him to go back home before long."

Johnny continued, "Monday, Thursday, and Friday she runs around with her friends, so I get a pass to come here."

"Sadly, this is the best option he's got." Mace quipped.

"I tried golf, bowling, sailing, competition shooting and just about everything else. Found out most of those were boring without having a buddy or two to run around with. That's why I come here. My buddy is actually working, so he has to be here."

Mace poured a new Mangrove. "His wife is just as entertaining. She usually sits with us for a bit when she comes to pick him up."

Johnny took a sip of his fresh, cold brew. "She knows if I'm hanging out here with Mace, I'm OK. He does a good job of keeping me out of trouble. Not woman trouble mind you, just trouble from running my mouth. I tend to get into other people's business."

Tres sarcastically nodded. "I've noticed."

Their attention briefly turned back to the TV as the female newscaster came on with a report.

"It has been two weeks since the Large Hadron Collider conducted its latest experiment by smashing atomic particles together. Online speculation in the scientific community has exploded with talk of the first-time discovery of what is being identified as... dark matter. Our on-call science specialist, Dr. Jeffrey Moskowitz, will be telling us exactly what that means."

The reporter looked at the camera on a split screen as a new face appeared. *"Dr. Jeff?"*

The Dr. nodded. *"Thank you, Rachel. The LHC experiments have reached a new phase. If dark matter is the actual discovery this time around, it will move a whole field of study from theory to fact, transforming much of what we believe to be possible, into what we know to be true..."*

Two minutes of science speak later, the camera returned to the reporter. *"Thank you Dr. Jeff. You managed to put that into terms that even I understood. I think. Anyway... media relations at the LHC have promised us a groundbreaking story tomorrow at 3PM, Eastern Standard Time. Next up, will our local celebrity, Mr. Football, Ronnie Baines, make it to the pros after this fall season? We'll be right back with that and other sports news, right after these important words from our sponsors."*

Johnny shook his head. "The only dark matter I have an interest in comes out of that Mangrove bottle. And Ronnie... he will for sure be going in the first round."

Tres replied, "I don't know, that one... dark matter, is pretty big. It ties together a lot of the theories about gravity and the size of the universe. Kind of exciting stuff."

Johnny laughed. "Maybe if you're a physi-cisi-cist."

Mace pointed. "OK, that's it Johnny. Gonna have to cut you off."

"What? I'm only on number three. And it's not like I'm driving. Jane will be here to pick me up at eleven."

Mace shook his head. "It's not the beer. It's the bad jokes. I can't have you driving off my only customer with such."

Johnny looked around as he laughed. "Only? When did Marlene and Tracy slip out of here?"

The lone waitress, Vanessa, stepped up behind Johnny. "They've been gone for fifteen minutes. I see you're right on top of everything as usual."

Johnny pointed at the TV. "Hey, we've been discussing dark matter. Word is they'll be announcing a full discovery of it tomorrow."

Vanessa replied, "Pfft. Yeah right. Dark matter. The only dark matter you... oh never mind. That's not a discussion I want to get into."

Vanessa turned and walked toward the kitchen.

Tres looked at Mace with wide eyes. "Who was that? She works here?"

Mace leaned forward on the bar. "That's my daughter."

Tres pulled back. "Oh. Sorry. Didn't mean anything by that."

Mace returned a smug laugh. "Just pulling your chain. Not my daughter. Just our waitress."

"She here every night?"

Johnny half frowned. "I wouldn't get my hopes up if I was you, Pancho. She's likely way out of your dating league. We've seen a few of the guys she runs around with. Big lanky fellas, Hollywood types with fancy cars."

"Well, maybe she needs someone to take her away from all this."

Johnny grinned. "Oh yeah? To where? Down to the Dortmer? Hahahaha!"

"Hey, I've got a few things I'm working on. If they pan out, she could be on my arm."

Mace smiled, then smirked. "Probably more likely to be in your wallet than on your arm. She's a good kid, but pretty full of herself at times."

Vanessa yelled from the back. "You know I can hear you, right?"

Johnny laughed. "You know we love you like family! That's all that matters!"

Vanessa poked her head out the kitchen door, pointing her finger as she smacked on a fresh stick of gum. "Just remember, I see all and I hear all."

Their attention was again diverted to the TV as another report flashed on the screen.

"*We have new information regarding the crash of the Air Tratta flight traveling from the Cook Islands to Auckland four days ago. The Civil Aviation Authority of New Zealand has just released word that the twenty-nine passengers and three crew aboard that flight... are missing. I repeat, for the second time in four days, we have an airliner that has gone down with no one aboard. We'll be going live to the news desk for a report on this new information following this break.*"

Tres gestured toward the TV. "See. This is why I don't fly."

Johnny poured down the rest of his beer, setting the empty mug on the counter as he gestured for another. "Gentlemen, we have a mystery that needs solving. And I'm going to have to side with Tres on this one. Starting to look like abductions. The question is... are they little green men or little gray men?"

Tres replied, "Who says they're little?"

Johnny laughed. "Maybe they got swallowed up by the dark matter!"

Vanessa came from the back, plopping herself on a stool next to Tres as she leaned on the bar. "You following the plane stories? Two of them now."

Johnny made a curious face as he pointed at Tres. "He thinks it's aliens."

Tres defensively protested. "I was making a joke."

Vanessa put her hand on Tres' shoulder. "Don't sweat it. I don't pay much attention to anything these two say. Everything's a conspiracy with them. I'm Vanessa, by the way."

Tres held out his hand. "Tres."

There was an awkward silence for several seconds as Vanessa stared at the outstretched hand.

Johnny said, "Watch out for this one, Vanny, he's a smooth talker."

Vanessa took his hand for a short shake. "Don't mind Johnny. He's proof that money can't buy you manners."

Vanessa looked at the tip jar. "Or make you a decent tipper for that matter."

Johnny frowned. "Hey now, let's not get personal."

Power to the building flickered and went out. A single emergency light kicked on, illuminating the floor near the doorway to the parking lot.

Vanessa stood. "Third time this week."

Johnny said, "Grid in this area needs a major overhaul."

Tres scowled as he looked at his near empty glass. "I suppose that soda fountain requires electric?"

Mace nodded. "Yep. We had an old CO_2-forced system up until six months ago. Sorry. No power, no soda."

Headlights flashed on the front windows of the bar. Seconds later, a short blonde walked through the door.

Jane Tretcher held out her hands. "You people just sit around in the dark all evening?"

Johnny replied, "Power just went off. What's it look like out there?"

Jane walked up to Johnny's stool, placing her arm around and behind her husband. "Pitch black out. Except for emergency lights on a half dozen businesses. Satellite radio even has static."

Johnny pulled back. "Why would that go out? It's not wired to anything."

Tres shook his head. "No, but the signals from the ground up to the satellite are."

Johnny laughed with a slight embarrassment. "Oh yeah, well, tell you all what, if the power isn't back on in the next couple minutes, you're all invited over to our place. The beer is cold as are the sodas. Courtesy of our recently installed gas generators."

Vanessa let out a sigh as she looked at Mace. "What do you think? Not like we're rockin' the house tonight. And my date won't be here for another two hours."

Mace nodded as he locked the register. "I can give you a ride there and back if you want."

Vanessa smiled as she turned with an arm gesture toward the door. "Thanks. Johnny, lead the way."

Tres remained at the bar for several seconds, unsure of what to do.

Vanessa turned. "Well come on. We can't leave you in here."

Mace said, "I can bring you back with her if you want to ride with us. Or if you're staying there, Johnny can bring you back in the morning. He gets up early anyway."

Tres hopped off the stool.

Jane and Johnny pulled out onto the roadway heading south. Tres and Vanessa piled into Mace's four-wheel-drive. As they started down the road, Mace looked up at the sky through the windshield, taking notice of the blackness of the night. The low glow from the city lights was missing. A new moon had the normally washed out sky full of stars. The darkness was a sight they would soon have to get used to.

Chapter 2

As they pulled into the stone-walled property, Vanessa rolled her eyes. "Johnny lives here? I knew he had money, but this place is like... huge."

Tres replied, "Look at that fountain. Who has a fountain that big right in front of their door?"

Mace nodded. "He's never been one to flaunt his wealth. I prodded him about it once or twice, but he wouldn't give up any details. Said it wasn't important to who you were."

Vanessa laughed. "I'd say his lifestyle is a lot more important than mine. Ah! Look at those doors. That's something I would expect to see on a castle!"

They parked and hopped out onto the light-gray granite pavers that circled the fountain. Two marble lions graced either side of the entrance to Johnny and Jane's palatial home.

A valet opened the car door. "Ma'am, sir, will you be in for the remainder of the evening?"

Jane held out the car keys as she stepped out. "I think we're done, Dirk. You can take her around if you like."

The valet offered a slight bow as Jane strode past him on her way toward the large portico that led into the house.

Vanessa asked, "You have servants?"

Jane smiled. "Goodness, no. Only Dirk. I got fed up with maids and cooks years ago. Johnny does most of the cleaning. Strangely, he enjoys it."

Vanessa joked, "You need to get some girlfriends who'll come over and hang out. This place needs to be seen."

They followed Jane through the huge oaken doors.

Greetings were offered by two small dogs with wiggling tails and wide eyes.

"The Westie is mine. Her name is Molly. The doxie is Johnny's, Derwood."

Vanessa stopped just inside as she knelt to pet the dogs. "Whoa... this place is gorgeous! And, Derwood, who named you that?"

"Meh," Jane replied as she looked around. "It's kind of like living in a museum. Haven't touched a thing other than our room, the kitchen, and Johnny's den since we've been here. And that's been twenty-two years. And Derwood was named by my twelve-year-old husband."

Johnny reached down to pet his dog. "Twenty-three, dear. And Derwood is a classic name. Aren't you, Der-Der."

Jane sighed as she counted on her fingers. "Hmm. Twenty-three it is. Can I get any of you a beverage?"

Vanessa nodded. "I'll have something. Just about anything would be fine."

Jane pointed at each of the guests. "We have wine. A Mangrove. Mace? The usual?"

Mace nodded. "That would be good, thank you."

Jane turned to Tres. "And our friend whom Johnny refuses to introduce?"

"Hey now. We just got here. Jane, this is uno dos Tres. And he'll have a soda, if I'm not mistaken."

Jane held out her hand for a shake. "Don't mind him. He's not much for manners."

Vanessa laughed. "I just said that not twenty minutes ago."

Tres shook Jane's hand. "It's just Tres. And soda is good, thank you."

They followed Jane into the kitchen.

Dirk entered from another hallway. "Will there be anything else this evening, Ma'am?"

Johnny put his hand on Dirk's shoulder. "I think we're good here, but the power is out again. Looks like it might be out for a while. You can head home. Or if you want my opinion, you should go and bring Donna and little Dee back here for the night. You can take refuge in the front bedroom again."

Dirk smiled. "Thank you sir, but I believe we'll be fine."

Jane added. "Give Dee a hug for me."

Dirk bowed slightly and turned, walking down the hallway at a brisk pace.

He stopped midway to the end. "Anyone else have a phone signal?"

They each pulled their phones from their pockets. No one had a connection.

Mace said, "We didn't lose our phones during the last blackout. Must be something different this time."

Johnny looked over his smartphone as he walked to a cabinet filled with bottles, Derwood trotting after. "Can't say I like this."

Dirk waved as he pocketed the phone and turned back toward the door. "Thank you again for your kindness."

Jane poured two glasses of wine as Johnny pulled a bottle of rum from the cabinet. After receiving the drinks, the guests followed the hosts into Johnny's den. A large marlin, a moose head, and several elk heads lined one wall.

Vanessa sighed. "Really?"

Johnny laughed. "Relax, they aren't mine. I have trouble pulling fish in the boat. I love the challenge of it, but I always feel bad once they're in my hands. I tend to catch and release."

Jane said, "He's a softy. The trophies belonged to his uncle. Family heirlooms, if you will. That was the one wall in this room we didn't touch."

Tres stood in awe of the TV screen. "What is that? Eight feet?"

Johnny smiled. "It's ten. And it should be on by now."

The host picked up a tablet controller from a coffee table as they each took seats on the large heavy leather couches in front of the big screen. "Hmm. Says it's scanning for channels. Rarely see it do that. Internet and satellite must be down too."

Johnny swiped at several displays.

A broadcaster at an AM radio station came over the speakers. "*Again, the blackout has spread to at least a full third of the eastern seaboard, affecting phones, cable, satellite and surprisingly, over-the-air FM broadcasts. The initial reaction from authorities has been a single statement that we should all remain in our homes for the evening. I'm here tonight with Jim Mathers, our K101 engineer. Jim, have you ever seen anything like this?"*

The engineer replied, "*No, Dave, I haven't. Both communications and power appear to be out in the northeast region. This has affected both cell phones and landlines. The latter of which I don't understand.*"

The broadcaster asked, "*Any idea what might cause something like this?*"

Jim said, "*Could be anything from a nasty solar flare to an attack on our country. Could be terrorists.*"

Dave sighed. "*OK, just for all our listeners out there, that was only speculation. We are not under attack and there aren't any reports of terrorists on the loose. I think we'll go with the solar flares.*"

Jim yelled, "*Ow! What was that for? Stop hitting me, man!*"

The air was silent for several seconds. "*OK, folks, sorry about that. Jim will be returning to his regular duties of keeping us on the air. It's shaping up to be a quiet evening, so just stay indoors, stay safe, and enjoy listening to the music.*"

A tune from the fifties crackled over the AM airwaves.

Johnny laughed. "If we're back to AM only, it must be the apocalypse."

Mace jokingly said, "So we may be holed up here for a while. You ready for that?"

Johnny shrugged. "You're all welcome to stay. At least until the power comes back on."

Mace crossed his arms. "What if it never comes back on?"

Johnny frowned and offered a deadpan reply: "Then I chop you up and use you for fish bait. I gotta keep eating."

Vanessa said, "I thought you threw the fish back."

Johnny turned. "OK, that makes two of you for the chum bucket. Let's just hope the power comes back on."

Seconds later, a flicker told of the generators switching back over to the normal power input from the grid.

Johnny smiled. "Looks like you're both off the hook."

Vanessa said, "Still no phone signal."

Johnny swiped at his tablet until a screen of his home power system displayed. "Outside power is up. Internet is connecting, and... up."

Jane looked at her phone. "I don't show a phone signal either."

The power flickered, and once again went out, taking the internet connection with it.

"You two, follow me. I'll get the bucket." Johnny said as he stood.

Jane shook her head. "OK, enough of that. It wasn't funny to begin with."

"I have a phone connection. And data." Tres held up his cellphone.

Mace said, "Try to make a call."

Tres typed away. "Sent my brother a text. He's always watching his phone."

Seconds later a vibration told of a response. "He says power was off there—Michigan—for about twenty minutes. Is out in sections going from Virginia all the way up to Maine. No word yet on the definite cause, but they're saying there's a massive amount of interference wreaking havoc on mobile phone service just about everywhere."

Vanessa lit up. "Finally! Got my service back!"

She immediately sent a text to her date.

The power again flickered but remained on.

Vanessa received a reply. "Great. Canceled. We were heading up the coast, taking his parents' yacht across to Cape Charles from where it's moored. Now he says he's heading out to his grandparent's estate in Pittsburgh. Looks like I have a free weekend coming up."

Minutes later, one by one the broadcast channels began to come online. The talking heads took to their desks and the speculations as to what had happened began. A half hour into the highly varied stories, word came in of a train derailment that had taken out a main feeder line. The experts pointed at the loss of the feeder for the power outage, but remained baffled by the loss of communications.

"Brian, what I don't understand is our loss of mobile service. The towers are up, the backup generators, from what we've been told, continue to function. We've had word of some type of massive RF interference happening, but nothing definite. Perhaps the Russians or Chinese are testing some new satellite weapon?"

The news anchor held up a hand. "Let's not be too hasty with that one, Garth. Wouldn't that be considered an act of war?"

Garth Roberts shrugged. "Just not sure where else it could come from. If this was a solar event, we would have had a warning from the scientific community. They keep tight track of those things so precautions can be taken to prevent outages or damage. There haven't been any reports of solar flares of late. At least none that have been mentioned. And this is the second week of outages."

The power and communications again failed.

Tres threw his hands in the air. "This is great. If I don't have the demonstration line up and working by Monday we lose our shot at a contract. I needed tomorrow's time."

Speculation continued among the group as the evening turned into the wee hours of the morning. Jane offered rooms and beds in the main house to her guests. All were soon sleeping in comfort.

The following morning saw no revival of the power or communications. The guests were invited to stay the day. A hardy breakfast and a morning of chat led to Johnny firing up his barbecue and cooking up a load of steaks from his freezer.

"Sorry they aren't fresh from the butcher. For guests I like to bring home the beef that's been properly aged."

Mace replied, "I think these might be thicker than any I've ever seen."

Tres laughed. "How am I supposed to eat that? It weighs half of what I do?"

Johnny shrugged. "Split it with Vanessa. I've seen her tear into a burrito over at the bar. It was savage."

Vanessa scowled. "It was once. And I was hungry... hadn't eaten all day."

The afternoon was one of relaxation and chat. Attempts at fishing from the dock brought laughter as the beer and wine flowed. The warm afternoon soon turned to evening with the power remaining off.

Jane said, "Dirk? Why don't you head home and bring Donna and Dee back here. No sense in them sitting in the dark over there."

Dirk nodded. "If it wouldn't be too much trouble. Our neighborhood backs up to a less desirable part of town. We were kept up half the night with a block party of sorts that went until this morning."

Jane waved at the door. "Go. I'd love to see little Dee."

Dirk hurried for the door and was soon out of the drive and on his way home. Johnny continued to scan for TV and radio stations with no luck.

Another quiet night was followed by an easy afternoon. As the sun set on the second full day of outage, the group returned to the comfort of Johnny's den. Dirk made a run back to his house for supplies for the infant.

Several loud pops could be heard from outside.

Jane said, "That sounded like a .45."

Johnny shook his head. "Just kids out having fun with fireworks."

Jane replied, "That's heavy stuff if it's fireworks. Sounded substantial."

Nearly an hour later, Dirk returned with extra diapers and clothing for his daughter.

Johnny asked, "Any traffic out there?"

"I-264 is backed up. I waited for fifteen minutes just to cross under the overpass. If people were supposed to stay in their homes, they're not complying. The grocery store was being mobbed."

Mace said, "They had power?"

Dirk shook his head. "No, sir. Looting. Headlights lighting up the interior while mobs of people ran about. The windows were all smashed out. I heard several gunshots as well."

Johnny frowned. "It's only been a day. How quickly we devolve into being savages."

Dirk glanced over at the hallway. "I passed a group of fifteen or twenty on the roadway about a mile from here. They didn't look to be up to any good. I think some of them were breaking into a house. And I noticed the perimeter lights were not on outside. Perhaps we should brighten things up?"

Jane said, "I told you that was gunshots we heard. Might be time to secure this place."

Johnny stood. "Mace, Tres, Dirk, come with me."

They followed Johnny down the back hall, through an exterior door, and across a paved area that led to his massive garage. A broad door rose up as they approached.

Johnny smiled as he gestured toward a locked door just inside the garage. "Gentlemen, welcome to the ready-room."

The steel door was unlocked and opened.

As they came through, Johnny pointed. "To the left we have antiques. Most of those belonged to my uncle. I don't think we'll be needing those this evening. Straight in front we have handguns. Last count we were at ninety-six, I believe. If you're skilled at shooting, please help yourself. Smaller calibers start on the left, with a collection of .50s over here."

Mace looked to the right. "Are these legal on this side?"

Johnny grinned. "These are all fully registered and legal. And we have at least a thousand rounds of ammo for each weapon. Jane's a bit of a fanatic."

Tres stood in disbelief. "Are you expecting World War Three?"

Johnny laughed. "No. Jane and I spent several years as competitive shooters. We might have gone a bit overboard with our collecting at the time. A good bit of this was inherited. Jane still competes. I mostly just watch."

Jane stood behind them, with Vanessa, Donna, and Dee in tow. "Have you shown them the real stuff?"

Johnny hesitated. "Wasn't prepared to do that just yet, no."

Jane glanced around the room. "Can you all keep a secret?"

Each of the room's occupants nodded as Jane looked them in the eye.

Johnny frowned. "You think that's a good idea?"

Jane waved her hand as she walked toward a bookshelf that showcased several dozen revolvers. "These are all good people here. I'm sure they have no problem with weapons used for self-defense."

A hidden button was pressed and one end of the bookshelf slid out several inches. Jane pulled the shelf door wide open, exposing a smaller, neatly arranged room with more weapons.

Mace stepped forward. "AKs... is that a Thompson? And this? Not sure I've seen one of those."

Jane grinned as she pulled the sub-machine gun from its place on the wall. It's Israeli. Weapons in this room are all fully auto. And yes, they are against the law to own without the proper Federal permit. However, I have a dealer license and I'm a certified importer-exporter for each of the manufacturers of these weapons. I have all the permits to have them in 'inventory'."

Mace nodded toward the Thompson. "I'm not buying that you have a license to export that. They don't even make those anymore."

Jane smiled. "If you have the money, you can have an exact replica of virtually any gun made. You just don't talk about it."

Mace said, "Who still makes a full-up Thompson?"

Jane pulled the sub-machine gun from its perch on the wall. "This one isn't a replica. It was carried by Johnny's grandfather on D-Day. He was a paratrooper dropped into France. Did a lot of fighting street-to-street with it."

Jane placed the gun gently back on its holders. "We won't be using this today. I would suggest the Israeli model you were looking at."

Mace looked down at the large case on the floor. "What's in the box?"

Jane grunted as she slid the case out and flipped it open. "It's an old .50 cal. Also from WWII. Saw action in Europe. Johnny's uncle collected that one when he was much younger. He used to tell Johnny it was ideal for hunting buffalo. His uncle was a hoot. I only got to meet him a handful of times."

Jane lifted the Israeli gun from the wall, pulling back the bolt and inspecting the chamber. "The blue box, bring it with you. It has twenty thirty-round magazines. All loaded and ready to use. Today was gonna be a practice day for an upcoming meet. Dirk, for you and Tres, these AR-15's will do. Grab one of those green boxes below them if you would."

Vanessa stood with her arms crossed. "I've never shot a gun before. I hope you aren't expecting me to carry one of those."

Jane smiled. "No, you and Donna will be staying in the house, but I'm not leaving either of you unarmed. I have a nice set of .32s over there that are light and easy to use. Johnny, watch the house if you would."

They followed Jane to the other end of the garage and through another locked door. Down a handful of stairs, they came out into a dual-lane, indoor shooting range that stretched out over fifty yards. It had been dug below ground going out into the yard behind the garage, leaving it unseen from outside except for a well-hidden door on the other side of a shrub-covered hump.

Jane turned. "Who here, other than Vanessa, hasn't fired a weapon?"

Tres reluctantly held up his hand. "I've held a .45 pistol, but never shot one."

Jane stretched out her hand for the AR-15 Tres carried, taking it with a smile. "OK, for you and Dirk, these have suppressors. That means they will make a lot less noise. Let's you communicate with others while you're firing. Anyway, this is the safety. Flip it like this and you're ready to go."

Jane opened a green box, lifting a loaded magazine. "You have a thirty round mag. I just loaded them this afternoon in preparation for practice the next few days for a competition. I only load to twenty-eight so I don't wear out the springs. Turn it this way, stuff it up in there. First time loading may take an extra slap or shove. After that, simple and easy."

Jane handed the rifle and magazine back to Tres. "Go ahead, load it."

Tres fumbled with the weapon as he turned it in his hand.

Jane shook her head as she shoved the barrel down toward the floor. "First rule. Never aim that barrel toward anyone or anything you don't want shot. Hold it like this. Shove the magazine in until it locks. Pull back the bolt and let it slide forward. It's ready to fire.

"Now, if you aren't engaged, and you don't need to fire the weapon, make sure the safety is flipped on. And if for some reason you squeeze that trigger and nothing happens, check your safety. If it's good, pull back on the bolt to inspect the chamber. If a round is stuck, it should pop out the side. Release the bolt and you should be ready to go."

Jane took the weapon from Tres. "Stock in the shoulder, line up the sight, squeeze the trigger."

The safety was flipped off just before a round charged down the range lane, striking a ready target at thirty yards. A small hole opened in the bulls-eye. Jane flipped the safety on, handing the rifle back to Tres.

Tres nervously took careful aim, flipped the safety lever off, and squeezed off a round. The target in his lane, sitting at ten yards distance, showed a small hole in the outer ring.

Jane said, "Not bad. Now, five shots in succession. Should be about a half second pull of the trigger."

Tres held up the weapon and squeezed.

Brrrrrrff.

Two rounds made it into the third ring.

Jane smiled. "OK, flip on the safety. Either of those would be a decent hit. Might not completely stop someone, but you have more rounds if needed. Go ahead and empty that magazine now."

Tres nervously flipped off the safety, took careful aim and again squeezed the trigger.

Brrrrrrrrrrrrrrrrrrrrrrff.

Jane gestured toward the safety.

Tres flipped it and grinned. "That was both terrifying and awesome!"

Jane nodded. "It's a powerful and deadly weapon. Always treat it with respect. Who's next?"

The training went on for another twenty minutes before the range door was closed and locked.

Jane said, "Johnny, if you would care to take the ladies and watch the house, we're gonna walk the property. And go ahead and lock down everything but the back door. If there's trouble, try to make it to the boat. We'll meet you there."

Johnny frowned. "House duty?"

Jane smirked. "Who's the better shooter?"

Johnny sighed. "You are. I'm sure we won't have any trouble. If you like, we'll take turns watching the property on the cameras."

Jane nodded as Johnny left with the girls.

Mace turned toward Jane as they began to walk. "You're the better shooter? Something you aren't telling me?"

Dirk replied, "She's won several national competitions."

Mace returned a surprised look. "Is that true?"

Jane half frowned, seemingly hurt by the expression. "It is. One of the reasons Johnny gave up on target shooting. I have an iron stance and a solid aim every time. His is always good-day, bad-day. If you ever get into a ruckus, you'll want me to have your back."

The twelve acres surrounding the house took fifteen minutes to walk. A paved jogging track followed a zigzag pattern near the property line wall as it circled the inner perimeter of the estate. The occasional light in the shrubbery made for an easy trek around the track, bringing them back to the garage where they had begun.

Johnny was standing at the door to the house. "You know, we have full view of the property with the security cameras."

"It's nice out. Just thought it would be good for everyone to be familiar with the surroundings. Let's go see what the news has to offer, if it's running."

Several pops from weapons fire could be heard in the distance as they turned toward the back door.

Jane frowned. "Those are getting closer."

Chapter 3

Five loud pops from a handgun could be heard a short distance from the house.

Jane remarked, "That was no more than a few hundred yards. The Simpsons have that wide open gate. I hope that wasn't them. Either way, I'm calling in help. You and Mace should go over there to check. You can walk that in a couple minutes."

Johnny replied, "Outside the wall?"

Jane gestured toward the garage. "Don't be a wuss. Go in and put on the vests. And I'm showing phone signal again, so call me with status when you get there. I don't want to be left wondering. And don't engage. Just watch for the cops."

Johnny reluctantly smiled. "Mace? That sound like a good idea?"

Mace replied, "Might not be a bad idea to just wait here."

Jane shook her head, "Will take the police at least fifteen minutes. You can at least scout out the situation before they arrive. I don't like the thought of the Simpsons being on their own over there. You're both skilled shooters, you'll have vests. Just go see that they're OK."

Mace rubbed the goatee on his chin. "You don't think they'll take issue with us walking around with guns?"

Jane laughed. "The cops? No. Johnny knows half the force. You'll be fine."

Johnny and Mace walked back into the garage and into the gun room. The bookshelf was again opened. Two bulletproof vests were handed out to Mace.

"Strap one of those on."

Johnny followed with two pairs of night-vision goggles and the head straps to wear them. "This slide gives you a 3X zoom.

Just make sure to slide it back if you have to move, or you'll be tripping over everything."

With vests on, goggles mounted and flipped up, and spare magazines in small packs slung over their shoulders, the two started toward the front gate.

Johnny made a nervous statement. "Not so sure about this."

"Relax. I've been here before. We're just scouting. If things look rough we just come back. Where'd you get the night-vision equipment?"

"The goggles are new last month, not yet on the market. Jane is a certified tester for the manufacturer, so she gets lots of toys to play with. She's very blunt in her reviews and most of the reps respect that. The reset on these is thirty hertz. You won't get white-out if we're hit with bright lights."

Once outside the gate and into the darkness, Johnny donned the goggles. "On switch is to the right."

Other than the low lights coming from the path surrounding the Tretcher estate, they were walking into a black void. After several seconds of fumbling, Mace powered the goggles on. The street around him lit up.

"Come on. Try to keep up." Mace walked ahead.

"Right behind you."

"Wow, these are much better than what we had in the service."

Johnny glanced back to make sure the path behind them was clear. "You probably had Gen-2's. As I said, these aren't available yet."

After a short walk, Mace slowed and gestured for Johnny to move over by the brick wall that lined the outside of the Simpson estate. He peered around the corner of a pillar on the right side of the drive leading onto the property.

"I have one figure at the front door," Mace said. "Come on."

"Shouldn't we wait?"

Mace hurried through the open gate, sliding to the right behind a row of shrubs. Thirty seconds later, he stopped within twenty-five yards of the front door, crouching behind the shrub-line. Loud voices and glass breaking could be heard coming from the open front door of the large home.

Johnny slipped in behind his friend, whispering. "I better call Jane... great... no signal. She's gonna be pissed. We should go."

"Not yet. And she'll have to live with it."

He raised up slowly, looking just over the top of the hedge before dropping back quickly. "Guy at the door has night vision. He also has what looks like a 9mm in his right hand and another in his belt."

A scream could be heard coming through the open front door. "*No! Please leave him alone!*"

Mace scowled. "I don't like this."

Johnny quietly took a deep breath. "We need to get help. Greg and Martha... they wouldn't offer any resistance."

A gunshot rang out from within the house.

Mace grabbed Johnny's shoulder, quietly saying, "I'm going in. You can follow if you want."

Mace began to move and then stopped. "You ever fire on a live person?"

"No. Where would I have done that?"

"Then you wait here. I swept houses for two tours over in the Middle East. Cover my back—and don't shoot unless you absolutely have to. Taking a life is not something you'll ever forget. Even if it is just some scumbag off the street."

Mace moved down to an opening in the shrubs before peering around the edge at the figure guarding the door. It was a woman. He looked down at the ground, selecting a suitable rock to throw from the white stone that lined the shrubs.

A quick flip sent it over the guard's head and onto the roof. It clomped several times on the porcelain tiles before dropping off onto the grassy yard on the other side. The woman first looked up and then toward the sound in the yard with her weapon raised.

Mace shook his head as he thought, *"Too easy"*.

A quick, quiet sprint caught the woman looking the other way. A fist to the back of her head sent her sprawling. Her pistol, after leaving her hand, smacked the bricks of the front portico before sliding to a stop.

Johnny was quick behind with a nervous statement. "I didn't see any movement this way from the inside."

Mace whispered, "Get her weapon. There's another in her waistband. Toss them in the shrubs along with her goggles, then help me prop her up on that bench. If they chase us out of here, that might just give us a second or two of distraction."

Johnny did as Mace directed.

"Guess you really have done this before. Any other tricks in your black bag?"

"A few, but none that I care to talk about right now. And not something you ever want to have to do."

Johnny patted Mace on the shoulder as they moved back to the front door. "Should I wait here?"

Mace stopped for only a moment. "Just watch my back. Make certain they're hostile before you pull that trigger. You can't bring those bullets back once you let 'em loose."

"Understood. Lead the way."

Mace closed his eyes for a quick prayer before removing the goggles. The Simpsons' home had generators; several lights were on inside. He slowly moved through the front door into the darkened but grand foyer. Swirling mahogany staircases flowed up either side, rising sixteen feet to the second floor. He gestured for Johnny to wait at the base of the right staircase.

A formal parlor room was on the left and a study to the right. Two rooms above on the second floor showed lights. Mace continued to creep along the right wall of the foyer, passing the rail of the staircase going up.

Voices could be heard coming from the rooms further into the house. *"Look. I know people like you keep cash. Just tell us where it is and we'll leave."*

Greg Simpson pleaded, *"I've given you everything we have..."*

"*I know you have a safe! Where is it?*"

"*In my office, behind my desk. But there's nothing in there of value to you. Just papers. Life insurance, will... no cash.*"

As Mace peered from the darkness of the foyer he could see a dark haired man with a frizzy black beard hoisting the elderly neighbor to his feet. Blood dripped from a swelling cut on the old man's forehead. Two men stood behind him with evil grins on their faces as a fourth stood in front of the gray-haired Martha.

The man in front of the terrified woman said, "How'd you and him get a place like this? No way you came out of the hood."

The old woman shook in terror, unable to answer.

Mace crouched behind a short white marble pillar that held up a bright green fern as the aggressor and his two thugs took Greg Simpson to his safe, passing from Mace's right to his left down a wide hall. He had clear view of the foursome as they came to a stop in the elderly man's office.

The voice of the bearded man boomed. "Pop the safe or we cap the old lady!"

"OK." Greg nodded. "Please, just a moment."

After opening a panel in the bookshelf behind his desk, the safe was revealed. Greg worked the dial, his thin fingers trembling. Seconds later, a click was heard and the door to the safe opened.

The leader of the attackers looked inside before pushing Greg to the floor with an angry expression. "You lying old bag of bones."

The bearded man pulled two jeweled watches from the safe.

Greg held up a hand, pleading. "I'm sorry. I forgot those were there. I never wear them."

The angry and scowling attacker slowly raised his gun toward the cowering old man. "Davis! Pop a cap in that old bag! We got us a liar here!"

In an instant Mace was confronted with a dilemma: save the old man or save his wife. As he watched, he could see the expression on the bearded man's face change. He had seen it before—as an innocent Arab boy was killed for potentially revealing information about his neighborhood. At the time, Mace Hardy had been under orders to not fire as the execution went down.

It was a flash moment of evil that had since haunted his dreams. Here, he had no such orders. He took careful aim at the bearded assailant and pulled the trigger.

Zzzt. Zzzt. Zzzt.

The three men fell as three short bursts left the Israeli-made rifle.

Brrrfff.

Mace turned back in time to see the fourth man fall to the side of a blood-spattered Martha Simpson. Johnny was crouched several feet away with a hard look on his face.

A voice called down from the stairs above. "We have a jackpot of jewels up here!"

Johnny whispered for his neighbor to remain calm before he stood, frozen in thought of what to do. Mace turned back to the stairs leading up to the second floor. A man and a woman could be heard celebrating their haul.

Mace gestured toward the Simpsons. "Keep them quiet. I'm going up."

Mace crept to the top of the stairs. A third figure was standing in the hallway with his back facing him.

The man looked into the room where others were pillaging the old couple's belongings. "Oh! Bring daddy some of that sugar!"

As a giddy girl stepped out of the bedroom door in front of her man in the hall, wearing a stash of the jewelry she had just acquired, her expression quickly changed. Mace was standing behind him in full view.

The butt of the Israeli rifle sent the man hard to the floor. The girl stepped back, pulling a pistol from her waistband.

Zzzt.

She fell silent.

Mace entered the room. Her fellow assailant was standing with gold chains dangling from his hands, holding them out to his sides. His grin quickly soured as he looked behind Mace Hardy at the body of his dead accomplice. The man dove to his left, stretching for the pistol he had left on top of an ornate dresser.

Zzzt. Zzzt.

The robber slumped to the floor behind a grand mahogany poster bed. The veteran Army Ranger stepped forward to check for a kill.

Brrrrrffff.

The man hit by the butt of Mace's rifle fell through the door onto a fluffy white rug that covered the dark marble floor. Blood began to seep from several holes in the center of his back.

Johnny stepped into the doorway behind him. "He had you dead."

"Thanks. Go back and keep the Simpsons safe. I'll clear this floor."

Johnny turned back toward the hall.

Boom! Boom! Boom! Boom!

The big man fell back into the room as four slugs from a .45 impacted his chest.

Brrrrrrrffff. Brrrrrrffff.

Mace heard the whump of two bodies falling on the stairway.

Jane called up, "Who's up there! Throw down your weapons and come out!"

Mace dropped to Johnny's side and yelled back: "Just us in this room! You have the Simpsons?"

"We got 'em. Cops are on their way! Where's Johnny?"

"He's on the floor! Took two to the vest! Doesn't look all too happy at the moment! No penetration! I think he'll live!"

Jane sprinted up the steps and through the door, squatting by his side. "Big ape. Why didn't you call?"

Mace replied, "We lost signal."

The Army Ranger stepped out into the hall as Jane knelt over her grimacing husband.

He pointed at the bodies in the room and the one in the hall. "Check these three. Should be dead, but never can be sure. I'll clear the rest of this floor."

"Greg said there were at least ten. Three here, two on the stairs, four downstairs. That leaves at least one."

Mace asked, "No one outside?"

Jane shook her head. "Not when Tres and I got here."

"Take Johnny down and keep your eyes peeled. Turn the other lights in here off when you're leaving and wait down in the foyer."

Jane nodded as she attempted to help a wincing Johnny to his feet. Mace moved down the hall, sweeping each of the fourteen upstairs rooms.

Jane called down the staircase. "Cowboy, were coming down!"

When Mace followed, Johnny was talking. "Thanks for cleaning up my mess."

Jane smiled. "That's what I signed up for twenty-three years ago. Not gonna quit now."

A wide-eyed Tres was crouched with the Simpsons behind the same white marble pillar Mace had used as cover.

Mace asked, "You gonna be OK?"

Tres half smiled as he noticeably shook. "Not quite the same as the movies. And you look so calm."

Mace gestured toward his head. "I've done it a hundred times. I keep the fear locked away in here now. Just keep down and keep your eyes open. I'll be done with this floor in about thirty seconds. We can take the Simpsons back to Johnny's to wait for the cops."

Johnny winced as he tried to laugh. "Make it quick. I gotta pee something fierce."

After a quick sweep of the lower floor, they were on their way. The pops from additional gunfire could be heard in the far distance as they made their way back to the estate.

Tres said, "Didn't think Norfolk would be this bad a place. And you two. That was bad-ass back there."

Jane frowned. "I'm shaking on the inside. Never done anything remotely like that before."

"My brain is in a fog right now," Johnny added. "My mind is racing from the adrenaline pumping. That and the bruised chest."

Mace nodded. "You both did well. Better than my first few times out. I threw up after coming back from my first fight... once I had time to think about what had just transpired. Got a lot of support from my squad mates, but a lot of ribbing too."

Minutes later, when they had settled into the den, Vanessa tended to the Simpsons. Jane looked over her husband as she helped him remove his vest.

Mace collected the guns. "I'll be back in a few. Gonna swap out the full auto on these for semi. The cops will be wanting the weapons we used and we aren't looking to get ourselves in trouble."

Johnny pushed away Jane's probing hands as he grimaced with her every touch. "Go with him before you kill me. I'm fine."

Jane frowned. "Hang on Mace, I'll give you a hand."

Greg Simpson grabbed Mace by the arm as he passed the couch where he sat. "Thank you. They would have killed us."

Mace patted his hand. "You're welcome, but you should thank your neighbors here. They're the heroes."

Once in the garage, Jane unloaded the rifles, inspecting each before setting them on a bench. "Put the ARs over here when you're done. I'll take yours."

As Mace broke down the rifles in his care, he glanced over at Jane. In seconds, the trigger mechanism of the Israeli-made rifle lay exposed.

"Where'd you learn that?"

Jane smiled. "Shooting competitions often have side competitions for building up and breaking down the weapons being used. I finished first with this one in the four competitions I used it in. Just takes practice, something Johnny and I have a lot of."

Mace smirked. "How'd he get so lucky to find you?"

"We went to the same college. He had a football scholarship and I was on the swim team."

"A swimmer huh?" Mace stopped. "Wait, Johnny played college ball? Why hasn't he ever talked about it? He didn't wash out, did he?"

Jane shook her head as she broke down a second rifle. "No. He was actually All-American in high school. As a freshman in college he was a starting linebacker. First game he busted through a block, sacked the quarterback and broke his leg. Bone was sticking out."

"That had to hurt. He couldn't come back from that?"

Jane again shook her head. "Wasn't his leg that snapped. It was the quarterback's. He took it hard, deciding he didn't want to hurt anyone else just for sport. He dropped off the team mid-season. Jane paused and took a deep breath."

"You OK?"

"Just trying not to think to hard on what just happened. I know we were in the right, protecting our neighbors and all. But still..."

Mace took in a deep breath. "Never gets easy, but you'll learn to live with it. He never said he went to college, or got a degree. Did he finish?"

"He aced every test before the accident, struggled some afterward. I think he lost his concentration. Has a degree in chemical engineering with a minor in astronomy. Went back for a Masters in astrophysics but lost interest and never finished."

Mace chuckled. "That's heavy stuff. Doesn't seem the school type."

Jane shrugged. "Our security system, the tablet that controls all the electronics in the house, he did that himself. When he sets his mind to doing something, he does a first rate job of it."

"How'd the two of you actually meet?"

Jane stopped what she was doing. "He went out with one of my roommates. She actually hated him for all the things I liked. He was a gentleman, he was patient. She said, 'Responsible and boring, not my type.' He didn't actually have his money at the time. His aunt and uncle, the ones who owned this house, he was their favorite and only nephew. They left it all to him."

Mace pulled the thin plate from the AR-15 that enabled the full-auto mode. "What happened to his aunt and uncle?"

"Mauled by a pride of lions in Southern Africa while on a deep-bush safari. Killed them both while they slept in their tent. The locals hired as guards had fallen asleep.

"He took it pretty hard. That den had two lion heads in it from prior hunts. First thing he did when they told him the house was his: he took them down and burned them in a bonfire out back. Even though he doesn't like the other mounts in there, he left them up in their honor. Just couldn't stomach the lions."

Jane glanced back at the main house. "He pretty much grew up on this property. His dad was in the Navy and often out to sea. His mom worked most of the time and was happy to let him hang out with her brother and his wife."

Mace prodded, "His uncle earn the money or it come from his aunt?"

"You sure are nosy aren't you?"

Mace laughed as he snapped the last piece of a rifle together. "Just like to know my friends, that's all. I already trust him with my life, and after tonight, I owe him for it. As nervous as he was, he saved Mrs. Simpson too."

The rifle was checked over before being laid back on the table. "I switching these back is necessary, but why'd you give them to us that way in the first place? Semis would have done the trick."

Jane smiled. "What good are toys if you can't share them sometimes? Besides, would you have ever thought we would actually have to use them? I didn't."

Jane looked over the five rifles they had adjusted. "OK, think we have it. Let me lock these plates up. You take these and we'll go back in. Oh, and if you don't mind, please don't mention our talk here to Johnny. If he didn't tell you any of that, he might have his own reasons for it."

Mace nodded. "Not a problem, I owe him. Besides, I have enough secrets of my own."

Jane glanced back. "Not me. I'm an open book."

Mace chuckled. "Like I said, Johnny's a lucky man."

Chapter 4

Forty minutes after the call to the police a single cruiser showed at the entrance to the Tretcher estate. They met the officer at the front gate.

Johnny was the first to speak as he held out his hand. "Dontell."

The police lieutenant looked at the rifle in Johnny's other hand as he reached back for a shake. "I heard the Simpsons were attacked?"

Johnny gestured down the road as he nodded. "We came in, Mace, Jane and I, just as they were about to be executed. You'll find nine bodies down there. One ran off."

The cop pulled back. "Whoa. Wait. Nine bodies? Anyone else hurt?"

Jane walked up behind them. "Greg Simpson got pistol whipped, but he'll be OK. We have them both inside. We tried to call for an ambulance, but the phone was out. What gives with all this?"

The cop shook his head. "Shut down the power and communications and all the loons come out. Never seen anything like it. People just have no sense of right and wrong anymore. Gangs have hit at least seven other communities. That's just in and around Norfolk."

Jane asked, "Where they coming from? We don't have that kind of a problem here do we?"

"In my many years on the force this has always been a peaceful place." The police lieutenant took a deep breath. "Criminal activity has been picking up in the last few months, but nothing like this. Captain thinks it's gangs coming up from Miami, as many as fifty to seventy-five people. Savannah had a bad spate for a while, followed by Charleston and then Wilmington."

Johnny said, "That's a big group to be moving around."

The lieutenant nodded. "If it's the ones that hit those other cities they're well organized. No power and with communications being down... makes just about any city a playground for a group of thugs like that. Captain was expecting them to show up here at some point. Guess they finally showed."

"Well, our valet said he saw at least two dozen people grouped up on his way in. We encountered ten. There may be another horde out there of equal size."

Jane nodded. "We heard other gunshots back up that way. You're gonna want backup. They were all armed."

"Not sure what I'll get at the moment," Dontell replied. "Captain's been trying to call everyone in. Phones haven't been working. Didn't even have comm to the car until on the way here. Your call had to be hand walked to me out the front door of the station. To be honest, I wish I was home with my wife and her mother about now."

Mace said, "Lieutenant, I wouldn't go down that way by myself. If you need backup, I can lend a hand."

Johnny nodded. "I'm with you too."

Jane stepped up. "Uh, no, you'll be going back in the house. He took two slugs to the center of his vest."

Johnny protested: "I'll be fine. Just a little bruising."

Jane shook her head. "Dontell, Mace and I would be glad to accompany you up the road for a check if you like. Mace was special forces in the Army, and well, you know my background."

Mace asked, "You know these two personally?"

"I played high school ball with Trenchfoot Tretcher. He's good folk. Give me a second to check on that backup."

The lieutenant clicked on his shoulder mic. "This is 442. I'm out on Halloway. We have nine dead bodies down here with possibly eleven or more armed assailants on the loose. Requesting backup to this location as soon as possible."

Only static came back from the radio. From a distance of about half mile, three moderate caliber gunshots could be heard, followed by two from a different weapon.

The lieutenant shook his head. "I'll follow you're advice. I'm not heading in there without backup."

Jane said, "That was less than a mile. Lieutenant, we need more of you out here."

Half a dozen muzzle flashes danced from the darkness of the woods across the street from the other side of the cruiser. Mace, Jane and Johnny ducked behind the safety of the car as Dontell dropped to the ground. The veteran officer emptied his revolver into the treeline.

Mace grabbed the passenger door, pulling it open and diving inside as Jane and Johnny blasted away at the darkness. The roar of gunfire was deafening as at least a half dozen more handguns opened up from the woods.

Mace climbed across the seat. Reaching out, he grabbed the moaning officer by the back of his shirt collar, dragging him up and into the car as bullets penetrated the rear and side windows. He felt the hot burn of a slug as it flew through the vinyl front seat of the cruiser, striking his upper arm.

As he pulled the officer out the passenger door, the gunfire suddenly stopped. Footsteps could be heard moving away as Johnny and Jane sprayed the darkness. The attackers had fled.

Johnny said, "Let's get back to the house. We can defend from there. That stone on the exterior is six inches thick and the windows are all triple-pane tempered glass, hurricane rated."

Mace said, "Help me get the lieutenant up on my shoulder. I'll run him in."

Mace hustled off on his body run as Jane and Johnny watched his back. Before they reached the house, the door of the cruiser slammed shut and the rear tires spun as it headed off on a joyride. Once in the house, the front gate was signaled to close. They entered Johnny's den.

Jane said, "You're bleeding!"

Mace nodded as he laid the lieutenant out on the floor. "Came through the seat. Just a hard graze."

Mace looked over the fallen officer. "Tres, Vanessa, keep pressure on these two. We have two in the legs and... hmm, right in the shoulder joint. We need to get him to a hospital. The leg wounds aren't bleeding bad, but this one is a mess."

Jane sprinted off.

Johnny said, "I have signal again!"

An emergency call was placed. "This is Johnny Tretcher of 2225 Halloway Road. We have an officer down with multiple gunshot wounds. I repeat: an officer is down!"

The dispatcher replied, "Are there any other injuries?"

Johnny replied, "What? He's bleeding like a stuck p—he's bleeding pretty bad. His shoulder is shattered. No. He's the only one."

The dispatcher replied, "Emergency vehicles are all out on calls. You'll have to take him to Mercy Point. The ER there is accepting patients. Downtown is overloaded from that bus crash on I-664."

Johnny huffed. "We can't move him. We have a dozen shooters outside who say we aren't going anywhere."

The dispatcher acknowledged. "I'm sorry, sir. All vehicles are out. It's like a war zone out there and we just have a few officers coming in now. I'll send the first available your way."

Johnny thought for a moment. "No, no, no! We have a dozen armed men out here shooting up everything. Unless you're bringing the Army, don't send anyone!"

The dispatcher said, "You just asked for an ambulance."

Johnny sighed, "Yeah, well, we're in the middle of a war over here. Things are a little out of control. Don't send anyone until you have at least a half dozen cops with them. And make sure they know what they're heading into!"

The dispatcher replied, "I have you as an emergency response priority—multiple armed assailants and an officer already down."

Johnny shook his head in frustration. "Not just multiple! At least a dozen shooters! You send two officers and you're sending them to their death. Got it?"

The dispatcher replied, "I have it. Sorry for all the confusion, sir. Things are heated at the moment."

Johnny ended the call. "We're on our own."

Jane turned back from a view of the security system. "Grounds are clear at the moment. Gate is closed. Dirk, can you keep an eye on this for us?"

Dirk nodded as he took control of the tablet.

Jane said, "You think Don Rogers has his 'copter running?"

Johnny nodded in response as he brought up a number on his phone, selecting 'Call'.

"Is this Cam? Is your father in?"

Johnny glanced at Jane. "We'll know in a moment. Putting him on speaker."

"*Johnny?*"

"Hey, Don. I have an emergency going here. Dontell Williams has three bullet holes in him. He's bleeding pretty bad. The cops and emergency people can't get here. We can't get out on the road. And we have an armed gang running wild over here that we're having to deal with. Is your chopper running? We could use a lift to get Dontell to Mercy Point."

"*Be right over.*"

"Land in back by the dock. We'll be waiting. And go lights-off as you're coming in. Don't wanna make you a target. Dock and property lights will be on. Should be easy to see us."

Johnny looked up as the call ended. "Let's move him down by the dock. Don will be here in ten minutes. Dirk, you see anyone coming in the front or over any walls, you let us know. Tres, come with me out to the garage. I have a few old army cots out there. We'll use one of those for a stretcher."

Johnny turned toward Mace. "How's he looking?"

Mace said, "Bleeding has slowed. I think we stopped enough that he'll make it. At least for a short while."

Jane stood over them. "Vanessa, first room down on the left, go in to the right and you'll find a closet with a belt rack on the wall. Grab three or four of the belts."

Jane turned toward the door. "I'll get a couple hand towels. We'll make some tourniquets before transporting him."

Jane worked to clean and secure his legs as Mace kept pressure on Dontell's shoulder wound. "Mr. Williams... we're gonna get you out of here."

The groggy officer asked with a half smile, "What was your name again?"

"Mace Hardy."

Dontell slowly nodded. "You take care of Jane and Johnny, Mr. Hardy. You won't find much better people in this world."

The officer grabbed Mace with his functioning hand as he grimaced in pain. "Oh, and if you catch up to those assholes, get my car back!"

Mace smiled and nodded as Johnny returned with the cot. Jane applied her tourniquets. Seconds later the four men of the group were hustling toward the dock, carrying Dontell on the makeshift stretcher. Several minutes passed before the sound of a helicopter engine and the wash of rotor blades could be heard coming across the water.

The illuminated green grass of the lawn whipped and swirled as the four-passenger helicopter landed. Cam Rogers, the teen son of Johnny's friend Don, emerged from the front passenger seat. The back door was pulled open as the teen waved them over. Dontell's stretcher was lifted and slipped into the back. The 'copter rose quickly, turning back over the calm night water of the inlet.

As the group turned back toward the house, a loud crunch, coming from the front of the property, was followed by the clang of metal mixed with the sound of shattering auto-glass.

Chapter 5

Jane yelled from the back of the house, "They crashed the gate!"

Mace was the first to run that way, with Johnny close behind.

Johnny veered toward the garage. "Dirk! Tres! Come get a vest!"

Mace met Jane at the door as she switched the tablet to the security displays. "I count thirteen. Plus one still in the car."

Mace replied, "Never would have expected anything like this. This is just complete madness."

"Yeah, well, we have this property lit up like a Christmas tree. Were probably asking for it."

When they entered the den, the inputs from eight cameras were showing on the big screen.

Jane said, "I'll be up on the roof with the tablet. Watch the front door. And what on Earth is Johnny doing out there?"

Mace replied, "He's getting vests for the others."

Jane pulled her phone, opening a line to Mace before attempting to three-way connect with her husband. "Come on, pick up."

Johnny answered: "We're on our way!"

Jane shook her head. "Send the other two back and make it quick. You stay with those weapons. We might need more ammo than what we have. Lock down that garage."

Johnny hesitated before taking a deep breath. "Will do. And, Jane, don't take unnecessary chances, you hear me?"

"Got it." Jane nodded. "Going up on the roof. And I have the tablet. Mace is covering the front door. Dirk and Tres will watch the back. Vanessa, take Donna and Dee upstairs!"

After hurrying up the steps, Jane sprinted across the flat rooftop, slowing to peer over the edge. "I'm in position."

Johnny said, "Dirk and Tres are in the house. I have the back door covered from here."

Jane replied, "I saw five heading to your side. If they get behind that garage, you're gonna have to button that place up!"

Johnny cut the lights on the front of the garage. "Got it. If boxed in, I can go out the back of the range."

Jane took careful aim.

Brrrff. Brrff.

"John, scratch two of those coming your way."

Seconds later a mass of gunfire could be heard. Three of the cameras went offline. A fourth camera now pointed up at the blackness of the night.

Jane yelled, "We just lost half our eyes!"

Mace took cover behind a short wooden bookcase stacked high with magazines. "I have a view of the front doors. Two shadows are lurking out there."

Johnny said, "Remember, triple pane tempered glass. Depending on what they shoot, it might take several rounds to penetrate."

Mace replied, "Looks like they're moving toward your side, Johnny."

Brrrff.

The sound of suppressed weapon fire came from the roof. "We have one more down. Leaves ten. Wait. Number eleven is getting out of the car."

Brrrff. Brrrff.

"This is my house asshole! He's down."

Gunfire could be heard coming from the back left of the house toward the garage.

Johnny rolled onto his back as the big door came down from above. "They just unloaded on me! Took a shot to the ribs. Garage is shut off."

Another barrage of gunfire could be heard.

Jane yelled, "I can't get a clean shot at anyone down there. The blasted oak is in the way!"

Johnny replied, "They're shooting from right under it. I'm heading into the range. Weapons rooms are locked down tight."

Mace called back to Tres. "Come up front and cover this door!"

Tres was soon squatted behind him with a case of spare magazines. "Tell me what you want."

"Anyone comes through that door without a safe-word, shoot 'em.

Mace spoke over the open phone connection. "Everyone, listen up. The safe-word is cowboy. I repeat cowboy. Say it back to me."

Johnny replied, "Cowboy."

Jane followed: "Cowboy."

Mace said, "Dirk?"

"Cowboy," was the reply.

Mace looked at Tres.

"OK, cowboy. I heard you."

"Never forget your safe-word. It applies to you too. If you're heading back to join Dirk, use it."

Tres nervously nodded. "I understand."

Mace stood, speaking into his phone: "I'm going around the left side. Jane, try not to take out any singles that you can't identify."

"Got it."

Mace slowly opened one of the giant oaken doors, peering out onto the brightly lit front drive. After several seconds of scanning for movement, he slipped outside, crouching as he moved toward the corner of the house. He dropped to the ground, crawling on his belly through a low row of shrubs. Two figures could be seen directly under the large oak that faced the garage.

Mace whispered. "Jane, I have two in front of me. If I spook them out and you have a shot, take it. Johnny, is that hump out in the yard your exit from the range?"

Johnny replied, "It is."

Mace said, "There's a—"

The phone disconnected. Signal strength dropped to zero. Communications had again been lost.

Mace took aim at one of the figures behind the tree.

Zzzt.

As the figure fell away from him, the second figure bolted around the tree. Gunshots could be heard coming from the back of the house.

Jane yelled down. "They're rushing the back door! I can't see. They're under the covered porch area! I'm heading down!"

Mace stood and sprinted to the tree. A single figure could be seen crouching near the side of the garage, under a carport where Jane could not have seen. Mace came around the tree in a rush, diving onto the ground as he moved within fifteen yards.

Zzzt. Zzzt. Zzzt.

The crouched attacker rolled backwards behind a stack of materials before exiting around the back of the garage. Mace pulled himself up and ran the five yards to the back corner of the house. As he popped his head around the corner for only a second, five loud shots rang out. Chips of rock splintered from the corner of the house where his head had been, spraying his face with shrapnel.

Brrrff. Brrrff.

Mace yelled up. "Jane? Was that you?"

No reply returned.

As he crouched by the wall, he could hear voices coming from the front of the house: "No. Andreas said around this side. Come on!"

Before Mace could react, two men were standing beside his dark silhouette, looking into the back yard. "What we got? We going in?"

Mace waved them forward.

Zzzzzt. Zzzzzzt.

The two men fell to the ground. As Mace celebrated his small victory with a smirk, a figure rounded the back of the garage into the open carport. From that position, Mace was crouched in the wide open. A rifle was raised to take aim. He expected the worst...

Johnny quietly called out. "Cowboy... Mace, over here."

Mace let out a deep breath. "Can you see the back door?"

"Not from here."

Mace moved up to the corner, sticking the barrel of his weapon around and squeezing off two bursts.

Zzzt. Zzzt.

A hail of gunfire returned, again spattering his face with tiny pieces of rock and sand from the corner of the house.

He shook his head as he spoke to himself. "You've got to stop doing that."

Johnny waved him over. "Over here! We'll go around back!"

"You go that way—see if you can cover the back door from that end! I'm heading back to the front."

Johnny held up a fist. "Got it."

Mace sprinted back toward the front, diving over the small hedge and rolling out on the stone of the portico. No slugs came his way.

He stood and hustled to the big oaken doors, opening one only a fraction. "Cowboy!"

The inside of the house was silent.

Mace whispered as to not draw attention from anyone hiding near his surroundings, "Tres? You in there?"

Tres replied, "Yes..."

"Why didn't you respond to the safe-word?"

"You didn't say I should respond."

Mace shook his head as he began to pull on the door handle. "I'm coming in. Try not to shoot me."

Mace stepped through the front door, pulling it closed behind him. The back of the house erupted in gunfire.

Mace's ears rang as three rounds from an unsuppressed AR-15 impacted the immense wooden door beside him.

As he dropped to the marble floor, Tres blurted out. "Sorry! Are you OK? Those shots freaked me out!"

"Thought you had a suppressor?"

"I just took the gun I was handed."

Mace yelled over the noise of the battle that was now underway at the back of the house, "Just keep watching that door! I'm going back!"

As Mace approached the den, the lights were off. "Cowboy, cowboy!"

Jane fired off two bursts toward the back door.

Brrrff. Brrrff.

"Dirk is down, but we have them pinned!"

"How many?"

Jane took a deep breath as Mace crouched beside her. "Four, maybe five. Tried to count muzzle flashes. They were just spraying everywhere randomly."

"If you return fire at any point, immediately move. They'll be targeting your muzzle flash. Fire and move, fire and move."

"Got it."

Mace glanced around the room. "How solid is that wall they're behind?"

Jane thought for a moment, before whispering. "Can't be certain, but probably ship-lap and plaster. Fifty-fifty whether or not you get good penetration, but by all means, if you think it might help, have at it."

A loud voice came from around the corner. "Might as well give up. I promise we'll let you live."

Mace shook his head in silence before whispering to Jane, "I just need a distraction to get over there."

The pitter-patter of little dog feet came up from behind him. The moment of silence was shattered by an ear-piercing series of barks from Derwood as he charged past Jane and Mace, heading for the intruders. Commotion and yelling, followed by gunfire, could be heard as the short-legged dog attacked.

Mace took a step back and dove across the open floor. Shots again erupted as the darkness was eclipsed by muzzle flashes.

"Gah! Get this dog off me!" was shouted by an intruder as Derwood tore into his forearm.

Mace rolled up behind a heavy leather couch, raising up, he unloaded waist-high on the wall shielding the attackers.

Zzzt. Zzzt. Zzzt. Zzzt.

Voices yelled as the last few gunshot rounds entered the den.

"They're running!" Jane yelled.

Mace sprinted from behind the couch, peppering the other side of the wall where the men had been. Two muzzle flashes sparked in the hallway beside the back door.

Again Mace cut loose, downing the last man as he exited.

Zzzt. Zzzt. Zzzt. Zzzt.

Derwood barked a continuous shrill warning. A new magazine was slapped in place. As Mace reached the still-open door, he dove behind the body of a dead attacker, landing hard on the pavement outside. With the adrenaline pumping through his veins, he didn't feel the skin scraping away from his exposed elbows.

Zzzt. Zzzt. Zzzt. Zzzt.

Two men fell by the back corner. As Mace took aim, scanning for a target, the low sound of boots scampering across the grass was all he could hear.

He lay frozen for several seconds. "Cowboy!"

Johnny came back. "We're clear back here. Those two are likely almost at the gate by now."

Mace stood as Johnny hustled up to him. "Dirk's hit. Don't know how bad."

After a quick scout of the back yard, they hurried into the house.

Mace grabbed Johnny, holding him in place as he stepped in the back door, yelling out, "Cowboy!"

Jane replied, "Cowboy. Come on!"

Johnny flipped on the lights before crouching beside Dirk. The valet was lying on his back on the floor.

Jane pulled back from the wound. "Passed through his thigh. Not much blood."

Johnny gently took Dirk by the shoulder. "Come on, let's get you up on the couch. Jane, get a couple of those pillows."

Tres stood in the hallway going toward the front, visibly shaking from what he had just been witness to. "Two men went out the gate."

Mace said, "You OK?"

Tres nodded. "Just a bit intense for me, that's all. We don't get much of this in the brewery business. You three are like superheroes or something."

Mace gestured toward the stairs. "Hardly that. Bring Vanessa and Donna back down if you would."

Jane placed several pillows behind Dirk. "Hold on, Tres. We might want to clean this mess up some. Little Dee doesn't need to see any of this."

Mace shook his head. "Sorry, you're right. Tres, just tell them we're all OK. And don't mention Dirk. She'll know when she sees him. No need to have to worry before then. Tell them we're just cleaning up."

Tres headed for the stairs.

Johnny turned his attention to his panting dog, rubbing the Dachshund's head. "I heard the Der-man teaching the bad guys a lesson."

Jane replied, "Your dog is insane. This whole night has been insane. The world has gone insane."

Mace said, "He attacked those men straight on. Not sure how he didn't get shot."

Johnny grinned as he squeezed his excited and wiggly companion. "You make your daddy proud."

Chapter 6

Johnny glared at his phone. "Mace, yours up? Mine lost signal in the middle of all that."

Mace pulled it from his pocket. "Nope. Says 'No Service'."

Johnny nodded. "You have a different carrier. Looks like they're all down."

Jane wrapped a cloth and a belt around Dirk's injured leg. "We should get him to a hospital when we can."

Johnny sat on the arm of the couch. "Without a phone I can't call Don. And I don't know that I feel safe driving out there."

Dirk replied, "Other than a numb pain, I'm OK. I can wait until dawn if you have anything that will take the edge off."

Jane asked, "Any allergies?"

Dirk shook his head. "No."

Johnny stood. "I'll get it."

As Johnny walked toward a cabinet in the kitchen, he continued to talk. "Had a tooth extracted last year. This will make you feel a bit loopy, but it will definitely take off the edge."

Johnny returned with a pill and a glass of water. The pain pill was downed and their attentions turned toward the dead assailants.

Jane said, "What do we do with this crap after we drag it out of the house?"

Johnny looked at Mace.

"We take 'em to the curb for trash collection. You have a wheelbarrow?"

Johnny replied, "Better. Drag these two out the back door. I'll meet you there."

As Mace pulled the second body from inside the house, he heard a small engine start up. Johnny emerged from the garage on a four-wheeler with a small trailer in tow.

"Load 'em up."

Mace hoisted the first body, dropping him onto the trailer with a thud and a clang. As the fifth carcass was stacked on top, Johnny started to pull away.

Mace yelled, "You need a hand offloading?"

Johnny looked over his shoulder. "Nope. Tilt trailer. They should slide right off."

The four wheeler screeched to a halt as Jane stepped in his way. "Take him with you. Those other two might still be out there."

Johnny nodded. "Good point. Mace, you heard the lady. Bring your party popper with you."

Ten minutes later the four-wheeler was stowed. They returned to the house. Jane had a bucket out, mopping blood from the floor.

Johnny cracked: "A woman's work is never done."

Jane stopped. "All the bodies moved?"

Mace nodded.

She gestured toward the stairs. "Might as well tell the others to come on down."

Johnny looked over the displays of his four still-functioning cameras. "I've got number two aimed right at the gate and the alert turned on. If anyone moves out there, we'll at least have a brief warning."

As Mace walked toward the stairs, he stopped and turned. "I have to say: the both of you sure were calm during that whole fight. Most of the men I fought alongside weren't as poised after their first few times out. Including me."

Jane frowned. "My insides are like spaghetti right now. Give me a little time to think about what just happened and I'm sure I'll be in a panic."

Johnny shook his head. "My hearts hammering at a thousand beats a minute."

Jane pushed the mop once and stopped. "Was it anything like this when you were overseas?"

Mace sighed. "Sometimes for weeks on end. When we finally had a day for rest, we went nuts with nothing to do. Take a soldier off the line, with all that adrenaline pumping, and put him in a box of a room with nothing to occupy his mind and he's likely to explode. I saw that a number of times."

Jane asked, "That why you got out of the service?"

Mace took a deep breath. "No. It's a long story though. I'll tell you later."

Mace stopped at the bottom of the stairs, yelling up: "Tres, you can bring 'em down if you want!"

Tres yelled back: "Cowboy! Be right there!"

Mace walked back into the den. "Any spare cameras we can remount?"

Johnny nodded. "I have a couple in the garage. We can do that if you don't mind holding a ladder."

Mace laughed. "You can stand on my shoulders if that's what it takes."

The two headed for the garage. "How're your bruises?"

Johnny flinched as he pulled back on his right shoulder. "The first two, I can feel 'em, but they aren't painful. That last one I took right in the ribs, though... hurts like all get-out."

"You did two tours, right? Never got hit?"

Mace laughed. "Hang on, I'll show you when we get in the garage."

The former Special Forces Ranger loosened the catches on his vest, pulled it over his head and laid it on a table before removing his shirt. "Shoulder was first. Passed through. A week off the line and I was itching to get back out there. These two were second. This one was another all the way through. His brother nicked my liver. Thirty-six days in a bed due to an infection."

Mace turned to show his back. "Graze of the right shoulder was next. Followed by this meat sticker just above the kidney."

Johnny pulled back. "Bayonet?"

Mace shook his head. "Kid with an assault knife. Probably seventeen or eighteen. Jammed it right between two back plates on my vest. I spun and caught him with my rifle butt before he could go too deep."

"Killing a kid. That's gotta be tough."

"He lived. Rest of my team dragged him out to the street and gave him a nasty beating, though. War ain't a pretty thing. Sometimes those who've been led down the wrong path have no problem with killing, thinking it's justified for whatever lame reason. We did everything we could to bring everyone out alive, but it didn't always work out that way."

Mace pointed to his left thigh. "Shrapnel from an RPG in here. They didn't get it all and I have a hard time going through the detector at the airport because of it. Another graze on this thigh. Took another round through the meat of the left calf. And last but not least, I'm missing the tip of a toe on this foot."

Johnny frowned. "What happened there?"

Mace chuckled. "Drunk at a card game. Stepped hard on a piece of broken bottle with my bare feet. Sliced it right off."

"They couldn't sew it back on?"

"Not after my bunkmate stomped on it trying to be funny. After that... well, we had a local dog for a pet. That little guy pounced on it and ran off. I'm sure he enjoyed the snack."

Johnny tried to contain his laughter. "A dog ate your toe?"

Mace nodded as he smirked. "I did get a purple heart for it."

Johnny crossed his arms. "Huh, didn't know you got a purple heart."

Mace sighed. "Five of 'em. The last two, and the toe, I told them to take back."

Johnny shook his head. "Now I know why you got out. You're defective. You're full of holes and missing parts."

Jane walked up behind them. "Man's got his shirt off. Should I go get some dollars? Or just leave you two alone?"

Johnny pointed at Mace's shoulder. "The man's been shot more than that lot we just dragged out to the street. Four holes, two grazes, shrapnel from an RPG, and a dog ate his toe."

Jane looked-on in amazement. "Seriously? You took all that while you were in?"

Mace nodded before pulling down his cheek to expose the lower left side of his jaw. "Lost a tooth in a fistfight. They put in a post and a new one."

Jane shook her head. "Wow. I guess I don't have to ask why you left now."

Mace pulled his shirt back over his head. "Wasn't that. I lost my best friend to an ambush. We thought we had cleared a house. Last two coming out into the street were maybe eight and ten."

"Kids?"

"Not sure where he got it, but the younger one had a 9mm hidden in a stuffed animal he was carrying. I should have checked it. They came out of one my rooms. Anyway, long story short, Thomas, my buddy, took a slug that should have been mine. I was due to re-up in two weeks. Decided it was time to come home."

"Can't blame yourself." Johnny put his hand on Mace's shoulder. "Wasn't your doing. I had a life-alterer too, but not anything near that level."

For the next few minutes Mace stood with his arms crossed, listening to Johnny as he gave a repeat of his college mishap while Jane watched for intruders from the garage door.

"Like I said, not to the same level..."

Jane said, "Why don't we get back inside... see if the TV has any news."

Mace pulled out his phone, stopping in the drive. "Signal's back up. I'll give 911 a call about what to expect when they come this way."

Jane and Johnny continued inside.

After a lengthy talk with a dispatcher, Mace was forwarded to a police captain. He explained their first encounter, the episode with Dontell, and the big shootout that followed. He finished by telling the captain about the stack of bodies at the end of the drive.

"So the two individuals that remained, they left?"

Mace replied, "Yes, sir. We're prepared if they decide to come back, but it's probably advisable that you send someone to collect the dead. If anyone else were to come across that stack... they might be a bit stressed by it."

The captain sighed. "They're dead, Mr. Hardy. They aren't going anywhere. And as far as anyone coming across them, well, let's just say we have bigger fish to fry right now. The looters have been out in force tonight. We're hearing gunfire all over town and without comms we don't know if it's good guys or bad guys. This whole town has gone nuts. Hospitals are filling up."

Mace finished the conversation. "I've taken enough of your time, Captain. We'll be here whenever you can get someone out. And thank you for all you guys are doing. You'll have our full support when you get here."

Mace walked into the Tretcher home and down the hall to Johnny's den. The view of the security cameras had been moved to the top right corner of the screen. A local newscaster filled the rest of the display.

"*The Virginia National Guard has been called up in Norfolk and over in Richmond. The known problem areas here in town are in Ghent and Estabrook. It seems the lawless have converged on Lafayette tonight.*"

A second newscaster joined in. "*That's right, Gina. We have reports of looting, home invasions, and buildings burning from Kensington to Estabrook. There have been at least two fatalities reported. If you are somehow watching from your home, be safe, lock the doors and stay inside. We have reports of gunfire coming from across the city. Please keep safe* tonight." The second newscaster turned. "*Gina, I understand we have word from Washington?*"

Gina faced the camera. "*That's right, Dave. We've been told to expect a news conference from Homeland Security at any moment. We'll be switching to that, live, when the feed becomes available.*"

Tres said, "I just got a text from my brother. He said the blackouts have spread throughout Pennsylvania. And now South Carolina and Florida and over to Louisiana have also been hit. He said their phone reception has been going in and out, getting worse. Probably won't have it for long."

Johnny sighed as he sat. "This is getting real ugly. We're supposed to be civilized during something like this."

Vanessa replied, "How could it get worse?"

Johnny shook his head. "We live in an 'everything now' society. What happens when our food stocks run out? Heck, Dirk said they're already making runs on the grocery stores, and we're just a couple days into this thing. If it goes on much longer, what do you think happens when people need to feed their families?"

Vanessa got a worried look. "I don't know. The government should be able to take care of that."

Mace nodded. "They will, but it'll take them a week to get any kind of supply lines up and running and order restored. After that, if it stays this widespread, I doubt they can feed everyone for more than a month. And if they lack communications too, we're all in trouble."

Tres said, "If this goes for a month, we're not in trouble... we're doomed."

Mace leaned back on the leather couch, crossing his arms. "I'm betting these two have some dry goods stashed around here somewhere."

Jane sat beside him with a wet cloth. "Let me clean up that face. Then I'm putting a patch on that graze."

Johnny replied to Mace, "We do. Enough to last Jane and me about five weeks. Divide that by seven with everyone here and it'll be gone in a week."

Mace returned a sarcastic look. "We can always stretch that out with your fishing every day. Am I right?"

Jane laughed.

Johnny shook his head. "I hope it doesn't come to that. I love sitting out there on the boat, but I never have had a lot of luck reeling much in. We'd probably do better just crabbing off the dock."

Tres said, "Looks like I lost connection to my brother. Anyone have anybody out west?"

Mace nodded. "My mother, but I haven't been able to connect."

Vanessa replied, "I have a sister in San Diego. I'll give her another try."

After dialing the number, Vanessa made a scrunched up face. "It went right to a busy signal. She has call waiting, it should still be ringing. She still has a house line. I'll try that."

Vanessa's expression turned to one of worry. "Same thing."

Donna pulled her phone from her purse. "I have family in Montana."

After dialing several numbers, Donna frowned. "They're all the same. Instant busy signal."

Tres said, "It could still just be us. Maybe our calls aren't getting out."

Vanessa propped her chin on the palm of her hand as her elbow rested on the arm of the couch. "I shoulda just stayed in San Diego."

Tres asked, "What brought you out here?"

"Navy boyfriend." Vanessa sighed. "An officer, but not much of a gentleman. He had a temper and I put up with it too long."

"He was violent?"

"And then some."

She pulled up the right side of her shirt, exposing several of her ribs. "This scar, he kicked me. Broke a rib and pushed it through the skin."

Johnny winced. "I don't understand that kind of mind."

Vanessa smirked. "It's not my first time around that block. Boyfriend before him gave me a bloody lip once, and a black eye another time. I used to think it must be me driving them to it."

"No cause for that." Johnny shook his head. "And I can tell you, I've seen nothing out of you that would elicit that kind of reaction from any real man."

"Yeah, I figured that out... eventually. Stepdad was an alcoholic and he and my mom would brawl all the time. She dished out as much as she took, though, so I grew up seeing it as normal. I've got it figured out now. And that boyfriend I came out here with... dishonorably discharged. That's when I came to my senses."

Vanessa looked over at Tres. "Don't be giving me those puppy-dog eyes. I'm fine. I've moved on."

Jane asked a question. "So, Mace, any girlfriends we don't know about?"

Mace shook his head slowly as he smiled. "Not at the moment. You have anyone in mind?"

Johnny leaned forward. "Hey now, you keep your hands off my wife."

Mace laughed. "I wouldn't dream of touching her... at least not while you're still alive."

Johnny returned a sarcastic scowl.

The banter continued for most of an hour before Jane showed Donna and little Dee to their room for the night. Johnny popped the top on a Mangrove Dark as he offered everyone else a drink. Mace declined, choosing to lean back on the couch with his eyes shut. His mind raced as memories from his time in the service played themselves out for the thousandth time.

Chapter 7

Mace awoke as the mammoth display in front of them switched to an image of a podium. A spokesman for the Department of Homeland Security stood behind it.

"Ladies and gentlemen, good evening. I am Deputy Director Paul Hodgekins of the DHS. I come to you this evening to provide what news we have available to us at this time. As you know, power has now been out in the Northeast corridor for over fifty-seven hours. We have crews coordinating across the region to get these outages resolved as soon as humanly possible.

"As many of you may have heard or experienced, our communication systems have been hit by waves of intense interference coming from space. At this time we believe this phenomenon to be natural and not the work of another nation. Moscow, Beijing, and Tehran are all experiencing similar outages. This is a worldwide event and as intelligent Humans we'll just have to work our way through it.

"The effect on communications has been a complete disruption of service, not only for mobile systems and over-the-air broadcasts, but landlines as well. Again, crews are working diligently to resolve these issues. We don't yet know the full cause of this sporadic but extremely heavy interference; however, we and the other nations of the world are cooperating on solutions. The fact that you are witnessing this broadcast is evidence of this cooperation.

"As to our military, they have been ordered to remain in place and prepare. With the current chaos that is dominating our citizenry, we are left vulnerable to our enemies. The President has ordered all troops and reserves to report, but to remain in place upon arrival pending further orders.

"We ask that all citizens, except for police, emergency workers, and our military personnel... please remain in your homes. Please make every effort to keep our streets clear for utility work and emergency vehicles as they are moved about as needed. For now through Wednesday of this next week, the President has ordered that all civilian government offices be closed, I would expect the same for local schools.

"I realize this briefing has been, well... brief, but know that we are doing everything in our power to resolve these issues. That is all I have for the moment. And I must apologize as there will be no questions answered at this time."

The briefing room erupted in chatter from the handful of reporters who had been present. The director turned and walked from the podium as a myriad of questions were hurled in his direction.

A stunned reporter turned to face the camera. "As you heard, we are experiencing a worldwide event. Authorities are coordinating, but it appears they don't know much as to its cause at this time. Please hold... OK, I'm getting reports that the west coast is now without power and widespread looting is underway in Los Angeles. This along with earlier reports of violence and lawlessness in Detroit, Chicago, Houston, and even on the Washington Mall in D.C. Please remain in your homes if at all possible. Allow our police and emergency workers to do their jobs. This is Tawna Binkley reporting, BHCN News."

Johnny shook his head. "This is a mess. I wouldn't expect the cops to be here tomorrow either. We may have to take Dirk to the hospital by boat."

Dirk said, "Mr. Tretcher, it hurts, but not so bad that I need immediate attention. If I don't move it, there's not much pain at all."

Tres looked over at the valet. "Wounds have a way of getting infected. Did you know more soldiers in the Civil War died from infections and disease than on the battlefield?"

Dirk nodded. "Those were overwhelmingly from disease and not infection."

Tres smiled. "Finally, someone who knows the Civil War."

Johnny thought for a moment. "Yeah, well, Dirk, we aren't taking any chances. We'll run you over after first light."

The remainder of the night was spent flipping from channel to channel looking for news reports while watching the grounds outside. Two broadcasts, coming from over the air, were all that could be found. Both were showing the footage coming from the DHS spokesman on a continuous loop.

Mace was troubled in thought at how quickly civilization, with all its marvelous technologies, was coming apart. He didn't move from the couch until dawn was beginning to brighten from just over the horizon.

With weapon in hand, Mace stood. "I'm walking the perimeter. Be back in ten."

"Not alone." Johnny said. "Tres, walk with the man."

Tres nodded as he stood, pulling two extra magazines from an ammo box before following Mace toward the door.

Tres joked, "I can't believe I gave up a night at the Dortmer for all this."

"Can't say I have a good feeling about our situation. Happened with no warning. The government didn't know, because there was no preparation on their end."

Tres checked the safety on his rifle. "When the power comes back on, I'll bet everyone goes right back to work."

Mace reached over to pat Tres on the shoulder. "Let's hope so."

As they walked, a huge explosion of light flared in the distance, followed seconds later by a shake of the ground and a rumbling.

Tres stopped. "What was that?"

Mace thought for a moment. "I would have to say that's one of the tanks from Craney Island. There's a big Naval fuel storage facility there. If so, give it a few minutes and we'll probably see more."

They walked toward the dock.

"Radio interference wouldn't cause something like that."

Mace shrugged. "Who knows. Might just be from the loss of power and then some backup system failed. Answers are the one thing we don't have right now, and I don't think we'll be getting any anytime soon."

"Why would you say that? We have some broadcasts back already."

"We've become dependent on power for just about everything we do. If this is happening globally, I don't think it will be over tomorrow. Most people can scrounge enough food in their homes to keep themselves fed for a week. After that, civilized behavior will be thrown out the window. Nothing more dangerous that a man intent on feeding his starving family."

Tres half laughed. "Aren't you the glorious rainbow of hope this morning."

Mace frowned. "Think about it. We get our water pressure from the millions of gallons being continuously pumped up into storage tanks. No power, no pumps. The longer the power is out, the lower the water pressure we'll have. And what do you think happens when we run out of water? That's probably worse than food in the near term."

Tres answered, "I don't know, I think we can be pretty resourceful if we need to be. We can boil it if needed."

"Some can, yes. And this group, we'll be survivors if someone else doesn't kill us first."

Mace stopped on the first planks of the dock where it adjoined the land. "I think the further away from the city you are, the better off you'll be. These people we dealt with tonight, they were just scumbags who picked the wrong people to rob."

"Glad I wasn't at the Dortmer."

Mace nodded. "Give this a week or two to fester and you'll start to see neighbors killing neighbors over food. If this was just local, not an issue. Help would be streaming in from around us. But put this everywhere like it is... no help will be coming. At least not at first. And without comms, it will take the military a while to get organized."

"Why would they hold the military back from helping us?"

Mace shrugged. "They must perceive a threat coming from somewhere. Maybe this interference. Who knows what they aren't telling us. If they even know themselves."

Tres walked back toward the house, shaking his head. "You don't have much faith in humanity, do you?"

Mace sighed as he followed. "I've seen what otherwise normal people are willing to do when they feel trapped and hungry. Not all of those were ideologues."

Tres stopped. "I gotta believe most people are good and will do the right thing. Not saying bad won't happen—it might. Just that, well, we're a smart species—we adapt, we overcome."

Tres again walked and laughed. "Now stop bringing me down, OK? I don't have the training you do, so I need the fluffy bunny, everything will be all right, stories."

"Let's check on the others."

As they walked, a second storage tank at Craney Island blew. A huge fireball rose into the sky beside the existing pillar of billowing black smoke. Seconds later, the shock could be felt and the rumble heard. The others were standing outside by the back door.

Johnny asked as Mace stopped beside him. "Those the Craney tanks?"

Mace nodded. "Yep. Can't say that's an encouraging sign."

Jane sighed. "I'm not liking this, one bit."

As they walked back into the house, Jane continued with the making of a pot of coffee and the baking of cinnamon rolls.

Tres pointed Mace at the kitchen. "See, civilization continues."

Jane winked.

Johnny flipped through the TV channels, looking for more news as he glanced at Mace. "You've been in a downhill spiral all night. You gonna be OK?"

"I think a part of me is just trying to reject the rush of violent activity we've had, that's all. It took me most of six years to get that edgy feeling out of my head. And here in one night it's all back. Not sure I want to go through the mental come-down again."

Johnny gestured toward the kitchen. "Not that it's anything the same for us, but Jane's running on all twelve cylinders this morning. Of course, we did just kill about twenty people. I can see where that would take its toll if you let it."

Mace said, "You're looking at the first combat reaction of most soldiers right there. It's not something you can turn off or put aside. You seem to have a similar reaction as to what I initially did. I was nervous, but calm."

Johnny thought for a moment, returning a chuckle. "Crapping my drawers over last night won't make me a better person."

"I'm the same way. Only thing I would add— from what I've seen and experienced, people like her tend to deal with these things better. Anxious at first, but once they settle they don't have issue with it again. At least not to the degree that others like me have."

Johnny smacked Mace on the back. "You are one of the calmest, most put-together people I know. What you're describing is just being human. We all have our moments, and everyone deals with their situation in their own way."

Mace half smiled. "Yeah, right."

"All you need is something to keep you busy. So, what say we go fire up the boat and take Dirk across the inlet to the hospital? The ride might do you good."

Mace sat back on the couch. "Take Tres. And Donna and Dee. She should be with her father. I'll keep watch here on the home front."

Johnny stood and joked as he pointed at Mace. "You just keep your hands off my wife. I'm watching you."

"You weigh almost three hundred pounds. I'd be an idiot. Anyway, while you're out, do some recon. Think about what might be of value to us in the near term if power stays out. Not saying to go looting, but if it comes down to it, we'll want to have a plan."

Johnny nodded. "Cool, calm, collected."

"Jane, make a few of those to go. We're taking Dirk over to Mercy Point."

Jane replied, "The hospital's four blocks in from the marina over there. You might want to take your yard wagon for Dirk. He shouldn't be walking on that leg."

"Good idea. I'll get it directly. Tres and I will be taking Donna and Dee with us."

"Why?" Jane stopped what she was doing. "They would be safer here."

Johnny agreed. "They would. But if we have to leave Dirk, I don't want to split them up. Dirk would want them there with him. If we come right back, we bring them back with us. And if they keep him for a day or two, we bring them all back together then."

Jane half frowned. "Just think it's an unnecessary risk, that's all."

Johnny pulled her close for a hug and a kiss. "They'll be fine. Be back before you know it."

The wagon was brought around and Dirk loaded before being pulled across the lawn. The sun was just beginning to peek through the trees. The boat's twin diesel engines powered up, breaking the silence of the ultra-quiet morning.

Mace remained on the couch, flipping through the endless list of channels before finding another broadcast.

A local reporter was speaking: "*Looting in downtown and the suburbs seems to have subsided now that the sun is rising. Police and fire units worked through the night to restore order. We have reports from the governor's office that the first National Guard units will be deploying later tomorrow. We have been unable to reach Mayor Danford or his office for comment.*"

A second reporter added, "*Word out of Washington has been slow. Very troubling given the current situation. Hold on...*"

A staffer handed the reporter a note. "*OK, two tanks at the Craney Island storage facility are in flames. We are told Navy firefighters are on the scene and further explosions may be* possible, but are not imminent. We have no reports of related deaths or injuries, or of the cause at this time. And, folks, we apologize to those who are watching. We are trying to do our best to stay on the air and deliver the news to you as we receive it. Until such time as we have grid power back, those of you who can hear us, please stay in your homes and be patient. This is a worldwide event and we all need to do our part to see ourselves through this in an orderly fashion."

Jane handed Mace a cup of coffee and a hot cinnamon roll. "Not the Sunday morning I was expecting."

Mace said, "You should go get some sleep. Could be a long day."

Jane smirked. "Sleep, yeah. Like I would be able to do that."

Jane held out her hand. It was trembling.

Mace nodded. "Not uncommon for a first timer. I did that for three days after my first encounter. Just know what you did was the right thing to do, and it was within your legal rights. All we did was defend ourselves and rid the world of a little of its filth."

Jane took a sip of her coffee. "It's a lot easier to watch on that big TV than it is to deal with in real life. There's no 'pause' or 'rewind' or shutting it off. It's there, it happened, and it will always have happened."

The newscaster on the screen perked up as a new note was handed to her. "This just in. As has been reported, interference from off-world has been designated as the source of our current problems. Reports are coming in that the interference may be subsiding, and, if that continues, power may be restored over the coming days. Scientists at a New Zealand observatory claim the Earth is passing through a massive wave of electro-magnetic signals, origin still unknown, and when we come out from the other side of this wave, things should return to normal."

Mace took a bite of a cinnamon roll. "As hard as it is to survive down here, we forget we live in a big hostile universe."

Jane said, "Let's just hope those scientists are right. I think tonight might be worse for some than last night was."

The Simpsons emerged from their room.

Jane gestured toward the couch as she got up. "Have a seat. I'll get you a cup of coffee and a roll."

The Simpsons nodded in thanks as they sat.

Greg asked. "Any new reports?"

Mace scowled. "Just one. But it didn't tell us anything we didn't already know. They don't know anything. The government can't decide what to do."

"The explosions, was that Craney?"

"Yep. Couple of the tanks are burning."

Greg took a deep breath as Jane returned. "We can't thank you enough for your kindness."

Jane smiled as she carefully handed over two steaming cups. "You've been good neighbors for the past ten years, quiet and good. Just glad we were able to stop them in time."

Molly, the Westie, hopped up on the couch seeking attention from the elderly couple. It was the first smiles the Simpsons had offered since the beginning of the night before.

Jane asked, "Greg, weren't you a surgeon?"

Greg shook his head. "Goodness no. Nothing so glamorous. Just research. And mostly on fecal matter."

Jane grimaced. "OK, I'd stick with the surgeon gig if anyone asks. Didn't realize there was that kind of money in fecal research."

"We had several patented test procedures that netted a substantial sum when we sold my company. Martha and I have lived in that house ever since."

Jane asked, "Any children?"

"No," said Martha. "We talked about it, and even tried for a short period, but neither of us had the time. We were too wrapped up in our company."

Jane smiled. "You worked together?"

Greg kissed his wife on the forehead. "She was my chief researcher. I can't imagine having been successful without her."

Jane grinned. "Now I feel guilty for never having invited you over."

Greg smiled. "We're just a couple homebodies anyway. Probably would have bored you to tears. Speaking of homebody, I think it's time we headed back to our house."

Mace said, "We left it the way it was. It won't be pleasant in there."

Martha replied, "Mr. Hardy, we worked with fecal matter for almost forty years. Having to work with it one more time won't hurt us."

Mace laughed as he turned toward Jane. "I like these people. That was funny."

Jane said, "I'll leave a note for Johnny. We should all go. We can help you with the cleanup."

The four of them turned to face Vanessa where she was sleeping in a large recliner chair with Derwood on her lap.

Jane stood. "I've never understood how some people are able to sleep whenever and wherever."

Greg replied, "That's one of the reasons we wish to go home. Didn't sleep any last night."

Vanessa was awakened and the group of five made their way to the Simpson house. Bodies were dragged out to the roadway and bloodstains mopped or otherwise cleaned up. Jane offered weapons to her neighbors. The Simpsons declined. As they left the property, the large iron gate at the end of the drive slid shut and locked. It was the last they would hear from the elderly couple.

Chapter 8

Three hours passed before Johnny and Tres returned in the boat. Another news broadcast brought more evidence of looting and home invasions. Also with it: reports of how unready every government entity had been when it came to dealing with the crisis. Initial emergency response relied on a minimum of communications. The world had little to none.

Jane, Mace, and Vanessa met Johnny at the dock.

Tres said, "Hospital was crowded like you wouldn't believe. They were understaffed when we arrived. A lot of the nurses and doctors are just beginning to show up. They put Dirk in a holding room and said it would be several hours before they would have a chance to look at his leg, but they started him on an antibiotic."

Johnny added, "We also stopped to check on Dontell while we were there. He was critical but stable. Lost a lot of blood. Doctor said those tourniquets definitely saved his life. Don Rogers and his son managed to find Dontell's wife. She's there at the hospital with him now."

Jane gave her husband a kiss. "Just glad to have you back. We took the Simpsons home. Cleaned up the mess. They locked themselves in."

Johnny frowned. "I wish we could have talked them into going to the hospital to get him checked out."

"Butterfly bandage on that little split on his forehead was easily holding. They should be fine. They know how to care for a wound. He can see his doctor for a checkup once things return to normal. See anything else of interest while you were out?"

Tres answered: "We talked to another cop at the hospital. There were apparently a number of gangs out like what we dealt with. They would hit a house with a dozen people, take what they wanted, and move to the next place. They left a big trail of destruction, too. At least twenty homes were burned to the ground. Three firemen were shot when they showed up with a pumper truck. What we did here... well, what you did here probably saved a dozen lives up and down this street."

Johnny added, "We passed two grocery stores over at Mercy that were in the final stages of being completely looted. I mean everything. People were even in the parking lot picking up or fighting over scraps of anything that was dropped or spilled."

Tres gestured toward the boat. "Anyone want to give me a hand?"

Mace asked, "What you got?"

Johnny said, "A rental truck followed us to the marina. A family was loading up a houseboat with supplies. They had extra they were willing to trade for a weapon and a few boxes of ammo."

Jane's face filled with concern. "You didn't!"

"It was a family with five kids. They had no protection."

"Do I want to know where they got the goods you traded for?"

"They claimed it was from a distribution warehouse they owned. Can't say whether or not that's true. The gun I traded is unregistered and they never saw us get on the boat, so I think we're OK."

Mace asked, "They say where they were headed?"

"Down the Elizabeth and out to Knotts Island. They have other family there and they said the residents have blocked the bridge. Getting out of town might not be a bad option if this continues."

Mace took a package of dry goods from Tres. "This boat, how far have you gone on it?"

Jane replied, "Bahamas, Bermuda, and up the coast to Maine. Sleeps ten, but six is about the most you would want aboard for more than a day."

Tres said, "You took this little boat to Bermuda? I mean, not that it's little, but that's a big ocean."

Johnny nodded. "She can handle it with good weather. She's forty-eight feet stem to stern. Twin diesels don't have a problem."

Jane added, "We did it once. I told him never again. We hit a short stint of fifteen foot rollers on the way back. That was not a pleasant journey."

Johnny said, "Knotts Island wouldn't be a bad choice. It's pretty isolated, unless you have a boat."

Tres handed up another box. "How about somewhere inland?"

"Where you have in mind?"

Tres thought for a moment. "I don't know. How about Organ Cave?"

"Where's that?"

"West Virginia. It's out in the sticks. Nobody to bother you there."

Johnny laughed. "A cave? Really? We aren't being bombarded."

"It has fresh water. It was a secret hideout for eleven hundred Confederate soldiers during the Civil War. They spent three winters in there. I'm just saying that it would be defensible, and isolated."

Johnny joked, "And where are we going to park the boat?"

Tres shook his head as he reached for the last box of goods. "No boats. What we need is an RV."

Johnny gestured, "Like the one behind the garage?"

Tres stood. "You have an RV?"

Johnny smiled as he pulled on the wagon. "Yep. When did we last take that out? Three months ago?"

Jane replied, "Just about. Ray serviced her last week. She was all set for the Gerrardstown shooting championship this month. In fact, a week from Wednesday we'd have been heading that way. Now, if we wanted somewhere to take refuge, that place would be about as well protected as you could get."

Johnny stopped on the drive in front of the garage. "Let's take a look since we're out here."

A fifty foot awning covered the long, sleek motorhome.

Tres said, "Oh, that is awesome. I so want to be you when I grow up."

Johnny clicked a button on his key-fob. "Welcome aboard *Gertrude*. I wanted to call it *Silver*, but I got overridden."

Mace laughed. "Fancy the Lone Ranger, do you?"

Johnny grinned.

Jane said, "He wanted *Silver*, but I told him since it was his he should have named it *Scout*."

Mace asked, "Why's that?"

Johnny returned a sarcastic look. "Because she's the Lone Ranger and I'm just Tonto the sidekick."

Jane pinched his cheek as she climbed the steps of the RV with a smirk. "As a gag at one of the competitions, I put Lone Ranger on my nametag."

Johnny cut in. "I must have had a dozen people point out that if she was the Lone Ranger, I must be Tonto."

Mace laughed. "That's not so bad, everybody liked Tonto."

Johnny sighed. "Problem with a name like that at these competitions is that it sticks. I've been Tonto for the last six or eight competitions. Nothing but a sidekick I am."

Jane waved her hand. "Oh, don't be so dramatic. You love the attention. And who's the one telling the Tonto jokes at every one of those meets?"

"OK, I concede. I have had some fun with it."

Tres asked, "Slide-outs?"

Johnny shook his head. "No slides. We're on the road with her more than camping out. Slides are great if you park for long periods. With just the two of us, they weren't necessary."

Johnny stepped up. "She's built like a tank, though. Quarter inch plate all the way around. The glass is bullet resistant. And I had her built with a hybrid diesel-electric chassis. A one-of-a-kind. We thought it would be cool to take to the shooting matches. Who else has an armored bus for an RV?"

Jane sat in the captain's chair, flipping a switch that powered up the cockpit-like displays surrounding her. "Johnny designed the electronics package. We have a nav system that automatically switches over from satellite GPS to ground-based radio tower identification. Although, I don't know that either would be working at the moment... hmm... and they aren't."

Johnny pointed. "We have a third system that uses gyros and accelerometers. You need a starting point. After that, it's good for about a half mile up to a thousand miles of travel. Last time we used her, eight hundred miles got us to within three hundred feet. I thought about putting together a system to market to others, but it cost a fortune, so the market would have been extremely small. Besides, I kind of like having bragging rights."

Johnny turned, walking back and opening a door. "Check this out."

After squeezing his big frame into a closet, he pressed a button inside and a hatch on top of the RV opened. The closet began to lift.

Jane shook her head. "He has his own armored shooting tower."

Mace laughed. "And what does he plan to shoot from up there, snipes?"

Jane shrugged as Johnny yelled back down. "Indians! If we get ambushed!"

Vanessa said, "You were right. Johnny is stuck in seventh grade."

Tres glanced back through the cabin. "What else you got?"

Jane pointed at the lower part of the windshield. "See that plate, it opens to four square inches. You can poke a gun barrel out through it nicely. You'll find one in the back and another on each side."

The shooting tower lowered back into the closet. "We have wheel covers as well. Cover down to about an inch off the roadway. You have to bolt them on, but it's relatively easy to do."

Tres looked around the interior of the coach. "This place is too plush to be armored. This had to set you back a fortune."

Johnny sighed. "We've been blessed in that department. My uncle's estate earns us more each year in investments than we spent on this rig."

Jane looked back at the group. "It's true. When we first saw the numbers in the will we were flat-out numb."

Johnny cut in. "Come back out here, let me show you something."

A door opened on the side of the RV. "Fresh water tank holds two hundred gallons. And with this hose I can filter up to fifty gallons a day from just about any source. I know it sounds gross, but we could filter our pee water to drinking standard with this setup. Not that we'd ever need to, but we could by flipping a couple levers."

Vanessa waved her hand. "No. Not drinking anyone's pee-water."

"All water is pee-water, Vanessa." Johnny laughed. "Just think about it. Where do you think all those fish go? It all gets filtered before we drink it."

Vanessa frowned. "Thanks for forever ruining water for me."

Johnny took three steps toward the back of the rig, opening a second bay. "This is the air-bay. It has a self cleaning HEPA filter and electronically switchable gas-mask filters. These six, with the air already in the cabin, would give us about eight hours of clean air. The cabin seals pretty tight. Positive air pressure does the rest."

Tres stood, shaking his head. "I really want one of these. Have you ever thought about adopting?"

Johnny laughed. "Tell you what, if I die before power comes back on... it's yours."

Tres turned toward Mace and Jane. "You two heard that, right?"

Johnny walked to the back of the rig where a thirty-foot trailer was parked. "In here we have the toys. Tres, go pull that wagon around. We might as well park some of those supplies right here in case we need to take off for some reason."

Mace pointed as the door slid up to the top. "Those gun cases?"

Johnny stepped into the trailer, scooching past a four-wheeler. "Yep. This is where we carry the weapons Jane will be shooting. We usually take sixteen and a couple thousand rounds of ammo in the boxes. We have as much ammo as we need inside too. I just like to keep some locked up out here as well. And I got tired of lugging it back and forth after matches... there is that."

Tres returned with the wagon. "This whole setup is crazy bad-ass. I can't believe I know someone who actually has a rig like this."

Johnny gestured with his fingers. "Start handing me those boxes."

After setting the first box in place, he turned. "This whole customization started as a gag. I was having a conversation with friends at one of the meets and someone brought up an article about an RV that had been armored and made into an all-wheel drive. I think it was the brainchild of some prepper. Anyway, our talking about it led to joking about what we would do to one given the budget... and here we are."

Mace handed Johnny the next box.

Johnny glanced back at Tres. "Guess how many rounds of ammo we have in the garage."

"Five... no... ten thousand?"

Jane smiled as she leaned in on the doorframe. "As of last Thursday we had close to seventy thousand. I know it sounds like a lot, but we can chew through a few thousand rounds at the range during a good practice session."

Tres nodded. "You could start your own war with that."

Johnny took a box and winked. "The trick is to have enough to finish a war. Anybody can start one."

Jane reached out, taking Vanessa by the shoulder. "Come on. We'll see what food we can scrape together for the men folk."

As the girls went inside, the guys stood by the RV, talking about the morning's events and what they might do should the power remain off. Johnny continued to tout the coastal areas as Tres pushed for the mountains. Mace was expected to be the deciding vote.

"I think they both have merit. On the coast you have isolation, except by boat, and you have fishing."

Johnny replied, "Johnny likes to fish."

Mace continued: "A cave, with water, would be defensible. Plenty of room to store supplies, and a year-round temperature that's tolerable. Not that I'm a fan of being underground, but unless your island is five hundred miles from anywhere else, I think I would take the cave."

Johnny threw his hands up. "Sure. Take the side of the kid."

A finger was pointed at Tres with the straightest face Johnny could muster. "I don't know how you swayed him, but if I ever find out, I'm gonna—"

Tres stepped back.

Mace laughed. "Relax. He's all wind and no sail."

"You take all the fun out of it sometimes, you know that?"

When the trailer and RV had been closed and locked, they followed Johnny to the house. A rich breakfast of eggs, bacon, sausage, grits, and biscuits with gravy was on the verge of completion. Stomachs were suddenly growling.

Chapter 9

As they ate, the chop from a rotor wash grew louder as Don Rogers approached in his helicopter. They met him on the lawn as he hopped out of the craft with his son beside him.

"Just came from the hospital. Dontell went into cardiac arrest about a half hour ago."

Johnny crossed his arms. "What? No. We just saw him earlier."

"They operated on his leg this morning. He lost too much blood."

"It's a hospital, they couldn't give him more?"

Don pursed his lips. "Hospital was overloaded all night and the blood bank didn't deliver any this morning. Yesterday, they had three pints of O-negative, a rare type. It was all used on someone else just before we brought him in.

"They put him on a saline drip thinking they would be OK until the shipment arrived. Word came that it wasn't coming. They decided to operate to try to stop the bleeding... he didn't make it. The entire blood stockpile was being re-routed to the Navy base for redistribution from there."

Mace said, "Wait, they're taking control of the blood supply after a few days without power? That doesn't sound good at all."

Johnny took a deep breath. "Sounds like some bonehead is jumping the gun."

Don continued, "Gets worse. They're calling up all reserves. Ordering them to report in to their posts. Word has it that anyone with prior service will be called next. I've been listening over the shortwave, which has been functioning on and off.

"Anyway, London, Frankfurt, Moscow, Beijing, they are all without power. Australia seems to be a partial holdout, but the interference is building there as we speak. I have a connection in DC who says they're gearing up for the long haul on this. He told me it would be wise to stockpile what I could."

Tres asked, "Any word from other places in the US? I have people near Traverse City."

Don sighed. "Wish I had word for you, son. There's just not a lot of people out there that know anything. Most of my shortwave friends have been stuck to their radios just listening."

Don asked, "What kind of preparations do you have? I know you and Jane are active in the shooting community. Of everyone I know, I suspected the two of you the most likely to be preppers."

Jane walked up. "Don, Cam, what's happening?"

Johnny stepped over for a hug. "Dontell passed this morning during surgery."

Jane comforted her man. "Oh no. What happened? I thought he was in good shape."

Johnny shook his head. "He was O-negative. They ran out of blood for him last night and the blood bank didn't deliver any this morning. They attempted to operate but he went into cardiac failure."

Jane sighed as she hugged him tightly. "I'm sorry."

Johnny released her as he wiped a tear from an eye. "That's not all. Mace, fill her in."

"Power is out the world over, and the folks in DC seem to be circling the wagons for the long haul. Don's been on the shortwave, and the news from around the globe is not good. I think we need to look at either loading this place up with supplies or getting out of town."

"If the decision is to leave, I'll volunteer my helicopter. It's just Cam and me. And with the way things are sounding, someone might be looking to confiscate my bird, so I'd like to make use of it while I can."

Johnny said, "Surprised its still airworthy."

"I've been having trouble, but the flight controls seem to all be working. Electronics are in and out though."

Jane asked, "You had breakfast?"

Don shook his head. "Coffee and toast this morning."

Cam added, "I haven't eaten since last night."

Jane waved them in. "Come on, we've got plenty. We can talk as we eat."

Mace said as they walked, "We were discussing where we might go if we leave. Down the coast, maybe Knotts Island, or inland to Organ Cave in West Virginia."

Don replied, "I've been to Organ. Rented a farm from a friend online who lives about fifteen miles from there. Nice guy, loaned us a car for a day. I took his kids for a ride in the helo around the area. I can make that on a single tank."

Johnny frowned as he bit into a biscuit. "Nothing on Knotts?"

Don shook his head. "Flown over it. It's an isolated area, but I couldn't say much else about it."

Tres pointed. "Three to one!"

Johnny took a deep breath. "You better watch yourself when you're sleeping, little man. Johnny's gonna come down hard."

Jane said, "Shut up and eat your biscuit. We'll talk about *where* once we've figured out *if*. We're only a few days into this. Any talk of leaving for anywhere is premature. Why is it men always have these end-of-the-world fantasies?"

Mace laughed, "Probably from watching too much Gilligan's Island as a kid."

The discussion circled around for several minutes as Vanessa looked on sheepishly.

Jane put her hand on her shoulder. "Hon, if anything is bothering you, please speak your mind. We're all equals at this table."

Vanessa took a sip of orange juice. "I just feel like I'm some kind of baggage, that's all. You people know guns. And you have a helicopter. What worth am I to this group and why would you keep me around? If you leave, am I invited?"

Jane replied, "First, we aren't going anywhere... yet. Second —"

Mace held up his hand. "I'll take this one. Look, you are an equal member of this group. At the moment you might not feel like you contribute much, but your time will come."

Vanessa half frowned. "My time? What would I have to offer?"

"If this continues, whether it's fighting off intruders, cooking, harvesting food, or washing laundry, everyone here will be pitching in. And I know you'll do your best at whatever that is. You always worked hard and took care of business at the bar. I have confidence you'd do the same with any other task."

Vanessa looked around the table as she offered a half smile. "Anyone need a waitress?"

Jane said, "You like animals, right?"

Vanessa took a breath. "Yes."

"Well... there, if we make it to a farm, you can be in charge of the animals."

"Great. The most I've done with animals is pet them. I had a cat once when I was a kid. It ran away."

Vanessa began to tear up as she laughed.

Tres reached over. "Hey, your position isn't any different than mine. All I've done is follow these three around for the few days day. What kind of contribution is that?"

"Yeah, but you're a guy."

Tres pointed at Jane. "She's a girl. And I'm pretty sure she can kick my ass at just about everything."

"So?"

"So just do the best you can. Nobody expects anything more. Besides, I don't want to be stuck with only talking to all these old people. I need someone near my age."

Vanessa replied as she dried a tear. "You're sweet. But I'm older than you think. And with way more miles."

"How old?"

"Twenty-nine."

"What month?"

"June."

Tres held up his fork, swirling it around. "Big whoop. So you've got me by three months."

Cam frowned as he looked around the table. "So I'm the only kid here?"

Don replied, "You've got plenty of time to make friends. World's not over yet."

Cam picked up a spoon full of grits. "Girls at my school are all snotty anyway. What's in West Virginia?"

Johnny laughed. "Cows and coal. And lot's of both."

Mace said, "So... who thinks we should stay here and fortify this place? We'd have to repair the gate, but it's a quiet, out of the way street. And the seven foot rock wall surrounding this place would be an asset. As well as being able to keep watch from the roof."

Don raised his hand. "Ordinarily I would say to stick it out here for at least a week. I'm not so sure about that given the government response I'm hearing. The longer we stay, the harder it will be to leave. Government might even close down the roadways if things start to get way out of hand."

Johnny asked, "You were just up. What do the roads look like right now?"

"There are some jam-ups on the Interstates, but I could steer you around them. If you want, we can go scout that out now. Highway 460 runs all the way to Lynchburg. We can cut over from there by going up to I-64 or down toward Roanoke and through the mountains. Cam's stepmother was from Lynchburg. He's got step-cousins there he's never met. And for those who are curious, she ran off with my ex-partner. They live in California. Cam's mom passed away just after he was born, in an accident. So it's just the two of us."

Jane shook her head. "Sorry to hear that, Don. I didn't know."

Jane turned a nasty eye toward Johnny.

Johnny shrugged. "Sorry, Dear. Just not a gossip."

Vanessa laughed. "Since when?"

Tres said. "I'm for leaving now for Organ Cave, but I'll admit to being biased. That would put me a lot closer to home than I am here."

Johnny went next. "I love this house... and this town. But I have to say I'm for leaving if there's a chance we'll be trapped here. If we go and things settle out, we can come back. If they shut the roads though, we're not stuck. We can always take the boat."

Mace glanced over at Vanessa.

"I'm just along for the ride. I don't have anything to add."

Jane said, "You get a vote just like everyone. And don't be afraid to voice it."

Vanessa cleared her throat. "OK... if it was up to me, I'd stay. I mean, we have stores here, there are people... not everyone is bad."

The discussion continued for a half hour before a vote was called for. The group decided they would stay unless something new came to light. They had supplies, at least for the near term.

The remainder of the day was spent fortifying the estate. The night brought with it sounds of more gunfire. The day that followed saw all communications and power remaining offline. After a fourth night of looting, fires and robberies, a morning flight was taken in the helicopter.

Don and Mace flew over parts of the city. "Those highways are jammed with abandoned cars. And every grocery store we've been over has been looted."

Don replied, "Retail stores too."

Mace sighed. "The National Guard haven't deployed. Something's not right."

Don said, "What strikes me is there's not another bird in the sky. I would have expected Blackhawks to be flying around for military comms at a minimum."

Mace nodded. "None of this makes sense. Where's our government? The locals can't handle something this big without help."

The engine of the helicopter sputtered for several seconds before recovering.

Mace asked, "That's the second time. Everything OK?"

Don shrugged. "Whatever that interference is has been messing with the systems. They're shielded, but apparently not fully."

"Might be time for a second vote. I don't like the lack of response I'm seeing down there."

The helicopter landed in the massive back yard of the Tretcher estate.

Mace delivered the news from their scouting mission. After a quick vote, it was decided to take the opportunity to leave. The topic again turned to *where*.

Johnny said, "We can take the boat, the RV, and the helicopter to Knotts. If we head inland, the boat gets abandoned."

Tres replied, "I have a Masters in mechanical engineering with an undergrad in agriculture. If we go inland and need to grow anything, I know how."

Johnny countered, "Knotts Island is farms. Anything you can grow at Organ you could grow on the island."

Tres nodded. "I could, but we don't even know if the residents would let us on there."

Johnny returned a grin. "We were invited. Remember?"

Jane held up her hand. "I vote inland. Knotts will be hot and humid in the summer and loaded with mosquitoes. And I love the mountains, and it's closer to Gerrardstown if we decide to head there."

Mace nodded. "Sorry, Johnny, I'd have to go with Organ as well. Knotts is a bit close to here."

The diesel engines of the boat could be heard starting up. Johnny raced from the house as the boat pulled away from the dock at full throttle. A silhouette could be seen standing at the deck controls.

Johnny stood at the dock as the others gathered around him. "Boat's gone."

Tres replied, "Kind of makes the island useless."

Johnny turned with a scowl. "Who'd you pay?"

Jane said, "Let's finish this. We're wasting time."

They returned to the house.

Still in protest, Johnny shook his head. "And what happens if we get to the cave and it's locked up? Or worse, someone else has taken refuge?"

Mace said, "It's out in the country. If need be, we would camp out and keep looking for somewhere to shelter. If we make it to Knotts Island, we may not be able to leave. And we have the RV."

Johnny rocked back in his chair with his arms crossed. "Well, now that we no longer have a boat, I suppose I won't oppose Organ Cave."

He pointed around the table. "But I reserve the right to say I told you so if it all goes wrong."

Cam stayed with Vanessa to clean up from the meal. The rest of the group wandered out to the garage for a planning session.

Johnny said, "We take every round of ammo we can carry. And our reload equipment. And vests and goggles. And all the guns we can carry as well."

Mace asked, "You have containers we can pack all that in?"

Jane waved her hand. "Over here. The ammo is mostly crated already, so that's done. I think we pick through the arsenal and take at least three weapons each."

The door to the gun room was opened. The hidden bookcase door followed. Weapons were selected and stacked on the table in the garage. Jane began the process of packing spares with the help of Don Rogers and Tres.

Mace stood looking at the Thompson hanging on the wall.

Johnny said, "She's heavy. We have plenty of rounds that she'll shoot. She won't do you wrong in close combat."

Mace replied, "I'd hate to see a good gun go to waste in this situation. How about this, we put it on a maybe list. We might be overloaded with what we want to carry as it is."

Johnny smiled. "What the heck. We'll make room. If anything, we might be able to trade it for something else we need. Guns are going to be like gold if this all goes the way it's looking."

Mace stopped for a moment. "You know, since my father passed, I've always had that feeling that I didn't have anyone to fall back on in hard times. I hate to think about it this way, but it's probably a blessing for him to not be here. Mom's with Brad out west. He's a good man and will take good care of her."

Johnny said, "You have a brother don't you?"

Mace half frowned. "He's in Phoenix last I knew. A bum. Haven't talked to him since just after I got out."

Johnny took a deep breath. "I'm right there with you. And so is Jane. She was adopted, you know, and her adoptive parents were old when we first met. Mine were too. Our parents passed only three years apart and each within six months of each other."

Mace said, "Didn't know you were adopted."

Johnny half laughed. "I wasn't. Jane was at birth. My parents passed when I was thirty-two. I suppose she and I may now be lucky in that respect. They won't have to endure whatever it is that's coming."

Mace replied, "Sounds like you've already written the world off."

"Let's hope I'm just a fool in that regard."

Mace pulled the Thompson from the rack. "Well, anyway, I'm glad you decided to come into the bar on a regular basis. Sure made those shifts go by a lot faster with someone there to talk to."

Johnny grinned as he picked up a crate with loads for the older weapon. "I kind of had to come in there. Jane was tired of my talking at home."

Jane poked her head into the gun room. "Let's get a move on. You two can play grab-ass later."

The weapons and ammo were evenly split between the RV and the trailer, with a small cache going to Don and Cam on the helicopter.

Johnny said, "We're on day four and the world has gone mad."

Mace shook his head. "I don't get the response from the government. There aren't any planes in the air and our military appears to be confined to base."

"Maybe they're under orders."

"An order like that would have to come from the top. Why would the people in D.C. order such? This is all of our lives... everyone's. And when I was up with Don we hardly saw a truck on the road. New supplies aren't coming anytime soon."

Johnny nodded. "That makes the decision to leave all the more important. Water pressure's already dropped by about half. People are gonna start coming out of their homes pretty soon. And if we look like we have power... they'll be coming over that wall. Leaving is a good thing."

With the protection items stowed, attention was turned to food.

Jane pulled the wagon toward the house. "I'll empty the pantry. You take everything we have in the storeroom."

Johnny nodded. "Will do."

Tres said, "Trailer or RV?"

Johnny replied, "We'll stack it behind the trailer and divvy it up from there."

Mace took a deep breath as he reached for the first of the Tretcher emergency stash. The neat stack of boxes was carried to the back of the trailer.

Chapter 10

Vanessa ran past Jane, yelling, "There's a cop car at the gate!"

Johnny replied, "Mace, come with me. Don, Tres, move everything in that room to the trailer. Pack it all the way in the back as tight as you can."

Mace followed Johnny out to the drive. He approached the cop with an AR-15 slung over his shoulder and his hands raised.

The officer drew his weapon. "Hold it right there."

Johnny replied, "I'm the homeowner. Johnny Tretcher."

The cop gestured toward the wrecked police cruiser. "What happened here?"

Johnny said, "That's Dontell Williams' car. He came to help us Saturday night when a gang was trying to overrun us."

The cop scowled. "Where is he now?"

Johnny sighed as he began to lower his arms. "He—"

The cop stood firm. "Keep those hands up!"

Johnny complied. "He came after we called for assistance. The gang roaming this street shot him up pretty good."

The officer said, "What gang?"

Mace pointed at the pile of bodies stacked behind a large shrub just outside the gate.

Johnny said, "We managed to get Dontell over to Mercy by helicopter three nights ago. He died shortly after because they ran out of his blood type."

The cop looked on in disbelief. "The lieutenant is dead?"

Johnny lowered his arms, to the cop's protest. "Look, we're on your side. That pile of bodies you're looking at is the crew that assaulted us. They shot Dontell. If you're looking for corroboration, go next door to the Simpsons. They were here when it happened. You'll find more bodies over there."

The cop lowered his weapon as Johnny walked toward him. "Dontell was my friend. We went to school together at Sister Mary."

Mace said, "You went to a high school named Sister Mary."

Johnny looked back and shook his head. "Save it."

"Anyway, Officer, you have any word of what's going on?"

The young cop laid his pistol on the roof of his cruiser, easily within his grasp. "It's chaos. Looters, rioters. Neighbors shooting each other. It's like the world went insane overnight. It's calmed down a bit this morning, but if last night is any indication, the calm won't last. Gets worse every time the sun sets."

The cop gestured at Johnny's rifle. "That an AR?"

Johnny nodded. "Yep."

The cop sighed as Johnny leaned on the hood of his car. "Does everyone have one of those? That's the third one I've seen this morning. Thank goodness it was the good people who had them."

"You want one?"

"What?"

"You want an AR-15? I can give you one, along with three or four mags."

The cop grew nervous. "Why would you do that? What do you want?"

Johnny pursed his lips. "I want nothing. I have a spare if you want it. If all this clears up, which I don't think it will anytime soon, you can bring it back to me. If not, use it to protect yourself and your family. What's your name?"

The cop glanced down at his name-tag. "Danforth. Harry Danforth."

"Well, Mr. Danforth. If you want an AR-15, I'd be happy to give you one."

Johnny gestured toward the dead bodies. "You run up against a gang like that tonight and you'll be wishing you had one."

Harry Danforth shrugged. "Sure, I guess. I mean, I'll take one if you're genuinely offering. Not supposed to, but rules are kind of out the window right now."

Johnny looked back at Mace. "Go get the man one of the ARs, and four—no five, full mags."

Mace nodded.

After a short run, and an explanation to Jane. Mace returned with an AR and a box with ten full magazines.

Johnny looked at the cache of readied ammo. "Ten?"

Mace replied, "Jane insisted."

Johnny handed the rifle to the young officer. "You ever fired one?"

"About a half dozen times with friends. I'm familiar."

Johnny carried the box of magazines around to the trunk. "No, you know what? I would keep these on your passenger floorboard."

"Sounds good to me. I can't believe you're doing this."

"There's a war coming, son. Nobody realizes it yet, but things are spiraling out of control a lot quicker than anyone wants. Our government is holding back the military from assisting, for whatever reason. Get yourself a stash of food while you're at it. And if things get too bad, I would make a run for one of the military bases around here and try to join up. You got a family?"

"Two brothers and my parents. They live halfway to Richmond."

Mace said, "If you get a chance to contact them, take it."

Harry looked at them both. "The two of you are scaring the crap out of me about now, you know that?"

"That fear will serve to keep you alive. Be suspicious, and only fully trust those who you already know."

Harry glanced over at the bodies. "You already call those in?"

Johnny nodded. "We did. I don't think they believed us, or else they were otherwise too busy."

"Busy is right. Everything is being done by word of mouth now. A patrol goes out with a second car no more than a block or two away. We do a check on whatever the captain orders and then return to the station. It's a complete mess."

"Meanwhile, the thugs rule the streets. Especially after dark. A quarter of our officers didn't come in last night. Stayed home to care for their families. Tonight will probably be worse. Bad thing is, we don't even know to go out to somewhere unless someone comes to tell us. If you're more that five or six blocks from the station, like out here, good luck."

The officer again looked over at the dead. "What should we do with them?"

Johnny laughed as he spat in the direction of the pile. "Let 'em rot. Them and the other stack of 'em next door. If things settle, send out the meat-wagon."

Harry looked at his watch. "Hey, guys, I have to report in. You going to be here if I come back by later?"

Johnny shook his head. "Hopefully not. Want to get out of town as soon as possible. How the roads looking?"

"Highways are clogged, mostly abandoned cars, but we're trying to clear them. If things go the way you think, everybody will be looking to leave."

Mace said, "We should get back to work."

Johnny reached out to shake the officer's hand. "Take care of yourself, Harry. And let the guys at the station know about Dontell. Tell them he went out with a fight."

The officer's radio crackled to life. "All units report your status. Repeat, all units report your status."

Harry smiled. "Best sound I've heard today. This is Danforth in 419. Position is quiet, but I have about twenty bodies stacked up along the roadway from the first night's home invasions. Perpetrators are all dead or gone. And I have news about Lieutenant Williams. He passed away at Mercy Point from gunshot wounds during this fight. His cruiser was used to crash the gate of a home out here."

The dispatcher replied, "Copy that. We have had confirmation on the lieutenant. Will be sending another car your way."

Harry replied, "Negative, dispatch. This location is secure. Better to send out the coroner and tell him to bring lots of bags."

The dispatcher was silent for a moment. Another voice came on the channel. "This is Sergeant Digsby. How many did you say?"

Harry took a deep breath. "At least twenty, sir. From their dress and markings, looks like the gang activity we've been briefed on. Only problem for them is they picked the wrong homeowners. There's no longer a threat here, Sergeant, but we do need someone out to clean up."

Digsby replied, "Stay put, get statements, Coroner is on the way. And I'm sending out Detective Michaels. Gonna be a busy week."

Jane walked down the drive. "Power is on, as well as at least a half dozen TV stations."

Johnny smiled. "Finally we have some good news."

Harry Danforth picked up the AR-15, box of magazines, and a clipboard, handing the first two off to Johnny. "Guess I won't be needing that, but I truly do appreciate the gesture. I was getting pretty worked up with what you were saying about the government."

Johnny replied, "If things go south and you find yourself back this way, the offer still stands."

"Thanks. You have somewhere we can sit? I'm sure this is going to take a while. And when the detective gets here, you'll have to run through it again."

Johnny laughed. "Come on, we'll get you something to drink while we're at it. Coffee, soda, water, a beer? You name it."

"Water will be fine."

Johnny and Jane sat across the table from Officer Harry Danforth. Mace sat at the table's end. They told the story of coming home, of hearing the gunshots at the Simpson home, of the rescuing of the Simpsons, and then the grand battle at the Tretcher estate. Johnny had to take a moment to collect himself when he talked of his friend Dontell. They finished up the tale with Lieutenant Williams being flown to the hospital and Dirk being driven by boat.

Johnny added, "Oh yeah, someone stole my boat this morning."

Harry pulled a form from his clipboard. "Start filling this out."

The detective knocked on the door. Tres brought him inside.

"I'm detective Brad Michaels. Quite the mess out there on the roadside."

Danforth replied, "I have an outline of the happenings, Detective. We can compare notes when we get back to the station. I'll be going next door to talk to the neighbors."

Brad Michaels nodded. "Thank you. You do good work, Danforth. Might make a good detective someday if you choose that path."

Danforth offered a panged smile.

The detective sat at the table. "So, let's start at the beginning and go from there."

The story was repeated in detail, the second time just as the first. When the detective got up to leave, the coroner was just arriving outside. They followed the detective to the end of the drive.

The coroner raised his hands. "What am I supposed to do with this? I can't put down that they all died in this pile!"

The detective laughed. "Just take your photos and load 'em up, Bobby. These people check out so far. Given the circumstances of the last few nights, I'd say they did our job for us."

The coroner looked at the wrecked cruiser. "That the lieutenant's car?"

The detective replied, "Yeah. He put up a fight here, and these people got him over to Mercy. He passed Saturday morning."

The coroner frowned. "I just came from collecting him for his wife. I liked the lieutenant. Good man. Terrible loss."

The detective patted the coroner on the back. "Follow me down to the next drive. We have another pile for you down there."

The coroner stopped to look at them. "What in the blazes went on here?"

Brad Michaels urged him to follow. "Come on, I'll fill you in."

The detective looked back. "And the lot of you aren't planning on going anywhere, are you?"

Johnny said, "Power's on. We'll be here."

Johnny frowned as they walked back toward the house. "Was almost hoping the power would stay off. Detectives will be questioning us for months. And if the media gets a hold of this... they'll be following us around for a year talking about those poor innocent gang members."

Mace glanced over his shoulder at the bullet-ridden, wrecked police cruiser. "Can't say I like the sound of that. Although, might make business at the bar pick up."

Johnny stopped just before reaching the house. "I've been wanting to ask you again since that first night at the Simpsons. How is it you stay so calm through all this?"

"You still seem to be taking it all pretty good."

Johnny took a deep breath as he looked back at the street. "Maybe on the outside, but inside my guts have been in a constant knot. Please tell me again that's something you get over?"

Mace laughed as he patted Johnny on the shoulder. "Unfortunately, you will, with the more it happens. I was a wreck inside my first week. After that, I was always at this elevated level. You spend less time thinking about what happened and more about what you would do come tomorrow."

"I guessing that sounds easier than it actually is."

Mace nodded. "Bad thing is, it all kind of builds up inside you and you let it out when you come back here. I've talked to a few old vets from prior wars. Every one of them to a man, said the same thing. When you get back, you just have to put it out of your mind and get on with your life. The longer you're here, the easier that gets."

Johnny continued toward the house. "So all this has you twisted up inside?"

"Strangely, no. I actually feel calm right now, like I was fully justified in all that and not just following someone's orders."

"I can see where that might make a difference."

"What do you say we plop ourselves in front of the TV for a couple hours, pop a couple brews, and then get some sleep before it gets dark again?"

Johnny took one final glance back at the gate. "If I pop a beer right now I'm liable to fall right to sleep. We need to get back out there and fix up that gate. At least do something to block off that entranceway."

Seconds later, they were seated in front of his mammoth TV.

Jane joined them. "Detective leave?"

Johnny replied, "Next door at the Simpsons, along with the officer and the coroner. I'm hoping they load up those bodies before that smell gets worse. Coroner said stuffing them under that bush and the cooler weather the last couple days has kept the smell down."

Jane winced.

They turned their attention to the reporter on-screen. "*...communications remain spotty, as do power outages. This word just in: the electromagnetic storms that are sweeping across the planet are not a near term health hazard. Here for further word on why is our science reporter, Dr. Jeffrey Moskowitz. Dr. Jeff?*"

Jeff Moskowitz nodded. "*Hi, folks. I'm coming to you from Pittsburgh today. I've been receiving a lot of personal questions about this in the past few weeks since these outages began. These electromagnetic waves, even though intense, are not a health threat. Yes, there are some possible questions about long term exposure, but we are talking years, not hours. It is safe to go outside. However, given the current situation,* please remain in your homes so emergency, fire, and police vehicles can get to where they need to be."

The doctor then turned toward the other reporter. "*Toby, we do have some other big science news today.*"

Toby replied, "*Go ahead, Doc. Please tell us.*"

"*As expected, a spokesperson for the Large Hadron Collider has released their findings, and those findings indeed verify the discovery of dark matter. This will fundamentally change the way we look at the universe from now on. Of course it won't affect you in your daily lives, but it may lead to new discoveries that could influence everything from how we travel, to how we communicate and interact with each other.*"

Toby cut in. "*So you're saying we might all be getting flying cars next year. Is that what you're saying?*"

Jeff Moskowitz shook his head. "*I know you've had your heart set on one, Toby, but they are not quite here yet.*"

Toby's smile turned to an expression of sincerity. "*Doc, I've heard others mention that this interference may somehow be because of the collider experiments. Any possible truth to that?*"

Jeff again shook his head. "*That is highly doubtful, Toby. These experiments are happening on a very small scale. We are talking smashing one stream of atomic particles into another. Without the extremely sensitive, and consequently highly expensive, instrumentation they use to monitor these events, you would never know they ever happened.*"

Toby jokingly replied as he waved around his hands: "*So no rift was opened into deep dark space, causing all this interference?*"

"*No rift, Toby. Sorry. That's something more for a science fiction movie.*"

Toby Hannock began to read from a newly handed piece of paper. "*Ah, this is what we've been waiting for. The Governor will be holding a press conference in a half hour, at 5PM. And all schools will remain closed this week, giving our officials time to get things opened and back on a regular schedule. Looks like an extended vacation for the kids.*"

Mace glanced over at his three hundred pound friend as his eyes struggled to stay open. Jane stood behind him with a smile on her face and a finger vertically crossing her lips. Mace nodded in response.

Jane whispered, "If you want to take the second room down the hall for some shuteye, I'll keep an eye on things out here. Everyone else has gone off to their rooms."

"What about Don and Cam?"

The engine of the helicopter could be heard as it spun to life.

"Heading home."

"The power may go back out at any moment. They coming back if it does?"

Jane quietly replied, "Yes."

Johnny began to lightly snore.

Mace shook his head. "He do that every night?"

"Sometimes like a diesel engine. I shove him, he rolls on his side and stops."

"Why don't you take him to your room for some sleep? I'll keep an eye out here for any news."

Jane tilted her head slightly to one side. "You sure?"

"You've already done so much. You need sleep too."

Jane let out a long sigh. "OK, but don't hesitate to wake us if it's important. If we have to get up and go, I want to be on top of it. Can you give me a hand getting him up? Once he goes down he usually stays down."

"Absolutely."

The Army Ranger helped Jane wake a groggy Johnny. After muscling him to his feet, Jane shuffled him off in the direction of their room. Mace walked to the fridge, popping the top on a soda before settling back in front of the TV. Ten minutes into his mission of keeping watch, his eyes closed and he drifted off. It was a deep, dreamless sleep.

Chapter 11

Mace was awakened several hours later by Derwood licking his arm. The dog was excited and in need of his attention. After a moment of thought, he recalled a treat was rationed whenever the dog returned from doing his business outside. His paws were wet from the evening dew that had settled on the lawn. Mace looked at his phone. It was approaching 11PM.

"Come on. Let's get you your reward."

As Mace dropped a small bone-shaped treat on the floor, he took note of the TV. The station was showing static. He picked up the controller, scanning for stations. None were active. He walked down the hall toward the bedrooms, stopping at Jane's and Johnny's door.

He knocked on the door lightly. "Johnny? You up? Jane?"

Seconds later the door lever turned and a drowsy Jane Tretcher stepped into the hall. "What is it? Has something happened?"

"How do I know if the power is out? No stations are broadcasting."

Jane shuffled her feet while walking to the couch as she attempted to wake herself up. Her hair was disheveled, which Mace had never seen on her before. She picked up the tablet controller. With several swipes, she brought up the screen showing the house monitoring system.

Jane sighed. "It's out. When did the channels go out? What time is it?"

Mace half smiled and half grimaced. "Not sure. Kind of dozed off myself."

Jane chuckled. "Not much a watchdog, are you?"

"Apparently not anymore. I used to be able to do forty-eight hours without sweating it."

Jane patted him on the shoulder as she turned to go back to her room. "We're not the spring chickens we once were."

"Going back to bed?"

"I wish. I was sleeping good. No, going to wake Johnny. You might go wake the others if you would. You can be the bringer of bad news."

Mace said in a normal voice, "Hey."

Jane stopped and turned.

He pointed. "I like the hair."

Jane rolled her eyes as she turned back to her room. Five minutes later, the group of five was standing in the kitchen, all mumbling.

Mace said to everyone, "We need to decide if we're leaving or not. Power is out again. It's late. This might be our best chance to get on the road."

As Jane poured a cup of coffee for Johnny, she said, "We're not sure exactly when power went out. We do know that it was sometime after four."

The comment was followed with a sarcastic "You're responsible" look aimed at Mace.

Johnny picked up the control tablet. "Hang on. We can check the status logs as to when the generators kicked in."

Several seconds passed. "We lost power at 8:13PM."

The prop wash from rotor blades could be heard in the distance.

Tres looked out the window. "That must be Mr. Rogers coming in."

"Well, I say we put it to a vote. We can always come back." Johnny said.

Mace replied, "Do we want to fix up the gate before we go?"

Johnny took a swig of his coffee. "Uh, that burns. I guess we never made it to that, huh?"

"I bet we could rig something up in half an hour or so. Might be worth the wait to know we have a safe place to come back to if we can't get out of town."

Tres asked, "You have a welder?"

Johnny nodded. "That garage has just about every tool known to man."

"Acetylene?"

Johnny nodded again.

"I can't promise it will be pretty, but I might be able to fix that gate. Can you bring the torch out to the end of the drive? I'll go have a look."

Mace followed Johnny toward the garage. "I'll bring it out. I have a Mig and a Tig too, but my generator that will run those is on the fritz at the moment. Been lazy about taking it to the shop."

Johnny turned back toward the door. "Jane, can you bring Don and Cam in? Maybe get some food going for everyone?"

Jane nodded. "Taken care of. Vanessa, want to give me a hand?"

"Yes. At least that's something I can do."

Mace followed Johnny from the garage, pulling the cart that held the acetylene equipment.

When they arrived at the gate, Tres was waiting. "If we can drag that car back, I can cut here, here and here. We'll need to straighten these bars. I can heat them down here if you pull from up there. As I said, it won't be pretty, and it certainly won't be as strong or secure as it was. But at least it won't be wide open."

Johnny nodded. "We'll take the SUV with us, and we can park my Jag right across front. Make it look like someone is here."

Mace laughed. "You don't think the Jag will draw them in? That's kind of like saying *Come get me*."

Tres sparked up the torch. "We could go back to the bar and get my rental. I need to get my clothes out of there anyway. Who cares if we leave that."

Johnny smiled. "I like this kid. Have I said that before?"

Mace replied, "I don't believe you have."

Johnny looked back down the drive. "I'll bring the SUV back with a come-along. We can get that cruiser out of the mix while he cuts."

Tres pointed. "You notice? The bodies are gone."

Johnny replied, "Just glad Mr. Michaels didn't come back for a visit."

Mace gestured down the road. "I know we can't pick up everyone we come across to take with us, but I hate leaving the Simpsons alone."

Johnny said, "Go ask 'em while I get the car moved. If they want to go, it'll be tight, but we'll make accommodations."

Mace walked down to the Simpson estate. The gate was locked and the body pile had been removed. He climbed up and over, jogging the fifty yards down the drive to the front door. His knocks received no response. He yelled out several times, identifying who he was. Nothing returned but silence. He circled the house, knocking on all the exterior doors. The Simpsons had gone.

As Mace jogged back up to Johnny's drive, Johnny was busy pulling the wrecked cruiser back from the gate. After an adjustment, the dead vehicle was pulled to the side.

Tres waved Mace over. "Pull on these bars as I heat them up. I'll tack that top piece back on when we're done."

The welding job took another twenty minutes.

Tres lifted his helmet and shut off the torch as Johnny pulled the gate shut. "Wow. Closed first try. Heckuva job you did there, Tres. I'd have been out here all night."

"Ready to get my car? I'm dying to get a shower and swap clothes."

Johnny raised Tres' arm. "You could use a little deodorant refresh there too."

Tres sniffed. "What? I don't smell at all."

Mace gestured toward the last location of the body pile.

Johnny chuckled. "OK, maybe that's from the scumbags."

Tres shook his head as he climbed into the passenger seat of the SUV. "Man's trying to tell me I smell like death and decay."

Mace half frowned. "That's a smell you never really get used to."

The ride to the bar was short and quiet.

As Tres got out of the SUV, Mace said, "When we go we should we bring the Jeep."

Johnny nodded as Tres opened the door to his rental. "Can't hurt to have a couple spare vehicles going with us. Would give those in the RV some extra room while we're on the move."

As they pulled back onto the roadway, Mace looked in both directions. "You notice we haven't seen any cars? I would have expected we would at least see a couple."

"I noticed. Just as happy to not see any. We don't want any trouble from the cops or the bangers tonight."

Upon arrival at the Tretcher estate, Jane was waiting outside with Vanessa. "You need to take this girl by her place for clothes. She won't fit into anything of mine. Too tall."

Vanessa shrugged. "Five-nine."

Mace replied, "You're across the bridge, right?"

"Just on the other side."

Mace gestured to Tres as he got out of his car. "Come with us. We're going on a run to get clothes for Vanessa and myself."

"Sure."

As Vanessa climbed into the Jeep, Mace said, "We hit your place first. We need to get in and get out. You're looking for practical stuff only. No little black dresses and no heels."

Vanessa scowled. "Hmm. I hadn't thought about that. Guess we aren't going dancing, are we. Not sure how much I'll be bringing."

Mace said, "Pretend you're going camping and there are no restaurants or night clubs anywhere around."

"You make it sound so appealing."

Mace pulled back onto the roadway. "If we're lucky it will be nothing but peace and quiet."

Tres said, "Too many people in the world for that. Let's just hope that anyone else out there is reasonable."

The bridge going across the river was mostly empty, as were the roads leading to it. Only the occasional car whizzed by in the other direction. As they turned on the street that fronted Vanessa's apartment complex, the interstate came into view. It was packed bumper to bumper with cars. The glow of red taillights illuminated the road in front of the Jeep.

Mace stopped. "Those your buildings up there?"

Vanessa nodded. "Yep."

Mace took a deep breath. "OK, hang on. We're taking the sidewalk."

The Jeep was pulled up over the curb and began down the side of the road. Two walkers yelled as they jumped out of the way. They hopped the curb back onto the entranceway of the apartments. Five cars sat in a line beside them, attempting to get out onto the road.

Tres asked, "Where they going?"

Mace replied, "Must have opened the highway up or something."

"Doesn't look very open."

Mace pulled to a stop in front of Vanessa's building. "Don't think we care. And we're all going in."

They climbed two flights of stairs before coming to her door. It was ajar.

Mace turned to Tres. "Watch my back."

Vanessa tried to look into her apartment over his shoulder. "Kitchen and living room here. Single bedroom and bath straight back."

Mace slowly pushed the door open, flipping on a flashlight as he went. The refrigerator was open in the kitchen. An empty stand stood where Vanessa's TV had once been. A quick check of the bathroom saw open drawers and an open medicine cabinet. Mace moved into the bedroom and checked the closet. Clothes were on the floor. Dresser drawers were pulled out.

He stepped back into the doorway. "Tres, stay right there. Vanessa, come in and get what you can."

Vanessa walked into her room. "Uh. Why do people have to do this?"

She turned and looked into the closet. "Nooo. My dresses! And my shoes!"

"Won't matter where we're going." Mace pulled an empty suitcase from the closet. "Here, fill this up. Got any plastic garbage bags?"

Vanessa pointed with a look of frustration. "Kitchen cupboard. Yellow box."

"Undergarments, socks, anything warm, T-shirts, sweats, shorts and jeans. Grab all you can. If we have to later, we can barter for whatever else we need."

Tres poked his head in the door. "Someone's coming!"

Mace said, "Keep packing. We'll handle this."

He stepped through the doorway onto the concrete landing as the individual topped the stairs. "Dudes, what's happening?"

Mace said, "We're just picking up a few things."

The guy squinted as Mace shone a flashlight in his eyes. "OK, not my business. You wouldn't have any good buzz, would you? To sell?"

Mace said, "Buzz?"

The guy crossed his arms. "Yeah, man. You know... weed."

Tres replied, "We got no weed or any other buzz, now piss off."

The guy turned toward the stairs with a scowl. "Don't have to be so harsh, man. Whole world has gone crazy."

Tres shook his head. "What a waste. Just like my cousin. World is crumbling and all he cares about is getting high."

"He won't last long if this continues."

Tres glanced back into the apartment. "She doing OK in there? Looks like a mess."

"It is. Why don't you go give her a hand so we can get out of here. I'll watch the door."

Tres walked into the room. "Tell me what you want and I'll stuff it in one of these bags."

Vanessa pointed. "Just start pulling everything from those drawers. Who was outside?"

"Some toad looking to score weed. We sent him on his way."

"Tall, thin, sandy-blonde hair and a goatee?"

"Sounds like him."

"Then we really need to get out of here. He runs with a group of five or six guys that are always up to no good."

Three pops from a handgun rang up from the parking lot. Mace dropped to the concrete deck.

A voice yelled up. "Throw down your guns and we'll let you leave!"

Mace replied, "Not a chance."

He crawled up to the railing. The flash from a muzzle could be seen coming from behind a car as two slugs impacted the building behind him.

Mace yelled down. "I'll give you one chance to clear out before I come down there to kill you."

"Big talk coming from someone lying on his belly!"

Several laughs could be heard.

Mace moved back and pulled himself up into a crouching stance against the outer wall of Vanessa's apartment. "There aren't any ambulances going to come pick you up, you know! Just the coroner!"

The hallway echoed as two more slugs hit the side of the building.

Mace moved back into the apartment, closing the door to Vanessa's room to block any light from the flashlight she was using. Tres poked his head out.

Mace said, "I got this. Just help her pack."

He pulled the door shut, making the living room pitch black, before moving up to the windows that overlooked the parking lot below. Peering from the two-inch opening at the bottom of the blinds, he located the shooter and his two friends crouching behind an SUV. With careful aim, he placed a 5.56mm round into the shooter's left upper arm. He dashed out onto the stairwell and sprayed the SUV with a half dozen additional rounds. The thugs yelled as they grabbed their downed friend, dragging him off to behind a building.

Mace walked back into the apartment. "You two about ready? I'd really like to leave before they get stupid and bold."

Vanessa looked around the room with a sigh. "I guess. They aren't still out there, are they?"

Mace picked up two bags of clothes. "They are, and we need to go now before they come back with more friends."

They hustled down the stairs, throwing the clothes into the back of the Jeep. As they sped down the parking lot, four pops from a handgun sounded. Tres turned, peppering the corner of the building where the shots had originated.

The Jeep turned the corner into the entranceway and then jumped the curb back onto the sidewalk. The line of cars attempting to get onto the freeway was growing longer. At the end of the line, they cut back onto the road and headed toward the bridge to cross the river. Mace's apartment was on the other side.

Tres said, "What is wrong with people?"

Mace replied, "Don't know, but if you find the answer, please tell me."

At the bridge, Mace pulled to a stop. "Crap. Cops are blocking it off."

"Well, they're on our side. They'll let us through."

Mace slowly shook his head as he put the Jeep in reverse, backing into a driveway. "We can't risk it. We'll have to go down to the next one."

Vanessa frowned. "Isn't that like three miles?"

"It is. Let's just hope they aren't doing the same there."

After a short drive, they turned onto a four lane road that crossed the river. It was open, with several cars moving in each direction. Fifteen minutes later they were rummaging through Mace's apartment.

Vanessa said, "Man, everything in here is stacked, folded and pressed. I should have had you handling my stuff."

"Ten years in the Army. They don't like sloppy. I guess their training works, because I can't stand to have things out of place now. I find it irritating."

Vanessa asked, "Tres, what about your place?"

"I'm kind of a neat freak too. I have everything in my room arranged in its exact position. My brothers used to come in and move one or two items almost every day because they knew it drove me crazy."

Vanessa laughed. "Great. Looks like I'm stuck with a couple compulsives. Just don't expect me to keep my space organized, wherever that ends up being."

The remainder of the run went without incident.

Jane turned to Vanessa as she dumped her bags. "Got the clothes you needed?"

"Some. My door had been kicked in and the place torn up. They took all my nice stuff, which it looks like I won't be needing anyway."

Tres said, "Mace got in a gun battle with some locals. Shot one. They scattered and we made a run for it."

Jane shook her head. "What is wrong with people?"

Tres laughed. "That's exactly what I said. We should be helping each other right now, not robbing each other."

The clothes were sorted through by Vanessa and Mace. They each took what they fully expected to use, with the rest being discarded in a pile. After stowing the selected clothes in the RV, they gathered in Johnny's den.

Mace asked, "Still no broadcasts?"

Johnny replied, "Not a peep from anywhere."

Don Rogers said, "I could have the ham up and running in about fifteen minutes."

Mace leaned back on the heavy leather couch. "It's already after 1AM. I'm thinking we wait until four-ish before leaving. Should see the least amount of activity out there about that time."

Johnny stood, "Don, I'll give you a hand. Come on. Maybe we'll hear something useful."

Cam followed after as they walked to the back door, heading for the helicopter and the ham radio gear.

Jane smiled. "I'm glad you all are with us. And I have confidence, if we can stick together, we'll get through this... wherever it leads us."

Mace crossed his arms in silent thought. "I*s she right? Can we get through this? Is this group strong enough to protect itself?*"

He reasoned they had the weapons... and the determination, so they would find out soon enough.

Chapter 12

They scanned for information on the ham radio for most of two hours. The handful of operators they talked with had nothing new to add. Power and comms were out the world over. No one knew if anyone had successfully overcome the electromagnetic interference that had shut the world down.

Twenty minutes after their last connection, Don spun the dials on the radio receiver. "Everyone is off. All static. Interference must have spread to these frequencies."

Jane turned to Johnny. "I can't believe we're thinking of leaving without Dirk, Donna, and Dee."

Johnny slowly shook his head. "I tried to convince him this was the better option. He insisted on staying. When released, they want to try to make it to her mother's house in Massachusetts."

"Might be time to get on the road." Mace stood.

Jane sighed. "I say we eat, and anyone who wants one, take a shower. This might be your last hot water. The water pressure is dropping again, by the way."

"Surprised you two don't have a water well."

Jane frowned. "Too close to the ocean. Saltwater intrusion knocked out the wells around here decades ago."

Vanessa said, "I had a shower a while ago. I'll help with the food."

Don raised a hand. "I could use a cleanup. Got a bit busy when the power went out again."

Johnny pointed. "Down the hall to the right. Third door. Bathroom inside there. Should have towels, shampoo and soap."

Don looked at his son.

"Nope, I'm good," said Cam.

Johnny laughed. "What is it about teenagers and baths? Don't know about the rest of you, but I love being clean."

Cam replied, "I took one yesterday afternoon."

Johnny nodded. "Suit yourself. Any chance you get to take one on the road will likely be cold."

Mace said, "The RV has a shower. No heater?"

Johnny replied, "No, it has hot water, just not a lot of it. Two really short showers and it's out. Only gets luke-warm if you aren't hooked to the grid. And I'd rather us not be using our water for showers if possible. Might be in short supply."

Tres asked, "How long will it take us to get over there?"

Johnny thought. "Just over three hundred miles by I-64, but we aren't going that way. Takes us past Richmond. We'll be taking Highway 460. It cuts across the middle of the state. On I-64 we're talking five to six hours. I would add a couple to that going 460, and a couple more given the circumstances. Good thing is, we can stop and set up camp just about anywhere if we need to. Don't have to make it there in a single day."

Food was prepared and eaten, the kitchen cleaned and dishes neatly put away. Don and Cam walked to the helicopter as the rest of the group piled into the cars and the RV. Jane and Vanessa, with Derwood and Molly, would pilot the RV while Johnny followed behind in his SUV. Mace would follow them in the Jeep, with Tres riding beside him.

The helicopter lifted off, returning ten minutes later. Cam jumped out and ran across the grass to the waiting RV. The roads were clear all the way to Bowers Hill, where a massive jam of cars sat at a standstill. They would stop at Sandy Pines to determine a strategy for getting around it.

The transit through Norfolk went smoothly. Mace continuously glanced over at I-264 as it paralleled their journey, hoping to see traffic on the move. His desires were not to be met.

As they drove along, Tres commented. "Less than a week and civilization has fallen into anarchy."

Mace replied, "Being out of power for a short time, we can handle. Without communications, all security is local. Anyone getting within shouting distance under these conditions is a threat."

"I should have taken my car and driven home when this all started."

"That's a long ride. Might not have been able to get fuel. With power out, all the stations are closed."

"Maybe. I'd have found a way to make it work though. I can siphon with the best of them."

"People will shoot you for less. Tell you what, when we get settled, we'll see if we can stock you up with a car and sufficient fuel. Might take you three days to get there on the back roads, but it should be doable."

Tres nodded. "Thanks. I'd appreciate that."

The caravan stopped near an open field in Sandy Pines. Don set the helicopter on the ground. Mace drove the Jeep into the field to meet him.

"The interchange up ahead is completely blocked. We won't be getting through there anytime soon. I do have an alternate route, although I don't know how doable it is with that RV."

"Give it to me."

Don pointed toward the other side of the road. "Railroad track behind that neighborhood. If you can get on it, we can sail right past that fiasco up ahead. Best shot at doing so is at the crossing back on Greenwood. Gonna be a bumpy ride. You think the chassis of that RV can handle it?"

"It's essentially a bus chassis. Made to be durable, but I'll have to run it past Johnny. He knows that thing a lot better than I do."

"Let me fly down the track for a few minutes. If it all looks clear I'll come back and hover over here. If not, I'll just land until we figure something out."

Don hustled back to the helicopter as Mace made his way over to the RV. Johnny was standing in the doorway talking to Jane.

"Bad news is it's jammed up with cars ahead. Johnny, if you want to go with me, we can scout for a way through, maybe across a median or using the other lanes or something.

"If we're completely blocked, Don thinks he has another way around. We head back to Greenwood and get on the rail tracks that run through the neighborhood over there. We'd have to stay on them for a couple miles. Would be slow going and bumpy, but clear. You think she could handle it?"

Johnny shrugged. "I suppose. She's as good a driver as I am."

Mace shook his head. "No, you idiot. Can the RV handle it? I have no doubt Jane can."

Johnny laughed. "OK, thought that was an odd thing to ask. It's a million mile chassis. I think it will do OK. If we get stuck, gonna leave a big mess if a train comes through."

"I doubt they're running anything on those tracks with communications being down. They'd have to stop at every crossing without the signals working. Trains don't like to stop."

Johnny hopped in the Jeep and they proceeded up the road to the interchange. Several people stood outside of their cars, pinned in by those in front and behind them, the traffic going in each direction was completely stalled. The lanes were filled with cars who had attempted to get around the snarl. A rental truck lay on its side with a crowd standing around it. Blue lights of several parked police cruisers were swirling, adding to the chaos.

Johnny shook his head. "Median is blocked up going both ways. And those cops wouldn't be too thrilled about us jumping the curb with that RV to push a car out of the way. Let's hope Don comes back with good news on the tracks."

Mace joked as he turned the Jeep around. "Should have had that RV jacked up and all-wheel drive added. Couple feet of clearance and some big mudders and we'd be in business."

Johnny nodded. "You know, had you suggested that at the time I was designing it, I would have seriously considered it. What a big redneck bus that would have made. Would've been a big hit at the shows though."

Mace replied, "Yeah, well, I can't think of everything for you."

"Too bad we didn't meet in high school. I think we'd have gotten along great."

"Maybe. Always wished I'd played football. Growing up I was by far the fastest kid on the block. Instead, I played soccer. I think as a team we averaged about two girlfriends and four parents in the stands every game."

"We were merciless to the soccer players back then."

"Yep. Our football players hated us back then as well. And I can't say there was much love coming from our side either. They had the nice stadium and all the gear while we played our games on their practice field. Was more mud than grass."

Johnny squinted one eye in thought. "It wasn't the American sport thing to do back then. In fact, we used to shove the soccer frosh out into the hall naked on a regular basis."

"Yep, those were good times. At my school, there was a ditch outside the locker room. It was a ritual for the football seniors to throw all the freshmen soccer players into the ditch. Of course, at the time they ate their own young as well. Anyway, there was always about a foot of water and muck in the ditch. And it was usually almost freezing out. And the freshmen were usually naked when it happened."

Johnny nodded. "Sounds familiar."

"When they came for me my freshman year, I ran past them and jumped in the ditch on my own. I think they were so stunned after that they just left me alone. We managed to get them back a couple weeks later with the old itching-powder-in-the-jock-strap gag. I tell you, I never laughed so hard in my life. They ran out on the practice field, and within ten minutes half of them were clawing at their crotches. You should have seen them trying to run back to the locker room. I could have watched that on video a thousand times over and never been sick of it."

"I had a bit of hazing when I got to college. Three of the offensive linemen decided they were going to hold me down and put their own heart shaped tattoo on my shoulder. I mean an actual tattoo! Come on!"

"What happened?"

Johnny gestured toward his right shoulder. They pinned me down and made it about halfway through before I broke loose."

"And?"

Johnny laughed. "Let's just say I got in a few good body punches before they scrambled out of there. They came up and apologized the next day. I let it slide and they respected me for it after that.

"You know, at that age you're a mix between indestructible and can't-do-any-wrong. They were just having fun. And it worked out. I talked Jane into getting a half heart tattoo on her shoulder so we matched. She of course didn't know the story about mine at the time."

Mace laughed. "How sweet. Have you told her?"

"Oh yeah. She was a little miffed at first, but we laughed it off later."

Johnny was quiet for a minute. "You know, after I sacked that guy and lost my edge, I often wondered what it would have been like to have gone pro. Then I would look at Jane and imagine what life would be like without her. There's no comparison looking back now, but man, at the time, I sure missed it."

Mace pulled to a stop beside the RV. As Johnny climbed out, he looked up at a returning Don Rogers. The helicopter was positioned toward Greenwood Drive.

Mace shut off the engine and walked to the RV door. "Jane, this is our current option. We go back to Greenwood and get on the train tracks there. We can ride those for about two miles. That will take us past the block-up. It will no doubt be a bumpy ride. And it might be tricky getting on or off the tracks. You up for it?"

Jane grinned. "Off-roading in an RV? Heck yeah!"

"Well don't be too enthusiastic about it. We get stuck and it puts a big dent in our plans."

"We'll figure it out. We sit here long enough and we're itching for trouble anyway. Lead the way."

Mace turned to Johnny. "You go first, I'll follow behind."

Johnny nodded as he headed to his SUV.

The ride back to Greenwood was short. After a wide, slow, sweeping turn, Jane steered the RV carefully onto the tracks. She came to a sudden stop.

Mace parked and walked back to the RV. "Too wide?"

Jane nodded. "Looks like it. Those ties look like eight-footers. This rig is right at that."

Mace took a deep breath as Johnny stepped in front to assess the situation. "Well, we could unhook the trailer. I can pull it with my car."

"That trailer is loaded down," Mace replied. "You have enough power?"

"Always get a V8! We take that trailer load off, she should be able to run with one wheel on the ties and the other off. If we take it slow, there shouldn't be much danger of rolling. And the clearance should be adequate. Hopefully anyway."

Mace looked up at Jane. "Still want to off-road?"

Jane pointed at the tracks up ahead. "Not getting out of town just sitting here. Let's move out."

"Give me a couple minutes to unhook the trailer."

Mace said, "Tell you what. Back this rig up and let's find a big parking lot where we can hook you up. I don't like fighting this in the road."

After a swap of the trailer, the end-run around the traffic congestion began. Johnny, pulling the trailer, went first. Jane eased onto the tracks as Mace checked for clearance. As he walked back to his Jeep, he didn't have the most confident of feelings. The vehicles easily handled the bumpy terrain, but at a slow pace.

Tres said, "Lean isn't too bad."

Mace replied, "She only has a couple inches clearance over that left rail."

"How's Johnny look with the trailer?"

"It just fits on those ties. If he manages to keep it there, he'll be in good shape. Don't think there's much in that trailer that can break, just the trailer itself."

After a slow start, the pace began to pick up. The two mile run would take less than a half hour, if all went well. Luck was not on their side. The RV came to a complete stop.

Mace ran up to an open door. "Problem?"

Jane pointed. "Rock is getting really low on this side. Look up under the front for me. Tell me what kind of clearance I still have."

Mace bent over, inspecting the situation. "Hmm. You have about an inch at the moment."

Jane said, "The next twenty yards that rock looks lower."

"What about this side? If you get this wheel back up on the ties, you might be better off leaning over this way."

"Hop on. I know you won't believe this, but this rig is all-wheel drive. Let's see if that's doable."

The hybrid drivetrain offered a torque advantage over standard. The front left tire edged slowly up onto the cross-ties as the right wheel moved off.

Mace laughed. "You're right. I don't believe it. Who has a big RV that's all-wheel drive?"

"We do. Now get back to the Jeep and let's keep moving."

Mace climbed back into his ride.

Tres asked, "Trouble?"

"No. Just had to make an adjustment. Gravel on the left was getting spotty."

They passed the first two neighborhood crossings without incident. As they approached the third, Johnny had come to a stop. Again Mace exited the Jeep, running forward along a rail before reaching the SUV. A pickup was blocking the tracks up ahead.

Johnny leaned out the window. "I don't like the looks of that."

"Wait here, I'll have a look."

"I'll get your back."

They walked the fifty yards toward the pickup. Johnny stopped at twenty-five. Mace stopped at ten.

Four young men were sitting in lawn chairs in the back of the tall four-wheel drive. One held a shotgun.

Mace said, with his hand on his weapon, "You fellas mind if we pass?"

One stood, throwing a beer bottle in his direction. "You want past, you pay a toll."

Mace replied, not wanting trouble, "How much is the toll?"

Another asked, "What you got?"

Johnny yelled from behind. "Fifty bucks if you move."

The shotgun barrel was aimed in Mace's direction.

Mace held up his hand. "We aren't looking for trouble. Just looking to leave town."

The first responder nodded his head. "You pay the toll and you are free to go."

Mace asked again, "How much is the toll?"

The man in charge scratched the back of his neck. "Well, seeing as how we have something you desperately want—to get past here—I'd say that gives us negotiating power. Tell you what, we'll take... a thousand dollars. I know rich folk like yourselves are carrying plenty of loot, so a thousand dollars... and that gun you're toting. And don't tell me you don't have it. I know that helicopter up there belongs to you as well."

Mace glanced back at Johnny and then back again at the men in the truck. "Let me talk to my friend. He's the banker between us."

The man in the truck held up his hand. "You hold right where you stand. You want to talk, he comes to you."

Johnny yelled out: "I have a better idea. How about we trade out a few dozen pieces of lead for passage?"

The man grinned. "Well, boys, looks like we got us some kind of smart-ass comedian wanting through. Maybe a little rock salt will persuade him to pay what we ask."

Jane was soon standing beside Johnny. "Hey, fellas. Was just listening in. I have an offer for you. Line up six empty bottles on the roadway there. I get five shots to break all six. If I fail to do so, you can have your way with me. But, for each one I hit, you each have to chug a beer. And we'll throw in that thousand dollars you want."

The man slowly shook his head. "Not workin' for me. I mean, in this spotlight you ain't half bad, but I'm not one to trust people I don't know. How about this: you come forward with the thousand dollars, we'll have our way with you, and then I'll even split a beer with you. And your friends can then go on by 'cuz I know if you have some of this you're gonna wanna stay."

The men in the truck laughed.

Jane sighed. "Mace, you might want to hit the deck."

Four quick pops from Jane's AR-15 saw four men dropped in the back of the pickup. Cries of pain could be heard coming from the truck. A single hand raised up in surrender.

Jane walked forward with purpose. "You there, with the hand up, get in the cab and move that truck off the tracks. Do that and I let you all live!"

The hand waved, followed by one of the men slowly standing. He hopped over the far side of the truck holding his bleeding shoulder, climbed into the cab, and moved the pickup off the tracks and into the neighborhood.

Jane stood at the crossing. "Mace, you take the SUV, bring it past. Johnny honey, bring up the RV. And tell Tres to bring the Jeep. When you're all safely past, I'll join you."

Mace shook his head as he looked at Johnny. "She's just little miss take charge now isn't she?"

"When it comes to taking action, or to using guns, I defer to her judgment."

The taillights of the pickup disappeared into the neighborhood as they brought the vehicles past the crossing. Jane returned to her position behind the wheel of the RV. They continued on their way.

As Mace climbed back into the Jeep, Tres asked, "What happened? I couldn't see."

Mace shook his head. "Jane just plugged four drunk rednecks is what happened. That woman is starting to scare me."

The next stop, the planned exit, was where Highway 460 intersected Highway 13. When they arrived, Johnny snaked the SUV and trailer through the cars that partially blocked the path. Jane stopped, not having the room to maneuver through to exit the railway.

Mace walked up to an open RV door as Johnny waited just down the road. "What's the plan?"

Jane said, "This barge won't fit through that hole."

"Those two cars don't have drivers."

"Neither do the ones in front of them. Probably all up gawking at that rental truck on its side."

"Can you make room?"

"You mean push them?"

Mace nodded.

Jane grinned. "Get back in the Jeep. I might need to back up after. And we'll want to be right out of here when I'm done."

Mace hustled back, climbing up inside and closing the door.

Tres asked, "What's the holdup?"

Mace half laughed. "Watch and see."

The big RV rolled forward slowly, gently bumping the side of the first car. Again the torque of the hybrid drivetrain was put to work. The two abandoned vehicles were pushed off the side of the road as others watched from their cars. Jane backed up briefly, turning onto the roadway and proceeding out to where Johnny was stopped. As Mace and Tres passed by, two passengers from the car immediately following stood in cheer. Past the interchange, the highway was clear.

Chapter 13

Halfway to Windsor they pulled to the side of the highway, once again hooking the trailer to the RV. The ride to and past Windsor was peaceful, but soon the pleasant journey came to an abrupt end.

Don Rogers set his helicopter down in the road in front of them. Cam jumped out, running back to give status. The roadway, just over a mile ahead, was blocked.

Mace stood next to Johnny at the open door to the RV. "This state is just crawling with road agents."

Johnny gave him a curious look. "What the heck's a road agent?"

Mace placed his hand on Johnny's shoulder. "You grow up not watching a single western?"

Johnny shook his head. "No."

Mace laughed. "A road agent is what they used to call highway robbers back in the Old West. Go to Boot Hill Cemetery in Montana and you'll see the graves of six of them they hung in a single day."

Johnny looked up at Jane. "Road agent? Who named them that?"

"Wasn't there," Jane replied. "Couldn't say."

Mace glanced down the road. "Was hoping this drive would be peaceful."

"All the more reason for us to keep moving."

Mace turned to Cam. "How many would you say are up there?"

"At least a dozen cars and trucks blocking both sides of the highway. And two of them are sheriff's cars. Dad thought it was just a checkpoint of some kind until they pulled somebody from a car and started beating them. From what I could see, the guy had his wife and kids with him. They made them get out and then popped the trunk. Emptied everything from there and the back seat, shoved them back in the car and sent them on their way."

Mace scanned a Virginia map. "If we go back to 616, can we work our way past them on 617?"

Cam frowned. "Nope. They are parked all over that intersection at 617."

Johnny asked, "Any suggestions?"

Mace thought for a moment. "I'm probably sticking my head in the lion's mouth with this one, but let me go up and talk to them. If I'm not back in fifteen minutes, you know something is wrong."

"Doesn't sound like much of a plan."

Jane said, "How about this? If they shake you down, tell them an RV is stranded just down the road. If they send out cars to take advantage of us, we take them down and then use them as hostages to get you back and to get safe passage. These are probably townsfolk that all know each other. They would be willing to trade."

Johnny shook his head. "Can't say I really like that as a plan either."

Mace glanced back up the road. "We need to keep moving. I'm up for the possible trade if you two think you can handle it."

"We got our end. You just keep yourself alive."

Johnny said, "You left out one important part."

"What's that?"

"What if they let you through? How do we follow?"

Jane said, "Cam, did you see us push the cars back there out of the road?"

Cam smiled. "I did. We were wondering what you were going to do."

"You think I could push them out of the way if we roll through there slowly?"

"You'd only have to push one. They're kind of lined up crossways. One of them is a little red clown car. I know you could move that one."

Jane sat back in the captain's chair. "Well, Johnny? We could push our way through if needed."

Johnny frowned. "That's all good when you're riding in a hardened RV. That SUV doesn't offer much protection."

Cam said, "If you pull off just before you get to them, you could cut through a yard or two and a parking lot. You have four-wheel drive?"

"I do."

Mace said, "You follow Jane and peel off if she goes in for the push. They might be distracted enough to not bother taking a shot at you."

Johnny chuckled, "You people are dead set on confronting everything head on, aren't you?"

Jane replied, "We are... and we will. Let's get this cat show on the road. Day's not getting any younger."

Mace handed her his rifle. "I'll go in with the .40. No sense in giving up a good weapon if they decide they wanna take it."

Jane held up her hand. "Hold on. Vanessa, let's see that peashooter I gave you."

Jane handed over the .32 caliber pistol as she wiggled her fingers for the forty. "If they want one that bad, they can keep the .32."

Tres boarded the RV with several boxes of supplies from the Jeep. Mace pulled back onto the highway, following a pickup. When they arrived at the intersection, he stopped thirty yards back.

The truck was inspected and allowed to pass through. The sheriff, standing along with five others, waved Mace forward. He glanced up at Don Rogers and his son as they hovered several thousand feet above, wishing he had a similar vessel.

"What's going on, Officer?"

"I'm not an officer, I'm the sheriff."

He looked around the inside of the Jeep. "Can you step out of the vehicle for me."

It was an order and not a question. Mace complied.

"That weapon on your seat loaded?"

"Yes, sir. I've already been robbed once since this all started. Just want to protect myself."

The sheriff looked at Mace with a suspicious eye as two of his deputized escorts climbed into the Jeep. "Just where is it you are headed? And where are you coming from?"

"Just came from Norfolk, sir. Heading over to Charlottesville."

The sheriff put his hand up on the open door of the Jeep. "Why didn't you take I-64?"

"Interstates around Norfolk are all blocked. I figured Richmond wouldn't be any better. If you don't mind my asking, has something happened out here that you're stopping everyone?"

"Looters. Already confiscated contraband from sixteen cars this morning."

"Why is it the dregs come out when people are most in need?"

The sheriff gestured toward Mace's front plate. "You a vet?"

"Ranger, sir. Two tours in the Middle East."

The sheriff reached up, placing his hand on Mace's shoulder. "Thanks for your service, son. I was in for twenty-two years. Navy. Never saw action though."

"Consider yourself lucky, Sheriff. It's been six years and I still have nightmares. Wish it was avoidable, but I guess there's dregs the world over."

The sheriff spat and then scowled. "You got that right. Danny! Put the man's gun back. And, Bobby, let the man through."

Mace hesitated before getting back into the Jeep. "Sheriff? I have a favor to ask of you."

The sheriff put his hands on his hips. "Go ahead."

Mace gestured back down the road. "I have two more vehicles with me. We're just looking to get away from the bad guys. No contraband. Everything is ours."

The sheriff tilted his head in suspicion. "You say that with a look of apprehension."

Mace replied, "Well, we have supplies with us. A lot of supplies... and weapons. We're planning for the long haul and hoping for the best. We just want to pass through. Not looking for trouble or to make trouble for anyone."

The sheriff raised his chin in thought as he looked Mace up and down. "You've been honest and straightforward with me, Mr...?"

"Hardy. Mace Hardy."

"You bring your people up. If they look legit, I'll let them through. We aren't looking to rob anyone."

Mace offered a half smile. "Thanks, Sheriff. Glad to see that someone is still willing to take charge and do what's right. And just so you know, I think what you're doing here is exactly that."

The sheriff pointed to the back of a pickup stacked with boxes. "Just had a guy come through twenty minutes ago with sixteen cases of expensive liquor. Had the gall to steal it with his wife and kid in the car. Tried to claim it belonged to him. I knew better. We've had run-ins with him before. Anyway, bring your people up, Mr. Hardy. I'll wave you past."

Mace climbed back into the Jeep, turned and headed back.

Jane was waiting with the door open. "Saw Don coming back this way. We were just getting ready to move."

Mace said, "Just follow me through. Go slow. I think the sheriff is OK. Says he's looking for looters. The people he had with him looked like regular townsfolk. Just smile and wave as you go through."

"So, no stopping?"

Mace shook his head. "He said he'd let us pass."

The small caravan rolled up to the roadblock at a slow click. The sheriff waved them to come through.

As the RV rolled up beside him, the sheriff yelled out, "Ho! Stop right there!"

Mace glanced over at the .32 sitting on his seat, deciding to let it sit where it was. He opened the door, hopped out and walked back toward the sheriff as he gestured for Jane to open her window.

Jane leaned out on her arm. "Something wrong?"

The sheriff pointed. "You Jane Tretcher?"

Jane returned a confused look. "Yes."

The sheriff turned back to one of his townies. "Bobby, come here!"

A chubby looking farmhand wearing coveralls waddled over.

The sheriff pointed again. "That's her! The one I was telling you about from last year!"

The sheriff continued his grin. "I'm sorry, Mrs. Tretcher. It's just I never forget a face. I saw you shoot at two events last year. Recognized you because of the RV. This the armored one?"

Jane nodded. "That it is, Sheriff. Want to come aboard for a look?"

The sheriff high-stepped around to the door as Jane opened it. "Come on up. Have a look."

The sheriff topped the stairs. "Aw, now this is living."

Jane waved Johnny up the stairs. "Show them the tower."

"Excuse me, gentlemen, I need into that closet."

Seconds later, a hatch on the roof opened and a smiling Johnny Tretcher lifted up into the air in a basket.

The sheriff shook his head. "Ain't that somethin'."

When the closet had again settled to the floor, Johnny took the sheriff out for a look at the bays. "We can filter just about any water, fifty gallons a day. And over here, air filters, good for up to eight hours. Will keep out tear-gas and such. Actual smoke will cut way back on that eight, but it will give us options."

Johnny pulled a battery-powered ratchet from a holder, setting it on the ground beside a rear wheel. Returning to the air-bay, he pulled a round steel plate that was folded in half with a hinge. The plate was flipped open and hoisted into place beside the rear tire. The ratchet was used along with four custom bolts to attach the plate to the wheel hub.

The sheriff shook his head. "Would you look at that! You expecting a shootout?"

"I hope not, but it never hurts to be prepared."

As Johnny attached the plates covering the remaining wheels, the sheriff walked back to the RV door. "Mrs. Tretcher, thank you and your husband for the tour. Sorry to have taken up so much of your time."

"Not a problem, Sheriff. And watch out for yourself. We've already had some nasty brawls with some very bad people. If this power outage persists, they'll eventually be coming this way."

The sheriff smiled. "I appreciate the warning, Mrs. Tretcher. We're a pretty close group here, we'll be OK."

Mace waved to the sheriff as he climbed back into the Jeep. Tres joined him.

"Wish I could tell them more about what's possibly out there. Seem like good people."

Tres said, "We could always invite them to come along."

"Fat chance of that. This is their home. They'll be staying here and fighting for Wakefield."

As they passed through the town, Mace took note of the townsfolk who were out and about like it was a normal day. The stores were closed, but kids were riding bikes and the occasional car or pickup moved about, no doubt taking care of the day's business.

After Wakefield, they passed through Waverly and Disputanta. Both were small towns and both seemed at peace. As they approached Petersburg, Don Rogers again stopped their progress.

Cam came up to the Jeep. "To get through Petersburg you have to cross under I-95 and I-85. Both are jammed with cars in and around the interchanges. Dad thinks you should go south down Highway 156 and work your way back around and up to Sutherland. You can pass under both interstates without going through interchanges."

The roads on the Petersburg detour were narrow but passable. An hour was added to the journey west. It went by without incident. Once back on Highway 460, the ride to Burkeville saw little traffic. The locals, on their farms, were staying home.

Chapter 14

The caravan stopped along the roadway for a break and lunch. Don landed the helicopter in a nearby field, joining them in the crowded RV.

Jane pulled sandwiches from the refrigerator. "We have roast beef, ham and bologna. Who wants what?"

The sandwiches were handed out as Vanessa opened a large bag of chips. "Hope y'all enjoy these."

Tres asked, "Why?"

"Because they aren't making them anymore. Didn't you get the memo?"

"I guess that goes for just about everything. Food, clothes, toilet paper... I don't know that I like the sound of that last one."

Johnny nodded. "We're about to find out what roughing it really means. We have the luxury of this motorhome right now, but it will eventually need parts just like everything else. And those parts will be hard to come by."

Don said, "That's assuming that power stays out. I have to believe they will remedy that at some point. I don't think the generating stations are out, just the transmission lines."

Mace added, "Well, let's hope they do figure this out and our trip out here is only for a few days or weeks at best."

Jane said, "When we get to the cave, we should secure the area first. And then immediately begin a hunt for longer term food supplies. If we lock down those two things we should be in good shape."

"Don, you pick up anything at all over your radio?"

Cam answered, "I've been searching almost non-stop. I don't think anything is getting through since we lost the short-wave."

They were startled by a knock on the RV door.

Johnny pulled his weapon as Jane glanced out the window. "It's a kid. Maybe thirteen."

The door was opened. "Can I help you?"

The kid gestured toward a bicycle with a large basket. "Want to buy any eggs?"

Jane looked-on with curiosity. "How many do you have?"

"Five dozen. Truck didn't show to take them to Petersburg yesterday or today and we're overloaded."

Jane said, "How many more you got?"

The boy took a deep breath. "We usually sell five thousand a week. We've got plenty."

Jane asked, "How far you live from here?"

The boy pointed. "Just over that hill."

Jane looked toward the hill in question. "You vaccinate your hens for salmonella?"

The boy nodded. "Yes, ma'am, we do. Most people don't, but we do. My daddy says he runs a clean farm."

Jane turned back to face them. "I say we stop for some eggs. They'll stay fresh for two to three weeks at room temperature if the hens have been vaccinated."

Tres replied, "We've always kept ours out. It's a British thing."

"You do know that most eggs are refrigerated here in the States because the hens aren't vaccinated, right?"

Johnny laughed. "Now why would he know that? That supposed to be some kind of common knowledge?"

"The Brits don't refrigerate because their laws say you have to vaccinate. I read it in one of the prepper magazines. Anyway, We could take a dozen dozen and be in egg heaven for a couple weeks."

The boy held up his hand. "If you break 'em and mix in a little salt, they'll stay good in the freezer for a year."

Jane pointed to the box on the back of the boy's bike. "The eggs already packaged?"

"Yes, ma'am. Ready for transport."

"Johnny, I'll be back in a few minutes. Taking the SUV on an egg run."

"Hang on. I'll go with you."

Jane shook her head as she set the crate of eggs on the steps. "Stay here. It's a boy on a bike. I'll be fine and back in a few."

Johnny frowned as the SUV pulled away, following the boy as he pedaled his bike with all the power he could muster.

"Mace, you still want a strong woman? You know they can be stubborn, right?"

"She'll be fine. We're out in the sticks now. The people around here are busy with their lives."

Mace picked up the crate. "Where you want these?"

"Put them in the corner of our room."

Vanessa asked, "Brits don't refrigerate their eggs?"

Tres shrugged. "My dad never has. You all act as if that's shocking or something."

Vanessa replied, "No. It's just you'd think they would rot."

"I don't really know. I just eat them."

Don said, "Next closest airport is in Lynchburg. We're in OK shape with fuel at the moment, but I would like to top off if possible."

Mace said, "When we get close, come down and pick me up. I'll ride in there with you."

"Thanks. I'd appreciate that. Most aviators are reasonable people. Although, with the current situation, one never knows."

Mace looked over at Cam. "You play football?"

Cam shook his head. "Baseball. Second base."

Don said, "He made all-county two years in a row. Was hoping to get him in front of a few college scouts this next season."

The baseball talk continued for several minutes before the SUV screeched to a halt beside them. Jane jumped out in a rush. Mace opened the door.

Jane said, "Let's go. We need to get out of here."

Johnny put his hand on her shoulder as she sat in the captain's chair. "Whoa. Slow down. What's happened?"

Jane covered her eyes. Tears flowed.

Johnny knelt beside her. "What is it?"

"I waited in the drive as the boy went to the house. When he opened the door, a shotgun..."

Jane looked away for a moment. "He took a shotgun blast to his chest. I got out, caught two of them as they came out the front. Two others took off out the back in a pickup. They had a girl with them, kicking and screaming. I tried to get in a shot, but they were moving too fast. The boy was dead. I went inside. They executed his parents."

Johnny stood. "Mace, Tres. Let's go get 'em!"

Jane slowly shook her head. "I wanted to chase them down, but I couldn't decide on whether to or not."

"You did the right thing. Don, want to be our eyes?"

"Absolutely."

Jane gave a detailed description of the truck and its direction. Don and Cam were soon in the air.

Johnny said, "You stay here. Watch the RV and keep Vanessa safe. You've had enough excitement. Lock this place up tight. You should be able to track us from wherever Don is hovering. We'll be back as soon as we can."

Tres followed Mace to the Jeep as Johnny peeled off in his SUV. Within minutes, Don gave them a sign the truck in question had been spotted. They followed as he flew overhead.

Several minutes later, Don landed on the road in front of them.

Cam ran up to Mace's window. "They went down this road up on the left. Third one. Go in slow. You'll come to a small building on the left. Park there. There's a road that goes behind it. It's short and dead ends in those woods. I counted three trucks and four cars down at the end."

Mace nodded. "You two head back and keep an eye on the RV if you could. And thanks, Cam. You're good people."

Cam half smiled as he turned to run back to his father.

As they turned off the main road, Tres said, "Twin Lakes State Park."

Mace replied, "What? You been here before?"

"No, we just passed a sign."

As the mentioned shed came into view, Mace shut off his engine.

Johnny was standing beside the Jeep. "Hear that music they have blasting? I say we park my SUV over there, blocking their exit. Then we make our way through the woods."

"You go to the right, I'll work my way around to the left. Tres, you stay here with the cars. Give us three minutes and then lay on the horn a couple times. I want their attention to be focused on you. And, Johnny, take at least five mags with you. Seven vehicles. I'm betting we're dealing with at least a dozen people."

Johnny pulled a small bag from the back of the SUV. "I have a dozen full mags. Take half."

Mace nodded. "Kind of wishing I still had that Israeli gun. Was just getting used to it."

As Johnny started to turn away, Mace grabbed him by the shoulder. "Hey, don't take any risks. That vest only covers your chest. Look around for ways out as you go. If these people killed that kid like Jane said, they're as bad as they get. And whatever you do, don't shoot until I've started the party rolling. This is my game we're playing here. I'm trained for this. When I have their attention, you can pick away at them from behind."

Johnny nodded. "Let's do this."

Mace moved cautiously from tree to tree. Working his way around the left side of the gathering, he could hear loud voices over the music, along with a girl's screams.

As he closed, he dropped to the ground, crawling up behind the base of a large elm. Five men and two women were standing in a circle with beers in hand. Mace took off his hat, carefully propping it against the side of the tree where it was in full view.

A man yelled, "Would you cut that music in half! I can't hear myself think!"

When the volume dropped, one of the women could be overheard. "We keep her and make her wash clothes. I'm tired of being a slave to you monkeys!"

A male voice replied, "You gonna share your food and beer with her?"

The woman replied, "No!"

The man shoved her in the shoulder, nearly knocking her down. "Then shut up! You got no say! Get back to your tub!"

An angry scowl was returned as the woman spat on the ground next to him. Mace quietly crawled over to the trunk of the next tree.

The man said, "Now, since the question has been broached... who's gonna start the bidding? Tommy?"

A car horn sounded three times. The group's attention was focused on the road.

Mace yelled from his location. "How about I start the bids! You let her go and I let you live!"

The men scrambled for their weapons, taking refuge behind their cars.

The de-facto leader of the group gestured for two of the men to work their way around behind Mace. Each was quickly downed with a round to the thigh as they left the protection of the cars. Each crawled back to cover.

Mace again yelled, "That was a warning! Send her out or we start picking you off one at a time!"

One of the men pointed. "There! Behind that tree!"

The ground around the tree where Mace had been erupted in flying dirt and leaves as a half dozen guns were emptied in its direction. Two of the men fell from gunshots to their backs.

Another yelled, "They're behind us!"

Mace squeezed off three rounds. Two found their targets through a set of car windows, while a third found the center back of an unlucky man who had taken refuge against a far truck. All three men were on the ground and no longer moving.

Mace yelled out, "The rest of you can live! Just send out the girl!"

Another man yelled back, "How about this! You shoot another one of us and we kill the girl!"

Taking careful aim, Mace's next round found center forehead of the man who had spoken. Johnny picked off another from the other side.

Mace counted feet from under the cars. "Six of you left! Not too late for you! Send her out!"

The tree in front of and the ground surrounding Mace popped and frizzled as his location became known. He stood behind his thick wooden protector.

Slowly leaning out, he took aim at a foot as splinters flew from the tree in front of him. The trigger was squeezed. A man fell to the ground. Three hot rounds quickly found their way into his body.

Mace yelled out: "That leaves five!"

The engine of a truck started. Rocks and dust flew as one of the women attempted an escape. Mace's first thoughts were of an unready Tres waiting back at the cars.

The windshield of the trucked shattered as a half dozen holes found their way inside the cab. The truck rolled off the road, crashing into a tree as the driver slumped over the steering wheel. Tres had made himself known.

Johnny yelled from his position. "Four! Time's running out!"

Two of the men sprinted for the back woods, zigzagging as they ran. A dozen rounds from Mace and Johnny could not find their mark.

Mace yelled, "Johnny! Stay your ground! I've got 'em!"

With that notice, Mace vaulted from behind the tree. Several shots were fired in his direction before Johnny's work forced the remaining two back into hiding.

The woods quickly opened up onto a small lake. The two men who had fled had taken refuge in an aluminum boat they had launched out into the lake. Mace stopped behind the protection of a tree as one of the men took shots at his position.

He leaned around the tree with a single thought in his head. *Idiots.*

Four slugs found their way into the slow moving vessel.

One man yelled at the other. "Row faster, dumbass!"

Mace took careful aim, popping another three holes in the slowing boat. The man in back stood, wobbling from side to side as he attempted to bring an end to the assault. A quick burst of three rounds found the center of his chest.

As the man fell over the side into the water, the rower threw down the oars and began firing at Mace with his pistol. No hesitation was taken to bring the shooter's evil existence to an end. With the lake cleared, Mace hustled back through the woods toward the others.

He came to a stop behind a broad tree. "And then there were two! Send the girl out if you want to live!"

Johnny yelled. "Better yet, drop your weapons and come out in the open!"

The surviving man yelled, "You let us drive out of here and we'll leave peacefully. We'll leave the girl up the road with your friend!"

Mace replied, "Girl stays right here. You want to leave, that's up to you. We just want her safe return!"

The woman yelled back: "Deal! You can have her! Just give us your word that you'll let us go!"

Mace stepped into the open. "You have it. Now go before I change my mind. Tres! Let them pass!"

The man stood from behind a car, opening the driver's door. The woman crawled across into the passenger seat with the man right after. The engine started. As the car began to move forward the blast from a shotgun shattered the driver's-side back window. The woman slumped over.

Two shots from a pistol came back at the girl as she pulled the trigger on the second barrel of the shotgun she had picked up. It was a gruesome scene as blood, hair and brain matter splattered forward onto the windshield. The car rolled ten feet before bumping another vehicle and coming to a stop. The girl collapsed where she stood.

Johnny was the first to arrive. The girl had been hit. Mace made a quick check of the other culprits and vehicles. The area was secure.

Johnny said, "You're OK. We're here to help."

After a quick once-over, and with applied pressure to her obvious wound, Johnny asked, "You hit or injured anywhere but here?"

The girl slowly shook her head. "No, sir."

Johnny half smiled as he lifted his hand from a torn and bloody shirt. "Bullet passed all the way through. Gonna be sore for a bit, but you'll heal."

The girl looked up at Johnny's face before breaking down in tears. Johnny's heart sank as he thought about the horrors she had just witnessed. Her brother and her parents were dead. Evil had crept into her once peaceful world and taken the foundation of her security.

Mace placed his hand on his friend's shoulder as Johnny fought back his own tears, attempting to be strong for the girl. Tres pulled up in the Jeep.

Chapter 15

Jane rushed out to meet them as they arrived back. Johnny carried the girl up into the RV and back to the bedroom. The two began the task of dressing her wound.

Jane asked, "You have any other family here in town? Somewhere we can take you? A close neighbor maybe?"

The girl shook her head. "We just moved here three months ago from Montana. I have an aunt and uncle back there."

Jane sighed as she wiped blood from the girl's arm. "You're welcome to stay with us until we can get you out there to them. I don't think you should go back to your house. And there is no way I'm leaving you with the local sheriff."

The two dogs jumped up on the bed. The girl half smiled as they moved up to her with their tails wagging.

Jane said, "This is Molly and Derwood. They'll be keeping you company, should you decide to remain with us."

Vanessa added, "Yeah, you are more than welcome to stay. These are good people and have treated me with nothing but kindness."

The girl thanked Jane and Vanessa before once again bursting into tears. Johnny left the room, closing the door behind him.

Tres asked, "How is she?"

"Physically, she'll be OK. But she's just been through an emotional meat grinder. And she's got no one this side of the Mississippi to turn to. How are you doing? You just took a life."

"Shaking in my shoes still."

Mace said, "If she's staying with us, we should go to her house and bring back clothes. No way we can let her go back there with her family like that."

Mace grimaced in thought. He wanted badly to punch a wall. The world truly was coming apart at the seams. The crisis was only a week old and for the fourth time in as many days, a group of miscreants had attempted to rob or kill innocent people. Jane had come too late to save the girl's family. Johnny wondered how the girl could possibly recover.

Don came into the RV. "How is she?"

Mace said, "She has a gunshot wound to the shoulder. Physically, it looks like she'll recover."

"I have some antibiotics if you want them. Strong stuff, but only enough for three or four days."

Mace followed Don back to the helicopter. The pills were given to Tres to take to Jane.

Mace said, "I don't think we'll make the cave today. It's taking too long."

"We made the right move by getting out of town. As I said before, we're not picking up any communications anymore. Whatever interference we have going on is intense. The electronics in this bird are well shielded, even so my gauges have been acting flaky. Engine has skipped a beat or two as well. Not something you want when you're a thousand feet up."

Mace asked, "Have you seen any other planes in the air?"

Don nodded. "At least a dozen, all small, four military. Usually see the high altitude contrails from jetliners. Haven't seen any today. Other than those interstate interchanges, there hasn't been a lot of traffic on the road."

Mace gestured toward the helicopter. "Fuel still OK? This landing and the runs back and forth have to be taking their toll."

Don crossed his arms. "We're easily good until we get to Lynchburg. Let's just hope they have accessible fuel."

Johnny came out to meet them. "Jane wants us to go to the girl's house. We have orders to bring all the clothes we can, and to round up family photos if they have them."

Mace replied, "Let's go. Don, if anyone comes this way, get this bird in the air. We can't afford to lose it. And let Jane know where we went."

Johnny walked to the SUV, Mace beside him. "Mace, we get over there and I start to break down, keep me focused. I can't imagine what that poor girl is going through. I just don't understand what makes some people act like savages. The world has so much to offer, only some feel they have to take what everyone else has."

As they pulled away, Mace clicked his seatbelt into place. "I couldn't say what makes one person act with respect and care while others are so foul. It's like they don't value life, even their own."

"I'm still shaking about that girl blowing those scumbags away. Not that they didn't deserve it, but she doesn't need to be involved with that as a teenager."

"Well, she did the world a favor. Those two would've gone out and killed or robbed someone else. So it's just as well she put them down. If anything, she won't be left with the completely helpless feeling most victims have. She did something about what they did to her."

Johnny pointed toward the dead body lying at the front door as they pulled up to the house. "As I said, try to keep me focused."

"You'll be fine. Just think about caring for the girl and not about what just happened to her family."

"Shouldn't we bury them or something?"

Mace glanced over at the family's barn. "They have a back-hoe on that tractor. I'll see if I can find some keys. You get a suitcase or bags and get as many of her clothes as you can. We'll finish up with grabbing family pictures if we have time."

Johnny followed Mace into the home. The house, other than the invasion that had just taken place, was clean and well ordered. Knickknacks graced a large fireplace and curio in the family room. A flower covered fabric sofa sat in front of them as country themed paintings hung on the walls.

Mace pointed down a hallway. "One of those would be her room."

The Army Ranger walked into the kitchen, holding up his hand toward Johnny as the carnage of the invasion was further revealed. "Head down the hall, try to find luggage. You don't want to see what's here."

Johnny walked toward the back. Mace stepped over the body of the girl's father, opening a kitchen cupboard and retrieving a box of plastic garbage bags. A cork board on the wall held the key to the tractor.

Mace dropped the bags with Johnny and made his way out to the yard. The tractor started first try. He left it to warm up as he returned to the kitchen for the girl's parents.

He gently lifted her mother, carrying her out to the green grass of the well-kept yard, returning for the father, and then the young boy who had sold them the crate of eggs.

The back-hoe was moved to the lawn where three shallow graves were dug. Mace held back his own tears as he lifted each of the victims and laid them gently in the ground, taking a deep breath as each shovel-load of dirt from the tractor bucket was spread over them. He had taken the lives of many during his years in the service. These were the first he had personally laid to rest.

When the task was finished, Mace knelt and said a prayer for each of the victims. He had never been strong in his faith, but he somehow felt compelled to plead the case of the innocent to a higher power. He stood, again taking a deep breath before turning back toward the house.

The tractor was moved back onto the drive. After hopping off, he loaded the two dead attackers onto the curled up shovel. A quick run to the end of the drive saw their bodies dumped on the side of the road.

He looked over, spat, and scowled as he turned the tractor back toward the barn. "Hope the buzzards eat your faces off."

After parking the tractor, he returned the keys to the cork board. Johnny was coming out of the house with four trash bags stuffed with clothes and shoes.

Mace asked, "That it?"

Johnny shook his head, "Two more. Then we have family pictures. And we really need to get back on the road."

"I was just saying to Don that I didn't think we'd make the cave today. Just as well, we'll find somewhere to park for the night and pick up again tomorrow."

A quick roundup of family photos was conducted.

As they returned to the SUV, Mace pointed at the barn. "Should we take a couple crates of eggs?"

Johnny sighed. "I know it's not stealing, since we have the girl with us, but it doesn't feel right, does it?"

"No it doesn't, but we have to live, and if we leave them they'll just rot."

Johnny looked over at the three graves and asked, "What'd you do with the others?"

Mace half smiled. "Dumped them down by the road. That ditch wasn't deserving, but I figured we needed to leave them there so others around here would know."

Johnny said, "Maybe we should leave a note. Someone may come to check on them."

Mace thought for a moment. "Sure. That sounds reasonable. Don't tell them who she's with, just that she is safe and cared for and will return if the situation changes."

Johnny gave a half smile. "You're a good egg, Mace Hardy, I don't care what everyone else says."

He gestured toward the house. "Just get that note taken care of. I'll load us up with eggs."

As Mace squeezed the sixth crate into the back seat of the SUV, Johnny emerged from the house. A short ride later they were parked beside the RV.

Jane came down the steps as Johnny began to pull the retrieved bags from the SUV. "How many did you bring?"

"Five bags of clothes, one of shoes, and one of pictures and such from her room and the house."

Mace added, "We brought another six crates of eggs as well."

Jane said, "I gave her a little something to help her sleep, although I don't think she will. The dogs will be good therapy. They took right to her."

Johnny chuckled. "Those two would take to anyone that gave them attention."

Mace said, "If we stay around here much longer, we might have to deal with the sheriff. I can't say that would be a good thing."

Jane crossed her arms. "She says she wants to stay with us for now. I don't know how much faith I would put in her decision making at the moment though. I asked her about friends and she said she was looking forward to school starting.

"No close neighbors?" Johnny asked.

All they've done since they moved here is work on the farm. They have chickens, pigs, two dairy cows, and about twenty acres of beans. This was to be her parents' retirement gig. He was in finance, her mom was a nurse. They were tired of the cold winters around Butte and were looking forward to something milder. Wanted to live where they could farm longer but still maintain the seasons."

Johnny said, "Should we put leaving to a vote?"

Jane replied, "I say we just make the call here and now. The day isn't getting any longer."

Mace said, "I say we go."

Johnny nodded. "Go then."

Jane turned back to the RV steps. "Pack us up and let's roll."

The helicopter took to the air as the RV pulled back onto the highway. Their continued journey took them just south of Farmville and through numerous other small towns.

As they looped around the north side of Appomattox, Tres said, "This is where the Civil War ended."

Mace nodded. "That's what they taught us in American History class about twenty years ago. Have to wonder if they still do."

"They only brushed over it when I went through. I'm a Civil War buff, which is why I knew about Organ Cave. You know, after the South's defeat at Gettysburg, Lee moved his forces back down here. They wanted to make it to the train depot in Appomattox to ride the rails down to North Carolina... to link up with General Johnston's forces. The North cut them off before they could get here. That's when Lee surrendered. They say the war could have gone on for years had he made it through."

"What started you on the Civil War? Your family wasn't over here then."

"My dad took me to a local museum when I was a kid. It had a Civil War exhibit with the local soldiers who had served in the Northern Army of Michigan's lower peninsula. I just found it a fascinating piece of history."

"Can't say I would have wanted to fight through that war."

"One of my friends had a family member who died on the *Sultana* at the end of the war. I don't know, it just made me think about all those lives. Brother against brother and all that. A whole nation at war. And you should read about some of the battles and the mistakes that were made on both sides. Interesting stuff."

"Well, I can tell you firsthand, the fog of war can change an outcome all on its own. We were on the verge of taking this one village, only to have a freak sandstorm drive us back. Four days later we were fighting for the same buildings we had already cleared."

Tres nodded. "That was largely what brought about the South's defeat at Gettysburg. J.E.B. Stuart's cavalry rode around behind the North's position to attack from the rear. A group of five hundred northern cavalrymen, coincidentally led by none other than George Armstrong Custer, attacked the five thousand Southerners. Instead of Custer's men being crushed, Stuart's got divided, spooked, and retreated. If you've heard of Pickett's Charge, his infantry were supposed to get support from that cavalry. Had that happened, Gettysburg might have been a decisive victory for the South. Had the Southern generals known of that retreat, they probably wouldn't have attacked."

Mace took a deep breath. "Just hope you never have to be involved in any such thing. The movies can make it all seem glamorous, but even with the effects they put in nowadays, it doesn't come close to the actuality of being there, killing people who are trying to kill you. You should only go to war when there are no good options left."

Tres sighed. "Just learned that lesson."

The caravan came to a stop just east of Lynchburg. They pulled off onto the driveway of a small church. Don set the helicopter down in the field in front of the drive. Mace joined him for a ride to the airport at Lynchburg.

As they lifted off, Don said, "This is a regional airport. They will have fuel. The question is, will they sell any of it and what would they take as payment?"

"Johnny gave me a couple grand in cash. I would assume it's still good after only a few days."

"That should more than do it."

The helicopter landed at the airport to a greeting by a patrol car. Mace stepped out, leaving the AR-15 he had been holding beside the seat.

An officer rolled down his window. "What's your business?"

Mace said, "We need fuel. Are they selling?"

The officer asked, "Where you headed?"

"Over to West Virginia."

"You the owner?"

The Ranger shook his head. "No, he's flying it. That's his son in the back."

The officer looked Mace up and down for signs of a weapon. "I've been told there's a twenty-five gallon limit."

Mace replied, "Every bit helps. Say, what's the word around here? Power coming back on anytime soon?"

The officer let out a huff. "Government's got its head stuck up its... well, you get it. Nobody is in charge and nobody is taking responsibility. Interference from the sun *my ass* is all I can say. Somebody is responsible and they need to pay."

Mace slowly shook his head. "I don't think so. My friend has a ham radio, and power is out world over. Everywhere."

The officer looked up. "No kidding? I heard it was just this region."

Mace shook his head. "I wish I could tell you that was true, but it's not. If you haven't already done so, you might want to stockpile a few supplies for yourself and your family, just as a precaution. If this interference is indeed real, there's no telling when it might subside."

The officer pointed. "Go into that building over there. Tell them Jay checked you out."

The officer sped off toward the direction of the exit. Mace proceeded into the designated building.

Two men were seated at a service counter. "Who wants to sell me some avgas?"

One of the men stood. "We have a twenty-five gallon limit."

Mace said, "I have cash and I'll pay double."

The man looked over at the other, then back. "Still twenty-five gallon limit."

Mace offered, "Triple? Plus a hundred dollar bonus for each of you?"

The still seated man stood. "I think we can do business. We are talking cash though. Greenbacks?"

Mace nodded as he pulled a roll of bills from his pocket. "Greenbacks."

A fuel truck was soon parked beside the helicopter. After the top-off of the main tank and reserve was complete, the men were paid.

Don asked, "Hey, I know it's against regs, but I have three five-gallon jerry cans I'd like to fill. We have more cash."

One of the men looked at the other and shrugged. "Doesn't bother me. You willing to pay a bonus on that as well?"

Mace replied, "Will another fifty each do?"

Both men smiled. The tanks were filled and the threesome were quickly on their way back to the caravan.

After landing, Don looked over his maps. "I suggest we continue to Montvale, then head up and over the mountains to Buchanan. From there we cut under I-81 and head over to Marshalltown. After that it's on to Organ Cave. Now, given the daylight we have left, I think we might do good if we can make it just past Montvale. The valley just north of there should be peaceful. I can run ahead from here and scout us a place to camp."

Mace nodded as he stepped out of the helicopter. "Sounds like a reasonable plan. Check out what you need and meet us back on the roadway before we get to Montvale. I'll fill in the others."

Chapter 16

Highway 460 heading to Montvale was a breeze. The traffic had picked up but was well below what would have been considered normal. Just before arriving at Montvale, Don set down in a close field to deliver his observations.

Mace met him beside the helicopter. "Was beginning to think you kept going."

Don laughed. "You guys have all the eggs, so you don't have to worry about me running off."

"What's it look like?"

"The road is a two-laner, easily passable. I spotted a small church about halfway up through the valley. We set down and I knocked on their door. The pastor was very friendly and agreed to let us park there for the night. I wouldn't expect any trouble from there. Mostly small farms. Should only take you twenty minutes or so to get there from here."

As Mace walked back to the others, parked on the side of the highway, Don lifted off to return to the church.

Johnny was standing beside the open RV door. "Well?"

"We turn up Goose Creek Road at Montvale, couple miles. After that we look for the sign of a small church on the left. We can park there for the night. Don okayed it with the pastor."

Johnny looked up at the sky. "Probably be getting dark in an hour and a half. Let's get settled in there so we can stake out our defenses."

"According to Don, we shouldn't have any issues. But I'm with you, a little caution won't hurt.

Mace glanced up the RV steps. "How's the girl doing?"

Jane replied, "Still crying. Vanessa has been sitting back there with her."

"Did we get a name?" Johnny asked.

"Tonya Banning."

"Well... let's get off this highway before we draw in any unwanted attention."

They pulled into the church parking lot a short while later. The helicopter had landed behind the church building, making it hidden from the road.

As they walked to the front door of the building, the pastor was standing there to greet them. "Welcome. Y'all are welcome to stay as long as you like, although, you may want to move away from the front here as the congregation usually parks there. Tomorrow is our Wednesday morning service. We've just decided on twice a week to pray for power to be restored."

Mace nodded. "We'll be gone at first light. We appreciate the kind offer, but we're hoping to be back on the road by then."

"I'm sorry, I failed to introduce myself. Henry Hargraves. I'm the associate pastor at the moment. Our senior pastor decided to up and move to Roanoke about a month ago. We were expecting a visit from a prospective replacement this coming weekend, but it's not looking promising. You folks going camping?"

Mace shook his head. "In a way. We're coming from Norfolk. With the power out and no communications, things were getting a bit too unstable for us."

Henry gestured for the group to enter and have a seat at a set of folding tables. "I see. Unstable in what sort of way?"

Johnny replied, "As in looting, home invasions, kidnappings, robberies, murders, sort of way."

The pastor pulled back in his chair. "Oh my. I had no idea it was that bad out there. Any word on when the power might be back on?"

"That's the million dollar question. This is a worldwide event. National Guard and all have been called in, but we aren't sure the word has gotten out to most of them. And the government, so far at least, is holding them in place."

Jane said, "After the first few nights of unrest, we decided it was best to pick up and leave."

Henry asked, "You had trouble?"

Jane sighed after realizing the can of worms she was about to open. "We had a gang attack a neighbor's house. We went in to defend them and ended up killing ten."

The pastor again pulled back. "Killing ten? What?"

"All in self defense. These were extremely bad people who would have killed our elderly neighbors had we not intervened."

Henry Hargraves shifted uneasily in his chair. "That's... that's just shocking."

"One of them got away and brought back a dozen more. After a fierce gun battle at our house, they shot a police officer friend of ours. We killed them too."

The pastor sat with his jaw dropped.

Mace said, "Jane, you might want to let that soak in for a bit."

"He's an adult. I'm sure he knows the evil that lurks out there in the world. Anyway, in our effort to get out of town, we had four men who tried to rob us. I shot 'em. They'll live though. Pinned each one in the shoulder."

Henry Hargraves retained the look of shock on his face.

Jane gestured back toward the RV. "We made it to Burkeville and came upon another home invasion. A group of men killed the homeowners and kidnapped a sixteen year old girl."

Henry leaned forward. "Did you alert the police?"

Jane frowned. "No. But we were able to track them down. We rescued the girl, but not before killing another ten."

The pastor returned a worried look. "You're saying you've killed thirty people in the last several days? Since the power went out?"

"It isn't something we wanted to do. And it's been weighing on my conscience. Were we wrong to defend ourselves?"

The pastor stood. "I have to say, if what you're saying is true, it's a bit overwhelming. I mean, we hear about the occasional killing down in Roanoke, but this part of the country is usually pretty peaceful. I wouldn't have thought Norfolk was such a hotbed of crime."

Mace said, "You turn out the lights and the roaches come out, Henry. As Jane said, none of this was anything we went looking for."

Mace glanced back toward the RV. "We've got a young girl out there who witnessed her family being murdered. She didn't hesitate to pull the trigger on two of the attackers when we went in for the rescue. I know it's not the way most of us think or act, but the old adage of desperate times call for desperate measures has held true since we lost power."

The pastor stood and began to pace back and forth in thought. "That poor girl. You say she's with you out in the RV?"

Jane replied, "Yes. Her family had just moved to Burkeville. Her closest relatives are all the way back in Montana. We couldn't just leave her. And with all the chaos, we couldn't risk dropping her with the sheriff. My heart is aching for her right now."

Tres came in the door. "Hey, there's several cars pulling up out front."

The pastor held up a hand with a worried look. "It's OK. We were just going to share a dinner between families. Do you have food? You're welcome to share in what we have, but I would ask that you hold back on the stories. There will be young children."

Jane stood. "Mr. Hargraves, we would be honored to share a meal with you. I'm in need of being around good people for an evening. And we have food we can share as well."

The pastor gestured toward the tables where they sat. "Well, OK. If you like, you can set up right there. We'll put the food on these two tables over here. And later on, if you desire, we have a number of cots in back that you could use. We have a single shower you can make use of down at the other end of this room. Although we only have cold water now. This is our recreation hall. Picnics, weddings and such is what it usually sees. Oh, and Sunday school."

Jane smiled. "We thank you and your congregation for the kindness you're showing us, Pastor. I'm not sure what we could do for you as far as repayment other than a few dollars' donation, but if you have anything else you need, we're here for the evening."

Henry scratched his chin. "Well, any of you know mechanics? Our church van has been acting up, won't start. Kind of leaves me stranded here. And I have several elderly congregants that I like to look in on during the day, especially now that the power is out."

Johnny and Tres both held up their hands.

Jane said, "OK, you two go check out the van and we'll bring in some food."

As they walked back to the RV, Mace let out a chuckle.

Jane turned. "What?"

"You just fit right in wherever you go, that's all. Quite the people person you are."

"Me? No. That would be Johnny. He's a pleaser. Drop him in a crowd and he'll soon be right in the thick of any conversation. I practically have to drag him away from the shooting meets."

"Yeah, he's a talker alright. Glad he wandered into the bar when I was there. The both of you are probably the closest thing I have to friends."

Jane reached back, taking hold up Mace's upper arm and squeezing. "We're happy to have you around. Now, what's good for a church dinner?"

Mace watched in amazement as Jane whipped up two dozen deviled eggs and was hard at work on a pot of rice. He was given the task of stirring a large pot of pork and beans. Vanessa joined them from the back, quickly making a dozen sandwiches.

Jane looked over at Mace as he stirred. "You might want to eat hearty this evening. Another meal like this may not come for some time."

The church dinner was a reminder of how different the world, and the people in it could be. Singing, followed by conversation, and board games by candlelight, were about as far as one could get from the vicious, bloody gun battles of the days and nights before.

When the evening had settled down and the congregants gone back to their homes, Mace sat in a chair out under the stars, sipping on a cup of hot apple cider.

Johnny, Don, Cam, Tres and the pastor were sitting beside him. "Mr. Hargraves, thank you for giving us an evening of reality. Or at least what reality should be."

The pastor looked up at the stars. "You know, when I look up there at the heavens, I sometimes say a prayer of thanks for the life I've come to know. It's not without its heartaches and troubles as well, but they are different. We have two of our elderly members that are terminally ill right now. Neither have children that care, so I've been carrying them to their doctors and keeping them on their medications and such."

Mace said, "Giving care, it's a commendable profession you've chosen."

"It's a hard thing to do, watching someone you care about slowly die, but I feel blessed that I've been able to provide comfort for them in their time of need. And blessed that I got to know them."

Mace placed his hand on the pastor's shoulder. "The world would be a better place if it was filled with Henry Hargraves."

Johnny held up his cider glass. "Amen to that."

"Well, hold on. I'm not all that deserving. At eighteen, I held up a liquor store and shot a man. I was quite the thug coming out of high school."

Johnny said, "You? You hardly look the part."

"I spent five years in prison in Colorado. Came to know the Lord while I was there. Changed my life. Changed my whole outlook. Doors opened. And for the first time in my life, I saw people for their kindness. I wandered about for a dozen years after, finally ending up here eight years ago. The people took me in, even knowing my past, and I've been living my life ever since trying to repay them."

Henry looked at Mace. "What's your story, Mr. Hardy?"

"Army Ranger. Saw too much combat. I've been tending bar and doing construction work ever since. Johnny here, and Tres, are two of my patrons."

Johnny eagerly added, "Oh, it's not like I drink a lot or anything. Just a social thing."

Mace laughed.

Henry Hargraves reached out and grasped Johnny's forearm. "You don't have to answer to me, Mr. Tretcher. Besides, the Good Book has many examples of celebration. A little moderation is the key though, keeps you from going out to rob liquor stores."

As they sat in the parking lot talking, a meteor zipped across the sky, turning into an intense fireball before burning out.

Henry sat back in his chair. "I do love being out away from the city lights."

Johnny chuckled. "That puts you just about anywhere right now. Maybe that was your aliens coming in, Tres. Tres here thinks the interference is from aliens."

Tres shook his head. "It was a joke. He's just trying to steer you away from his drinking problem."

Mace stood. "That the van you're having trouble with?"

Henry nodded as he sat up in his chair. "Yep. I'm afraid it might need a battery now too. Just won't start."

Mace looked at Johnny. "You couldn't do anything with it?"

Johnny frowned. "Actually, we were just getting started when the call for dinner came in. Forgot we were looking at it."

"You have a good spotlight in the RV? Maybe we could fix her up."

"Sure. I'll meet you over there in a sec."

Johnny walked over carrying a bright light and a small toolbox. "See if she'll turn over."

Tres was given the task of turning the key. The starter turned the engine over slowly, but it wouldn't start.

Johnny laughed. "Sounds like a dying walrus. Let's see if she's getting spark."

A single plug was removed, reconnected to the plug wire and set against the exhaust manifold.

Tres was signaled and the van engine turned over.

Johnny held up his hand. "That's enough. She's getting spark. Let's check the fuel."

The plug was inspected before being returned to its respective hole. A screwdriver was used to loosen a clamp on the fuel line as it connected to the old carburetor.

Johnny waved back as he aimed the rubber line toward the ground. "Give it a short turn."

Again the van engine struggled to turn over.

Johnny held up his hand. "That's good. You see that? Barely dripped out. Next we take off the filter."

Thirty seconds later another wave was given to Tres. Gasoline pumped out onto the ground.

"Ho! That's enough."

Johnny connected the filter-less fuel line to the carburetor. "Padre, looks like you may just need a fuel filter."

Tres was signaled and the van engine slowly grumbled to life.

Henry smiled. "Oh wow, this is wonderful. I can't thank you enough."

Johnny held out the clogged filter. "You have someone that can install a new one if you get it?"

"I do."

"Take this with you to the parts store. Should only be a few bucks. And you'll want to replace it as soon as possible, as all the crud in the tank and line will otherwise get in the carb and that will cost you a lot more time and effort to fix."

Henry smiled. "I will take care of it first thing after morning service."

As time approached midnight, they moved back into the rec-room and onto the cots Henry had so kindly pulled for them.

Vanessa stayed in the RV with Tonya. First light would come early. Henry said goodnight and the candles were blown out.

Chapter 17

Mace was awakened just before the sun by a rooster crowing in the distance. He had somehow managed a deep sleep. He reasoned it was the familiarity of the cot, though it had been years since he had slept on one. He stood and stretched before noticing that Jane was not in the room.

Mace walked out into the parking lot as Jane stepped down from the RV. "Anything wrong?"

"No, was just worried about Tonya, so I got up to check. She and Vanessa are both sound asleep."

"Good. I'm glad she was able to get some rest."

Jane stood, looking toward the coming dawn with her arms crossed. "Gonna be getting cold soon."

"Can't say that it will make things easy, but I do love a good snow. I'm almost looking forward to it."

Jane frowned. "I'm good with it for about a week. Then I'm pretty much done, ready for the warm again. Of course, the only real time I've spent in it was out west skiing. You ski?"

"On water. Tried the snow once. Girlfriend broke her leg, ending our trip on the first day. Never had the money to go back, and then along came the Army."

"Johnny likes to cross country. I don't see the fun in it."

Mace opened the door to the rec-room. "Never tried it."

He looked around at the sleeping bodies before clapping his hands together and yelling: "Let's go Rangers! Time's wasting!"

Johnny slowly sat up, rubbing his eyes. "I don't remember signing up for this."

Mace laughed. "On your feet, soldier. There's a war going on out there and you're gonna be late!"

Tres sat up on his cot. "What's for breakfast?"

Mace pointed toward the RV. "Eggs. Just as soon as you get out there and cook 'em."

Jane held up her hand. "Sit tight. I don't want any of you chowder-heads monkeying up my kitchen. I'll call you when it's ready."

As they walked out the door into the parking lot, Henry was climbing into his van. "Y'all just leave everything as is. I'll be back in an hour or so. If you're gone by then, well, Godspeed to you and have a safe journey."

Johnny nodded goodbye as he held up a thankful hand.

Breakfast was prepared and quickly downed. As the sun began to rise over the mountains in front of them, they pulled back on the road. Goose Creek Drive wound back and forth through the miles-long valley going up an incline marking the valley's end. The ride up to Bearwallow Gap took only minutes. There, the road going north was blocked by an abandoned police cruiser.

Don landed the helicopter in a nearby clearing.

Mace pulled the Jeep close before hopping out. "Road blocked for a reason?"

Don nodded. "Train derailment. There's a dirt road that would allow you to go around, but it's blocked by a truck. We'll have to take a cutoff down a couple miles. Although, you'll have to get around that cruiser first."

Johnny answered from beside Mace. "Not a problem."

Mace followed Johnny to the RV. A floor jack was pulled from a side bay, rolled under the rear differential of the cruiser, and jacked up.

Johnny gestured toward Mace and Tres. "You two walnuts just going to hang around looking stupid or you gonna push?"

The cruiser was moved back. Jane drove the RV and trailer past. The jack was dropped and stowed and they were again on their way.

The cutback road was a sharp turn heading back in the other direction. After several attempts, the trailer was unhitched. Jane maneuvered the RV onto the new roadway and the trailer was reattached.

From Buchanan the road led to Springwood and then southwest to Fincastle. From Fincastle they would go up and over the mountains to Marshalltown. After Marshalltown, they would cross another ridge of the Appalachians before descending the other side into West Virginia. A final stretch would take the caravan to Union and then up to Organ Cave, a two hour drive on a normal day.

As they moved up and over the mountains toward Marshalltown, the sky turned a decidedly dark gray. The road was quickly obscured as a thick bank of clouds rolled in. Visibility dropped to near zero.

Tres said, "Winter's on its way. The first one of these cold fronts usually comes with about a fifteen or twenty degree temperature drop."

Mace replied, "The cold I don't care about. It's the not being able to see. The trailer is only twenty-five feet away from us and I can hardly see its taillights. This is gonna be slow moving."

Mace frowned as the RV came to a stop.

Tres said, "Want me to go check it out?"

"Please."

Tres returned seconds later. "Wow, I almost got lost coming back. That is some kind of pea soup out there. And it's definitely getting colder. You want a jacket? I can get one from the RV."

"Nope, I'm good."

Mace flipped on the emergency flashers. "But we might as well go up there where we have company. This doesn't look like it's breaking anytime soon."

Tres tapped on the door of the RV and it opened.

Jane said, "Never been in fog this thick. Looking down, I can barely see the road."

Johnny joined them. "Did we just land on another planet?"

Mace turned to face the kitchen, taking note of Tonya sitting in a chair with the two dogs on her lap. "You feeling better this morning."

Tonya nodded. "Yes, sir."

Mace smiled. "Call me Mace. We're all family here now. At least until all this is over."

Tonya began to tear up.

Mace sat beside her, hoisting an eager Derwood onto his lap and rubbing behind his ears. "Sometimes the world can be a terrible place. What you have to remember though is that it's not the world, it's just a handful of the people that occupy it. Most are like us, but some, well, they have nothing but evil in their hearts.

Mace handed Derwood over to the girl. "If you have anything that you want to ask, or anything you want to say to any of us, please just say it. We are all on the same side here. We can't replace family, but we're the best each other has got."

Tonya wiped her eyes. "Well, I am a little cold."

Jane frowned. "Oh, honey, why didn't you say so? We have plenty of blankets. Look, while you're here, treat this place as if you own it. If you're hungry, get or ask for something to eat. Cold, get or ask for a blanket."

Jane looked around. "I know it's not the same, but just try to treat us like family, maybe cousins or something. Just don't worry about offending us, and please don't feel like you're putting us out. OK?"

Tonya smiled as Vanessa wrapped a blanket around her shoulders.

They sat for twenty minutes before the clouds began to clear enough for them to see.

Tres returned after walking back to the Jeep. "Anyone leave the trailer open?"

Johnny scowled. "Crap. Out of my way!"

The lock had been clipped with bolt cutters. A dozen boxes of supplies, including ammunition, were missing.

Johnny said, "Right under our noses. Never heard a peep."

Mace asked, "You have another lock?"

Johnny nodded. "Yeah, and they won't cut through this one. I should have used it instead. It's just harder to get through the hole of that latch so I used the cheap one."

The lock was replaced and the caravan again rolled. At the bottom of the mountain they passed through Marshalltown. After moving through another valley they started up the next incline.

Tres looked back. "We've got two trucks that just came in behind us."

Mace frowned. "I saw them."

Tres glanced forward before looking out his window and up. "Wouldn't mind having Mr. Rogers up there scouting for us."

"That cloud bank is too low. My guess is he's gone on ahead to the cave. Hopefully the weather is clear there."

Tres pulled his weapon from the back seat, setting it in his lap.

Mace asked, "Safety on?"

Tres glanced down. "Yes."

"Full magazine?"

Tres nodded.

Mace gestured with his head toward the back. "Wanna check mine? Not sure I topped off that mag after the rundown in Burkeville."

Tres picked the AR-15 from the back seat. "Safety is on and... magazine is full."

The magazine was shoved back into its block and the bolt pulled back. "Round is in the chamber."

"Glad to see you're getting comfortable with that."

"Still scares the crap out of me, but I'll get over it."

The progress slowed as they approached a hairpin turn. The RV braked to a sudden stop.

Tres looked back. "Trucks are blocking up the road!"

Mace yelled. "Haul ass up there and get in the RV!"

"Where you going?"

"Just do it!"

Mace shoved the door of the Jeep open hard and bolted for the woods on the left side of the road. Pops of gunfire could be heard, followed immediately by the crackle and whiz of bullets zipping through and bouncing off the trees around him as he ran.

A voice yelled out. "Come out of them woods and we won't hurt ya!"

Mace stopped behind a tree, yelling back. "Get back in those trucks and leave I won't have to kill you!"

A single shot rang out, striking the large tree Mace stood behind.

The voice yelled, "Listen up! This is our road. Our mountain. You didn't ask our permission to use it, and that's gonna cost ya!"

Mace took a quick glance around the tree only to be rewarded with an arm full of splinters as a bullet skimmed the edge of the tree where his shoulder had just been. The attackers knew how to aim. Mace scanned the trees surrounding him, looking for a strategy. Gunfire could be heard from the front of the RV.

The Army Ranger estimated the position of his attackers as related to the tree before sprinting down a steep hill away from the road. Three shots blistered the trees around him as he ran.

A second voice could be heard. "Chicken ran off and left his friends. I'm going after him."

The first voice replied, "No, get the bolt cutters. Let's see what's in that trailer."

Mace continued his run, changing direction to parallel the road.

As he came to a stop, the first voice could again be heard. "Darryl, you and Sonny watch our backs. You see anything moving in the woods down there... shoot it."

A voice replied, "Dale, I don't wanna shoot nobody. Can't we just hit the trailer and go?"

The voice of Dale called back. "Anybody shoots at me, I'm shooting at you. Understand?"

Darryl scanned the woods and frowned. "Yes."

Again shots rang out from the front of the RV. Mace took another sprint, coming out at the road's edge a hundred yards behind the attackers. He crept slowly along the tree line until the tailgates of the two pickups came into view.

The voices of the lead attackers carried down the road from the back of the trailer. "What do you mean it won't cut?"

A second voice replied, "I'm just telling you, that ain't a normal lock!"

The first voice growled. "Just give me that, you idiot."

The second voice harped, "Oh, so what, you're stronger than me?"

The first voice smirked. "No, just smarter. I bet this latch ain't so tough."

The two men came into view as Mace peered around the left side of a tree. The second of the two men fell to the ground screaming as a round from the AR-15 pierced the back of his right thigh.

The bolt cutters dropped to the ground as Dale yelled back at the others. "Find him!"

The second man cried out: "Gah! It hurts, Dale!"

Dale crouched behind him, propping his rifle on the man's side, aiming down into the woods. "Shut up and stop squirming! I think I saw him move!"

Darryl yelled back from the trucks. "I can't see him!"

Mace cut loose with three bursts of three. Several of the bullets skipped on the pavement before impacting the back of the downed attacker. He stopped moving. As Mace looked through his scope he took note of the small gun portal opening up on the back of the bus. A barrel slowly poked through. A muzzle flash preceded the man named Sonny falling to the roadway as a bullet punched a two inch hole out the back of his skull. A terrified Darryl dropped to the ground, his rifle falling to the side.

Dale yelled out. "OK! You proved your point! We'll go!"

Mace yelled back. "Drop your weapon and stand up with your hands over your head!"

Dale replied, "I do that and you shoot me dead!"

Mace yelled, "Maybe! Or maybe I'll just let my friend standing behind you do it!"

The man named Dale spun around. Mace used the opportunity to send out another three-round burst. The first skimmed off the road, striking his dead friend. The second caught Dale's left ear, nearly tearing it from the side of his head. The third found its mark, entering the lower back of his neck.

Mace sprinted from behind the tree and was soon standing over a crying and groveling Darryl as he looked at the dead body of his cousin Sonny.

Darryl said, "Please don't kill me, Mister."

Mace gestured toward the road heading back to the valley. "You get up. Run as fast as you can back down that road. If I see you slowing down, or if I see you looking back this way, you'll get what Sonny got."

The young man nodded. "Yes, sir. I won't look back, sir. I just want to go home."

Mace shoved his arm with his foot. "Go then. And don't look back."

The young man got to his feet and started into a run, fully expecting to be shot in the back. Mace made his way toward the RV. He could see two more trucks blocking the road in front.

He yelled from behind the RV. "Get in your trucks and go or I'll do to you what I did to your friends!"

The door to the RV opened, Tres stepped out. "Jane already shot three up there. A fourth ran off into the woods without his gun."

Mace said, "Let's get these vehicles off the road."

Tres shook his head as they walked past the two bodies in the road behind the trailer. "What we do with 'em?"

Mace replied, "Drag them to the side of the road for the buzzards to peck at. Let's just get this done so we can get out of here."

Chapter 18

Keys were collected and the trucks moved to the side of the road. The bodies were dragged beside them and left for the authorities to deal with.

As Mace walked back past the RV toward the Jeep, Jane grabbed his arm. "Whoa. Hold on there, Champ. You're bleeding."

He glanced down at his arm with a sigh. "Yeah, forgot about that. Took some splinters from a tree."

Jane gestured for him to come aboard. "Let's get that patched up. No need to risk infections if we don't have to."

Three half-inch long splinters were pulled from under his skin. The area was thoroughly cleaned and a bandage applied.

Mace glanced up to see Vanessa sitting beside Tonya. "You ladies OK?"

Vanessa nodded. "I was just saying, we're turning into the rolling death-mobile. What is wrong with people? We should be helping each other."

"If the blackout continues, things will probably get worse. We're only a few days away from those normally helpful people starting to do whatever it takes to feed their families."

Vanessa replied, "I have to wonder if we just stopped and started helping people, you know, organized, would that be enough to make most people behave?"

"Anyone who tries to take an authority position will meet resistance from others who want to either be in control or be left alone. I don't think we'll see any signs of stability until the military makes a move. And right now they are just as much without communications as we are. Maybe if we can get established at the cave we can begin to organize a settlement of our own."

Vanessa sighed. "If there's anyone else left to join us."

Tonya timidly raised her hand. "Mr. Hardy, for what it's worth, I think you are doing what's right. You have to get yourself safe before spreading that around to others. These men here today, they didn't deserve to live."

"Well, we were only trying to defend ourselves. Others might view us as vigilantes. Either way, it's best we get off this highway."

Mace downed a glass of water before heading back to the Jeep. Tres insisted on driving. Mace was happy to give over control.

Johnny again led the caravan forward. The ride through the mountains took another twenty minutes before the group crossed the West Virginia line. Fifteen miles further found them on the road that lead to Organ Cave.

Tres smiled. "Almost home."

Mace frowned. "Sadly, you may be right."

As they approached the east end of the town of Union, the road was once again blocked. A deputy stood next to cars stopped in both directions with three other townsfolk. As the Jeep came to a halt, Mace hopped out and walked toward the deputy.

A townie holding a shotgun stepped into his path. "Hold it right there, Mister."

Mace nodded. "Is there trouble up ahead?"

The townie replied, "Just making sure there's no trouble here."

The deputy approached. "Can you get back in your vehicle, sir? We'll get to you in a minute."

Mace said, "These three vehicles are together."

The deputy asked, "What's your business in Union?"

Mace said, "We're on the road toward Fairlea. Came from Norfolk. Just wanted to get to somewhere safe and peaceful."

The deputy squinted one eye. "Trouble in Norfolk?"

Mace nodded. "Looters, thugs. We just thought it best to get away. The longer this goes, the crazier it will get in the cities. For what it's worth, I think you're doing the right thing here. We've met up with some bad people on the highway already."

The deputy gestured toward the bandage on his arm. "That from a run-in?"

Mace returned his best short laugh. "Just some splinters. Hurt like heck."

The deputy looked over at the RV. "I'll need to do a quick check of your vehicles."

"I'll be up front with you: we packed supplies for the long term, and we are heavily armed. And that's only intended to inform, not to threaten."

The deputy gave him a stern look. "A man's got to protect himself, right?"

"Yes, sir."

The deputy walked over to Johnny's SUV. "Pop the hood please, sir."

Johnny complied.

The deputy walked around back of the SUV. "Open her up please."

Again Johnny followed orders.

The deputy picked over the boxes stacked in the back. "OK, let's check the RV."

The Union cop walked the length of the interior of the RV as Mace stood by the door. "Wow, now this is nice."

Jane smiled. "Thank you. I do competitive shooting and this is what my husband and I travel in."

The deputy stopped. "Competitive? That's with like the targets and such?"

Jane nodded. "Yes."

The deputy asked, "You ever make it to the one in Gerrardstown?"

Jane smiled. "Champion in my division two years running."

"Well ain't that something. My cousin goes up there every year, but I don't think he's ever placed higher than sixth."

"We're still hoping this clears up so we can make this next one. Hate to lose the streak I've got going."

"Well, I can tell you're decent folk. I'll get out of your way. I'm sure you'd like to get where you're going."

Mace stepped onto the roadway, followed by the deputy. "What I said earlier, I think you are doing the right thing here. And you might want to start stockpiling and organizing your town for the longer haul. We had a ham radio up and running a few days ago. This event is worldwide."

The deputy looked at the ground in thought as he scratched behind his ear. "I appreciate the concern, but I think we'll be OK. Sheriff has things in order here."

"Just keep this in mind. When the people in the cities start running out of food, which will be soon, they're going to come looking for it out here. And a hungry man will do what it takes to feed his family. You're quiet and peaceful now, but that could change with one incident."

"You were in the military?"

Mace nodded. "Army Ranger."

The deputy patted him on the shoulder. "You look like the type. And that's not meant as a bad thing. Anyway, you folks take care of yourselves."

"If we happen back this way, can we count on being welcomed?"

The deputy half smiled. "Now that would depend on the situation at that time, wouldn't it?"

"I guess it would."

Mace walked back to the Jeep. The caravan moved forward at a slow roll.

Once past the barricade, Mace said, "That had me spooked. Any one of these sheriffs could turn out to be a bad element. Maybe only looking out for his townsfolk, but in a way that's very bad for us."

Tres asked, "What if he had demanded half our supplies?"

"I can't say that would've been a good thing for him to do. Not that we want to shoot up the good people of the world, but what's ours is ours."

A short drive later had them stopped at the property that held the entrance to Organ Cave.

Mace said, "Is this privately owned?"

Tres nodded. "Yes."

Mace winced. "And you think they won't have issue with us squatting here? If it was public property, that's a whole different matter."

"I guess I didn't think about it. I do have one other bit of news though that I forgot to mention."

"What's that?"

"The cave has a huge supply of saltpeter. During the Civil War, this single cave was said to have supplied three quarters of the saltpeter the South used during the war. We just need some sulfur and charcoal and we can make our own gunpowder."

Mace thought for a minute. "That might come in handy down the road. Although, we're pretty stocked for ammo at the moment."

As they rolled down the drive, they looked around at the buildings on the property. The door to a gift shop was open.

Mace stepped out of the Jeep. "Let's see if the owners are willing to take on some boarders."

Johnny joined him as he walked. "Place looks private. Thought it was a park."

An older man was sitting behind the counter. "Sorry, we're closed until we get power back on."

Mace said, "We're actually wondering if we can camp out here for a while."

The old man glanced out the window and shook his head. "We have RV slots, but no power... or water. And we don't have tank pumping either. You might try the RV park over in Fairlea."

Johnny said, "Well, we don't need power or water. Would you be interested in renting to us anyway?"

The old man shrugged. "Sure, I guess. Just there won't be any tours running until power is back either."

Mace smiled. "Not interested in tours right now. We mostly just want to get away from people."

The old man asked, "Where you from?"

Johnny leaned on the counter as Mace replied, "Norfolk. Things were getting a bit too unstable for us. We had the means, and we picked this place as a starting point for getting away from everyone."

The old man scratched his shoulder. "You got cash? Can't take credit."

Johnny nodded. "How much you want for two RV slots for a couple weeks?"

The old man crossed his arms. "For cash? A hundred fifty dollars. No refunds though. You leave, that's all on you."

Johnny pulled out a wad of bills. "How does four hundred sound for a month? We won't be any trouble."

The old man looked out the window again. "How many of you are there?"

Mace replied, "Eight of us. Youngest is fifteen."

The old man held out his hand. "Jasper Collins."

Mace shook it, assessing his firm grip. "Mace Hardy."

Jasper pointed. "You can pull the RV over there. The cars, heck, park them wherever you want for the moment."

Johnny asked, "You the owner?"

"For the last fourteen years. My father had it for the thirty before that, and his father for twenty-six before him."

They followed the old man out onto the porch of the gift shop. "Cave is over there. Please don't mess around on the walkways while we're closed."

Johnny asked, "How much would you want for a personal tour?"

The old man smirked. "I don't give tours anymore. I got a young staff that does all that for me. Without phones, wouldn't even know how to get in touch with most of 'em. You really didn't pick a good time to come here for a vacation."

Mace said, "That's OK. We aren't here for fun. Just trying to keep ourselves alive."

The old man waved his hand. "Oh pooh, they'll have power back on at any time."

Mace slowly shook his head as he walked down the three steps to the driveway. "I wouldn't be so sure. I hope you're right, but hope doesn't turn on the lights."

The old man tugged at his overalls in the back. "Sorry, been sittin' too long. You think this is permanent or something?"

Mace half frowned. "All we know is it's a worldwide event. Power and communications are out everywhere."

The old man leaned his head back, looking down his crooked nose at the two men. "Everywhere? I wasn't aware of that."

Johnny said, "In the cities they're looting and robbing. The cops are overwhelmed, as are the emergency workers. The government, without communications, has yet to organize any kind of stable response. People will begin to get hungry real soon. And when that happens, well, being in a city is not where you'd want to be."

Mace said, "If you want, we can provide you with security while we're here."

"From what? We got nothing here to steal. Gift shop has snacks and such, but nothing anyone would rob you for."

Mace replied, "Not that I'm looking to argue with you, but a starving girl and her father will beat you senseless for a candy bar. Hunger is a powerful motivator."

"Not worried about that out here. Neighbors can all take care of themselves. Other than that gift shop, all I've got is the cave. Don't see anyone stealing that."

Mace looked toward the entrance. "To be truthful, that cave is why we came here. It offers a defensible location, water, shelter, and from what I understand, saltpeter. If this outage continues, this cave would be an ideal place to take refuge."

"Well, the Confederates thought so. I tell you what... you keep this place secure—just turn anyone away that comes by—and I'll see about getting you a tour. But you gotta be polite. I don't want to drive people off. Just let them know we're closed."

Mace asked, "You had anyone come by since the power went out?"

"First day we had a school bus show up early on. Had to send them on their way without power though. We had a couple come in that afternoon, and one yesterday morning. Nobody since."

The old man fidgeted on the porch, undecided at which direction to turn.

Johnny laughed. "You wanting to go home?"

"That obvious? Just my arthritis in my knees acting up a bit. Without my pills it will spread to my hands. Pills are at home."

Johnny said, "Here, take another two hundred dollars. We'll pay to be your security team."

The old man turned a leery eye. "Why would you pay me for that?"

Mace stepped up. "He only meant that you can trust us, that's all. You've been kind enough to let us stay, he just wants to let you know how much we appreciate it."

The old man looked Mace up and down. "You in the service?"

"I was. Been out for six years now. What gave me away?"

The old man pointed. "Aside from your stance, it's that haircut. May not be how you wore it in the service, but it's not far off."

"Fair enough."

Jasper looked Johnny up and down with a squinted eye. "You... you ever in the circus?"

Johnny pulled back. "What?"

The old man reached out, slapping Johnny on the back. "Just joshin' ya. Tell you what, keep an eye out for me for a bit and I'll see what I can do about a lantern tour tomorrow. I should be back in a couple hours."

The old man pulled the door to the gift shop shut, locked it tight, checked it twice, then scurried down the steps and over to his car.

Mace glanced over at Johnny. "Were you ever in the circus?"

"I'm in the circus right now. Prefer to think of myself as the ringmaster and not one of the clowns. What about you?"

"Elephant trainer."

"That some kind of a big man joke?"

Mace smiled. "You tell me."

Chapter 19

Jasper Collins returned in less than an hour only to roll onto the drive in front of the gift shop and turn around. As quickly as he had come he was again out of sight.

Johnny said, "Trusting guy, huh?"

Mace replied, "Can't say I'd leave my fortune in the hands of strangers."

"It's a cave. He scared we're gonna steal his bats?"

Jane stepped down from the RV, with Tres following. "OK, what's the plan?"

Tres added, "Anyone else notice that we haven't seen Mr. Rogers and Cam?"

"It has me concerned," said Mace. "Not much we can do about it though."

Jane asked again, "Plan?"

"I guess we should think about a thorough recon of the area. Probably wouldn't hurt to have someone up beside the road, identify a way for them to signal us, or a trail for them to run down here with info if anyone is coming in."

Tres said, "I'd be happy to take first watch. If the job is to just watch and run back, I'm qualified for that."

"Consider it your mission. Let's go scout the road."

A short walk had Mace, Jane, Johnny, and Tres standing beside Highway 63, a lightly traveled road. Nothing moved on the blacktop but a slight cool breeze. The previously cloudy sky above had broken clear.

Mace turned toward Tres. "You'll need a jacket. Gonna get cold when that sun sets in about an hour."

"I've got a sport-coat to go over this one. I wasn't expecting cool weather over in Norfolk."

Jane said, "I'll hook you up with a good blanket."

Mace looked up and down the road and then back toward the RV. "I think you could park yourself here beside this building. Should keep you out of the wind if it picks up any. And you have a straight shot down through the trees if needed."

"If I stay out here closer to the road I can see what's coming better. If I wait over there for anyone to come around that curve, I may not know what we're looking at before I have to run."

Mace said, "That'll work too."

Jane pointed. "I don't think we have too much to worry about with anyone coming from behind us. They'd have to hike out of the mountains for that. If we cover this drive, we should be in good shape."

Johnny looked up the roadway going north before turning the other way. "Other end of this road is a little town named Caldwell. There's a short tunnel where the road goes under the railroad tracks. Only a nine foot clearance. If things get rough, we could block off that tunnel. That would leave the only way in as up through here."

Tres said, "We could blow it up."

Johnny laughed. "And how do you propose we do that?"

"We've got all the saltpeter we could want. You familiar with black powder?"

"I'm plenty familiar with black powder. It takes more than saltpeter to make it. Charcoal we can make ourselves, but I'm thinking we might have a shortage of sulfur."

Mace said, "If we have to make a few runs into the local towns, it would be worth the effort. Never know when it might come in handy."

Johnny quipped, "You expecting Yankees?"

Jane smacked him on the arm. "Enough with the smartassery. This is serious."

Johnny held up his hand. "Just trying to lighten the mood. Didn't know the comedy police were out today."

The comment drew a sharp poke in the ribs.

Mace said, "I think it best we all walk every inch of this property. I want to know where every rock or stump or divot in the ground is. If Jasper Collins allows us to stay, this will become our fortress. We'll need to know how to best defend it."

The final hour of daylight was spent circling the property. A path was laid out for a perimeter patrol and water sources were identified. Jane pulled an inflatable mattress from the RV trailer, laying it out neatly inside a tent. Johnny began filtering water from a small creek to fill it.

As Tres turned toward his post at the road, he stopped and asked, "Waterbed?"

Jane replied, "Nope. Water storage. We have eight people, we'll be going through a lot of water."

Tres frowned. "I'm not drinking from that."

Johnny laughed. "OK, but would you shower from it or flush a toilet with it?"

Tres nodded. "Guess I wasn't thinking that through."

Jane said, "I don't know about you, but I like to stay clean if possible. That RV tank is good for two short showers. With this we can stretch that to six. I have another air mattress we can make use of also. It's back in the trailer if you want to go get it for me."

Tres came back with the second mattress. "You do know that whoever sleeps on those is going to be freezing, right?"

"We have enough blankets to throw over them. We should be fine."

Tres shook his head. "Just saying, when the temperature drops, the temperature of those mattresses will fall with it. I had a waterbed once, and in the winter, in a heated house, I would sometimes freeze my butt off."

Johnny said, "Well, OK, you're the mechanical genius. Why don't you design a system that allows us to heat the water and circulate it through here."

Tres smiled as he turned back toward the road. "I'll do just that. It'll give me something to think about while I'm sitting up there."

Johnny said, "You make it to midnight and I'll come up to relieve you."

"Deal."

Mace finished setting up a third tent. "I've been thinking about our defenses. High ground surrounds this place. I don't know that we can defend it well from out here."

Johnny laughed. "I think the big reason for success for this cave back in the Civil War was that it was relatively hidden. Tres was telling me that Yankee troops camped out right up there one winter while the Rebs were still in the cave."

"Yeah, well, the Rebs weren't driving a big shiny RV. If we go out traveling this area, we should look for a way to camouflage it. I don't think your bright red tents here are doing us any favors either."

Johnny stood from a filled mattress. After tossing the hose to one side, the water from his filtration system poured out on the ground.

Mace said, "Are we wasting that?"

"Reverse osmosis. If we wrap a cloth or two around the intake we should be good for quite some time. The system is self cleaning."

Jane walked to the RV steps. "Vanessa and I will get started on some dinner. I think tomorrow we should take a serious look at our supplies. Decide on what we will be needing more of in the short term."

Johnny watched her with a smile as she climbed the steps into the RV. "I do love that woman."

Mace replied, "She's a gold mine."

"Just wish she appreciated my humor more. Those little fists hurt when she punches."

"Yeah, well, be happy she's not a constant giggler. I dated one once, and I can tell you it gets old quick. At first I was like, 'Wow, this is great, somebody that gets my jokes.' A few weeks later I realized she was giggling at everything anybody said. She even laughed when I told her I didn't think we were a good match."

"Vanessa seems to like you."

"Yeah, don't think that's a good match either. She's a sweet girl and all, but we don't have anything in common. I don't have an issue with getting down and dirty if the situation calls for it. I don't see her doing much more than stirring a pot or painting her toenails. Maintenance is what I see. Besides, given the situation, I don't think this is the best of times to start a relationship."

Johnny sat on the end of the trailer. "I don't know, shared experiences are the best things about relationships, and I'm sure we're gonna have a lot of close sharing if this thing continues."

"Anything else we need out of there tonight?"

Johnny turned his head around to look. "Might throw a couple more of those blankets into the tents."

"How many can we sleep in the RV?"

"Six is pushing it. When we designed her, we compromised on extra sleeping space to get things the way we wanted them in there."

"OK, the rest of you can stay in the RV. I'll take a tent where it's less crowded—and where I don't have to listen to your snoring for another night."

Johnny laughed as he leaned toward Mace. "I'm not the snorer, that's Jane. But don't say I said anything. She would kill me if she found out I ratted her out. She's like a buzz saw sometimes."

"You really are a bad liar, you know that? I know for a fact that was you snoring. I actually got up last night and walked over to see if I could get you to stop. You were *this* close to receiving a gut punch."

Johnny shrugged, trying to restrain the grin on his face. "Nope. You must have been sleepwalking. When I sleep, I'm like a little mouse deer staying quiet so the mountain lions don't find me."

Mace shook his head as they stepped up into the RV. "You are about as far from a mouse deer as anyone could get."

Jane said, "What are you boys talking about?"

"Deer hunting," Johnny replied quickly. "Should be good in this area."

Jane turned a piece of meat on the gas grill burner in the RV kitchen. "I'm portioning out four ounces of steak for each of us. We'll be needing to keep up with our protein intake. Mace, you ever gutted and cleaned a deer?"

Mace shook his head as he glanced over at Johnny. "Never shot one."

Johnny pointed to himself. "Well don't look at me. I have a hard time killing a fish."

"Wow. Didn't know I was going on survival with a bunch of wimps. You know, we can only get our nutrition out of a box or a can for just so long. You two are gonna have to man-up if we're gonna make it out here."

Johnny frowned in jest. "Such a harsh taskmaster. Tell you what. You shoot a deer, we'll figure out how to clean it."

Vanessa said, "If you need help with it, I know the basics."

Johnny chuckled. "You? You're telling me Miss Priss has killed and cleaned a deer? I thought you were a big animal rights person?"

Vanessa pulled a tray of biscuits from the small RV oven. "My father was a hunter. Insisted that I go with him and insisted that I help gut the deer we brought back. I never shot one. Could have, but missed on purpose. Anyway, it's been a long time, but I know how."

Johnny replied, "Huh. Never would have taken our little forest nymph for a butcher. You just never know about some people."

"I quit going with him in high school. I've been pro-animal ever since. And before you say anything, Johnny, I am a realist. I don't have any desire to shoot any of the little forest animals, but I will if I have to eat."

"I thought you had never shot a gun."

"A handgun. Plenty of rifles, but not for a long time."

The meal consisted of rice, beans, the small steak portions, and biscuits with honey. Before they sat to eat, Vanessa prepared an extra plate.

Carrying her food and the spare, Vanessa headed for the door. "I'll run this out to Tres. Go ahead and eat without me."

Johnny leaned in. "See, you're missing your chance, bro. Tres is already working on your woman."

Jane asked, "What are you two whispering about?"

Johnny cleared his throat. "Just saying what a sweet girl she is."

Jane returned a suspicious eye.

Mace turned toward Tonya. "How's the shoulder?"

"Better. If I don't move, it just has a dull ache. I just wanted to say thank you to all of you. I just—"

Mace held up his hand. "You've already thanked us enough. Tell us something about yourself. You have any hobbies, play sports? Draw?"

"I was on the swim team out in Montana."

Jane jumped in. "I swam in college! I miss it, but I don't miss the early morning practice. We had to swim for an hour every morning before school."

Tonya frowned. "Left a lot of friends back there. Only thing I've done for the last three months is tend to our chickens."

Johnny took a bite of his steak, consuming half of his portion at once. "We could use some chickens around here. I could build a coop and a fence. You could be our chicken tender."

Johnny laughed to himself.

Tonya asked, "What's so funny?"

"I said chicken tender. Kind of made me hungry for a whole basket of them with some honey-mustard sauce. Pop a top on a Mangrove Dark, now we're talking about a good meal."

Jane sighed. "You have two cases of beer in the trailer and a half dozen in the fridge. If you get started on those, what are you going to do for beer tomorrow?"

"Hey now. I don't drink that much. Besides, what do you expect? I weigh three hundred pounds."

Mace asked Tonya, "Were you a good swimmer?"

"Came in second a lot. My best friend was like this swimming machine. She would beat me by eight lengths in the hundred meter. The colleges were all recruiting her."

After consuming most of a biscuit, Johnny asked, "You have any college aspirations? Any career you thought you might want to pursue once you were out of high school?"

"I don't know, maybe something in the medical field. A nurse or even a doctor maybe."

Jane said, "Either one of those is a good choice for a profession. Nurses or doctors can work anywhere. You don't get squeamish from shots or getting blood drawn, do you?"

Tonya shook her head. "No. My friends said I was weird for it, but I liked going to the doctor. My doctor always made the visits interesting, explaining the cases she had seen since the last time I saw her. I think she loved her job and was happy to have somebody who was interested in hearing her talk about it."

Johnny laughed. "OK, you can be our chicken tender / doctor. How does that sound?"

Tonya half frowned. "I've had my fill of chickens."

The door to the RV opened. Tres came up the steps breathing heavily.

"Car coming up the road. It's turning in."

They scrambled for their weapons. Mace sprinted across the lot to a position he had identified beside the gift shop building. Johnny and Jane headed for a mass of trees while Tres pulled Vanessa into the RV, closing the door and assuming command.

The car pulled slowly up in front of the gift shop before coming to a stop. The engine continued to run for almost a full minute before shutting off. Jasper Collins emerged from the driver's seat.

Mace stood. "Jasper. We were wondering if you were coming back tonight. That's a different car."

The old man waddled around to the back of the new car, popping the trunk before holding out his keys. "Do an old man a favor and go unlock that door."

Mace took the keys, hopped up the three steps and twisted the key in the lock. The door to the gift shop creaked open.

Jasper waddled up the steps, carrying a small crate.

Mace asked, "What you got? Can I help?"

Johnny and Jane joined them.

"Two more boxes in the trunk. You could bring them in."

As they climbed the stairs, light from a battery lantern dimly lit the gift shop.

Johnny looked into the box he carried as he set it on the counter. "Liquor?"

Jane said, "Oh my gosh. Your eye? Were you in a fight?"

Jasper nodded. "Yep. Got home and my grand-nephews were in my liquor. We squabbled, one of them punched me."

Jasper held up his right hand. His knuckles were bruised, with one bleeding.

Johnny said, "You fought back?"

"Punched my nephew Charley in the nose. He went down like a sack of potatoes. Brent came at me. I swung at him and missed. Hit the wall. He backed off, collected his cousin and left. I didn't think it was a good idea to stick around."

Jane said, "Your family attacked you in your own home? That's awful."

Jasper waved his hand. "Not my home. Belongs to my sister and her husband. Anyway, they'll be OK tomorrow. They had a bottle half empty and was just being teenagers."

Jane asked, "Where are their parents?"

"At their home up in Lewisburg. I rent from my sister. Anyway, they was just being kids."

Jane turned to Johnny. "Go bring me that little medical kit."

As Johnny stood, Jasper said, "Now hold on, you don't have to do that. I'm fine."

Jane insisted. "Bring me the kit please."

Johnny looked at Jasper. "Sorry, I gotta do what she says."

Jane asked, "You aren't planning on staying in here tonight, are you?"

Jasper looked toward the back. "I got a padded chair back there. I'll be alright."

Jane shook her head. "Nope. We've got a bed you can sleep on. Johnny and I can sleep in the spare tent tonight. I'll let Tonya and Vanessa have our room and you can sleep in the cabin with Tres. Plenty of room."

Jane stood. "Now, have you had any dinner?"

Jasper returned a sheepish grin. "No."

Jane took his arm. "Come on. We have a little extra."

Johnny hopped up the steps with the medical kit as they came through the door.

Jane pointed, "We're feeding him and he's going to stay in the RV tonight."

Johnny turned around. "OK."

As they walked, Mace moved up close to his three hundred pound friend. "No seconds for Johnny tonight."

Johnny whispered back, "I was already told that earlier. This survival stuff ain't quite the fun and adventure I thought it would be."

Chapter 20

Mace woke in the morning to Jasper standing in the doorway of his tent. "You city people gonna sleep all day?"

Mace rubbed his eyes. "Not even light out yet."

The old man looked up at the sky. "If you come now, I'll give you a personal tour of the cave. Will have to do it by battery lantern."

Mace sat up. "Let me get the others."

The old man shook his head. "Nope. Just you and me. You people were kind to me last night and I want to show something to you, but not everyone."

Mace stood, dropping a blanket as he attempted to shake off a chill. "Cold this morning."

The old man laughed. "This ain't cold. Wait 'til just after Christmas. When we hit zero, you'll be saying it's cold."

He followed the old man to the gift shop, where two battery lanterns were retrieved. They walked to the ramp that led down into the cave.

"Watch your step. Can be a little slick in the morning."

"Must have been fascinating growing up here as a kid."

"Had its perks. My favorite days were the middle of winter when we didn't have visitors. I would sneak over here after school and go exploring with my friend Billy."

Jasper stopped and shook his head. "Billy, he was a hoot. We brought girls in here, had our own little hideaway. Had some good times."

"Billy still around?"

"Nope. Lord took him nearly forty years ago. He got drunk one evening and decided he was gonna ride a bull around the pasture at his daddy's farm. That was a mean old bull, and I guess Billy thought he was meaner. Anyway, it was standing by a fence, he jumped on its back. It bucked once, throwing him onto a little rock outcropping on the ground next to him. Broke his back."

Mace grimaced. "Wow. Tough way to go."

"Not what killed him. It was the goring he took after reaching over and slapping that bull on the leg. Doc's said he would have recovered from the fall. That bull tore into him something fierce. Just glad I wasn't there when it happened or I would have jumped that fence and probably been dead too."

"Even tougher way to go. I lost a good friend over in the Middle East. Kid came out of a room I had just checked and shot him in the face. I got out of the service shortly after."

Jasper stopped. "I ran the scenarios through my head for months about why I wasn't there, and if I had been what I would have done. There are just things in this world that you can't control and you have to accept. We all live and we all die."

He began to walk again, shuffling his feet. "Doesn't take much effort to postpone that death if you have a desire to live. Losing Billy was hard, as was your friend to you I'm sure, but living, that's something else. There is just so much to see and do. So many interesting people to meet."

"You love giving tours of this place, don't you."

"The people are what give this cave life. They're what gives me life. Without the people it's just a big hole in the ground, with bats. I'd still be giving tours if I didn't wear out so fast."

They walked into the area of the cave known as the Chapel Room. It was huge. It was easy to see how it had held so many soldiers during the civil war. Mace followed the old man as they walked back through twists and turns. A short climb took them down another passage, where again they ventured off on several splits.

When they reached the destination Jasper had in mind, he walked into a small room and turned to face Mace. "This is it, mine and Billy's place. That slab was his, this was mine."

The old man sat down on the carved out rock, looking around the room. "Haven't been in here since Billy died. Just couldn't make myself do it. I passed that entrance once, but couldn't make myself look in."

Mace smiled as he sat on Billy's bunk. "Glad you showed it to me. Wish I had somewhere like this to come when thinking about Harry. I've got no desire to go back to the Middle East."

"Wanna see what we used to do to the girls when we brought them back here?"

"Not particularly."

Jasper flipped off the lantern. It was the blackest black that Mace's eyes had ever been witness to.

"You scared?"

"Getting there."

"You bring a girl back here and turn out the light, she'd let you grab just about anything you wanted just to get herself back out of here. Of course, you try that now and you get arrested. Back then you either got lucky or got slapped. I got one of each. Not that I'm some pervert or anything, we was just dumb kids fooling around. Word about it got out quick and we never had dates that came in here again."

"You can turn that light on again anytime you like."

Jasper laughed. "You worried I'm gonna grope you?"

"I wasn't until now."

Jasper chuckled. The bright light flashed in his eyes.

After a moment of getting used to it, the old man stood. "Come on, Missy, let's get you out of here."

Jasper stopped at the hidden room's entrance, grabbing onto Mace's arm. "Thanks for coming back here with me. It's something I haven't been able to get myself to do. I appreciate the company."

As they walked, Mace said, "When I told you yesterday about this place being our destination for a reason, I was serious. I don't think power is coming back. And people aren't far from attacking one another over food."

The old man stopped, shining the light in his eyes. "Tell you what: the lot of you can stay so long as the power is out. You can make yourself at home, in the cave if you like, but you can't be doing anything destructive. If the power comes back, I gotta make a living, you know."

"How about this: we'll provide you with security and food so long as you give us free run of this place. We may move a few things around, but we'll be careful to preserve what was there."

The old man again held the light up to his face again. "Deal. Just wanted to see it in your eyes. You can read a man's soul by looking deep in his eyes."

When they emerged from the cave, the sun was just about to rise over the trees. Johnny and Jane were standing beside the RV. Tres was up at the road.

As they approached, Jane scowled. "You can't just run off like that. We had no idea where you two went. Tres looked down into that cave entrance and there were no lights."

"Jasper just took me on a quick tour, that's all. We discussed our use of the cave. We have his permission to use these grounds and that cave so long as we respect it. And protect and feed him."

Johnny yelled. "Hey, Tres!"

A voice came back from near the roadway. "Yeah?"

Johnny yelled again: "Come on down here for a sec! We've got some news!"

Tres hustled through a pack of trees and down a short leaf-covered hill before stopping in front of them. "What's up?"

Johnny gestured toward the cave entrance. "You got your cave. You win."

"What do you mean?"

Mace replied, "We have full use of the property. All we have to do is keep Mr. Collins fed and secure."

"Sweet! So we can go in the cave?"

"Just treat her nice. She's my life and livelihood."

Tres looked off at the cave entrance. "Oh, you don't have to worry about that. This place is like a historical shrine to me. I can't wait to get in there. You giving tours?"

Jasper Collins rolled his eyes. "Sure. Just give me a couple minutes to evacuate my bladder. Getting old has its penalties."

Minutes later, Tres and Vanessa followed Jasper toward the mouth of the cave.

Mace turned to Johnny. "I think our coming here is going to work out. The old man is good stock. Today we—"

The chopping sound of rotor blades could be heard echoing off the hills. Seconds later, Don Rogers' helicopter popped over a ridge, swept in, and settled in a nearby field. As the blades came to a stop, Cam jumped out, his father right behind.

After a short jog, Don Rogers said, "Glad you made it. That weather front threw us for a loop. We had to go down to Roanoke and set down for a while. Was able to fuel up again, but we had to leave last night. Some kind of ruckus kicked up."

Cam nodded. "We could see the muzzle flashes from gunfire. Half a dozen trucks busted through the main gate."

"We think they were looking for either a plane or a helicopter, so we got out of there before they came our way. We spent the rest of the night in a big field about fifty miles south of here before a farmer chased us off. Thought he was gonna start shooting at us."

"Glad you made it," said Johnny. "We had another gun battle of our own coming through the mountains. More hijackers trying to rob people."

Don shook his head. "It's like somebody let all the nuts out at once. Oh, and we took a ride up to Lewisburg and Fairlea. Looks like the exits off I-64 are blocked, as are the bridges and roads in and out of those towns. The locals seem to be taking charge in the smaller places. Didn't see a single police car in Roanoke. I'm sure they were there somewhere, but the roads were peppered with accidents. I-81 is a complete mess in and around the city. I would expect that we'll see a steady stream of cars heading out looking for food or shelter. Still no sign of National Guard being rolled out. When we passed the armory at Bedford yesterday, there was activity there, but it didn't look like they were ready to go anywhere."

Johnny shook his head. "The insanity grows."

Don looked around. "You just take the place over?"

Mace replied, "Better. We made a deal with the owner. We'll protect his property and feed him. In exchange, we have free rein to do what we want."

Don gestured toward the roadway. "First thing you're gonna want to do is block off that entranceway. We need to do something to let people know this place is off limits."

"My concern with that is if you block it off, and people are out looking for food, they will stop and ask. And I don't know about you, but if we get a bunch of families coming down the road just trying to feed their kids, it will be hard to turn them away. For me at least."

Cam asked, "How's the girl doing?"

Jane pointed toward the RV. "Go in and ask her yourself."

"I don't know her. What do I say?"

Jane laughed. "You say, 'How are you feeling?' Can you swim?

Cam replied, "Swim? Yes."

"Well there you go. You both have something in common. Just go in and say hi. You aren't asking her on date, are you?"

Cam turned a slight shade of red. "No. Was just wondering."

"Go in, get a soda from the fridge, ask how she's doing."

Cam half smiled. "I can do that."

As the teen disappeared up the steps of the RV, Jane turned to Johnny. "Were you like that back in high school?"

Johnny shook his head. "Not me."

Jane looked at Mace. "At that age I was terrified up until my first girlfriend. After that I was OK."

Don said, "Don't look at me. I was married right out of high school."

Mace asked, "Any word from anyone of power or comms coming back up?"

Don shook his head. "I connected with another ham-head at the airport. He has a fifty foot antennae setup at his house. Said nothing was coming through."

Johnny said, "So, what do we do this morning for securing this cave?"

Mace replied, "We have six or eight neighbors surrounding this place. I say we enlist their help in our cause. If we can make their homes the first line of defense, that gives us a buffer. And it gives them a secure place to fall back to. When Mr. Collins comes back out, we can quiz him on the neighbors. He's been here his whole life, he should know who they are."

Mace turned to Don. "You flew up to Lewisburg and Fairlea. Other than roads being blocked, any signs of unrest?"

"There was a building smoldering in Lewisburg, but that could have been from anything. There are only three roads leading in here: straight down at Caldwell, 219 coming out of Ronceverte, and 219 coming up from Union. We have two bridges just south of here at Second Creek. There are other back routes, but those are the major ones."

Jane crossed her arms. "Maybe Tres' idea of blowing up bridges wasn't so bad."

Mace laughed. "OK, for the moment at least, we aren't blowing any bridges. We destroy public roads and we're begging for the National Guard or the Army to come take us out. Let's shelve that one until the situation starts to border the extreme."

Mace walked Don around the perimeter of the new domain. When they returned, Jasper Collins was emerging from the cave, with Tres and Vanessa at his heels.

Jasper walked up the steps to his gift shop, opened the door, and proceeded in with Tres still behind him. Tres came out seconds later, joining them at the RV.

Johnny said, "He kick you out?"

"Said I was asking too many questions."

Mace said, "Well, give the man a break. That's his second tour this morning, and I would bet he's a bit tired from it."

"Completely worn out is more like it. He had to stop and sit half a dozen times on the way out."

Mace began to walk toward the gift shop. "I'll check on him. Hope he's up for a few questions about his neighbors."

The Ranger hopped up the steps and walked through the door. Jasper was in his chair and already fast asleep. Mace turned, quietly making his way back to the RV.

"Poor old guy is out."

Johnny pointed at the trailer. "Why don't we look at emptying whatever we think we'll want to store in the cave. You can give Jane and me the short tour."

Vanessa said to Jane, "It's actually a cool place. You'll like it in there. Once we got down that ramp, Mr. Collins seemed excited to talk about it. He's crotchety, but very funny."

Johnny laughed. "I bet he's given that tour five thousand times."

Mace gestured toward the property entrance. "Tres, go watch the road for us. Vanessa, have a check on Tonya. Might be good to get her out here in the fresh air and sunshine. You two, come with me. I'll show you around."

Mace took the battery lantern from the counter in front of a sleeping Jasper. His tour lasted half an hour and was limited to the front rooms of the cave. Once back out in the daylight, he again checked in on their host. Jasper was staring at a shot of whiskey that sat on the counter in front of him.

Mace asked, "You OK?"

Jasper waved his hand. "I'll be fine."

"Kind of early for a drink, don't you think?"

"It's not for me. It's for Billy. I never said goodbye to him. Thought this would be a good time."

"I'll come back in a bit."

"No. No. You got a question, go ahead and ask. Billy can wait. He ain't going anywhere."

Mace leaned on the counter. "What do you know of your immediate neighbors?"

"What you want to know?"

"Are they approachable? Would they be interested in being a sort of perimeter watch if we provide a place for them to fall back to in case of trouble?"

The old man scratched his head in thought. "Let's see, we got three up here on the main road and three down the road behind 'em. One of the houses on the main road is empty and for rent. A trailer on this back road is the same. That leaves us with four. Three out of the four are elderly couples about my age."

Jasper thought for few seconds. "The fella on the main road closest to the entrance doesn't much care for me. We used to have summer concerts and picnics out here and he got annoyed by the music. Other than that, I wouldn't hesitate to knock on any of their doors. Just be up front about what you are offering. I'm sure most of them will just want to be left alone."

Jasper sat forward in his chair. "I really don't think you'll get much warning out of any of them. They might even be more of a burden than a help."

"How you figure?"

"Well, Jack Altman has Parkinson's. He don't move so well. His wife is barely able to drive him to the doctor now. The Bains rarely come out of their house anymore. In fact, you know, I think they might be down in Blacksburg with their daughter. They used to do that and come back about Thanksgiving.

"And Angus Parker and his wife Mildred, might be down in Florida by now. They go every winter. Not sure if they left yet or not. Might be too early. The grumpy one is David Davidson. He inherited from his parents about twenty years ago."

"The riding pen out there, you have horses? They might come in handy if fuel gets short."

"We've got one. Old Mag. She's just an old plow horse, mostly just use her for the kids to pet. I have a deal with several of the neighbors around here that manage the horse rentals and such on their own. We had six of our own at one point, but they were just too much to keep up."

"I really don't like where the RV is right now. Would it bother you if I moved it down here? Along with our tents?"

Jasper shrugged. "Don't mind at all. You're in charge, do what you want."

"I also want to move Johnny's SUV up to block the drive."

"You're in charge of security, Mr. Hardy. Move what you want where you want."

After a dozen related questions, Mace got to work screening the neighbors. All was as Jasper had said. The lone holdout was David Davidson. He was one of those people who had a constant scowl on his face. He wanted no part of whatever scheme the visitors had cooking. When Mace returned, the SUV was in the drive and the RV parked in the trees by the gift shop. Their tiny kingdom was slowly being secured.

Chapter 21

By lunchtime Mace found himself on the road in the Jeep with Tres. The ride to Ronceverte took all of eight minutes. The south side of the bridge over the Greenbrier River was barricaded with cones and blocked by two pickups.

A deputized townie came out to meet them. "What business you have here?"

Mace said, "Just looking to purchase supplies if possible. We have cash."

The man looked into the Jeep windows. "Can't let those weapons into town."

"Can we park and walk in?"

The man shrugged. "Sure, but the weapons still stay here."

Tres asked, "Any chance we can get a ride in? Twenty bucks to speed us on our way?"

A second younger man stood behind the first. "For a twenty I'll ride you around. My shift is up anyway."

Mace said, "One of those your truck?"

The man nodded. "Green one."

"For fifty would you take us around where we want and then bring us back here?"

The young man half smiled. "Seventy-five?"

Mace agreed. "Take us in. Oh, and for you, twenty bucks if you watch the Jeep. I would like our weapons to be there when we get back."

The man nodded. "They'll be there. Only been five cars through here this morning. But I'll take that twenty."

Mace parked the Jeep, peeled off a bill to the remaining townie, and hopped into the cab of the green truck. Tres climbed in back.

"Name's Mace. You got a name?"

"Friends call me Bucky. Had bad buck teeth before my braces. Name stuck even after they was fixed. It's what everybody knows me by, so I just roll with it. What is it you're looking for? Groceries is right here. All the meat's gone though. They just got a generator running this morning for all the coolers. They do have strict per person limits though. Only restocking is limited to farmers bringing in local produce."

"We're OK on food, but I would like to stop there on our way back. Wouldn't happen to have an Army-Navy store in town, would you?"

Bucky shook his head. "Nope. Closest one of those I know of is all the way down in Radford, below Roanoke."

"OK. How about somewhere that has plastic tarps? We want to cover a vehicle. Just don't want anyone bothering us."

"We have a home supply store. I can take you right there. I think they opened this morning. Oh, and everybody is cash only."

They arrived at the store to find a dozen other vehicles in the parking lot.

Once inside, they were directed to the tarps. A dozen large camo-green tarps were purchased and thrown in the bed of the pickup.

Mace asked, "Happen to know where we could get sulfur?"

Bucky turned. "Making your own gunpowder?"

Mace nodded. "Would like to have that option."

"Well, gun shop might have some. We got a lot of black powder rifles around here. If not the one here, we got a shop up in Fairlea or even further up in Lewisburg."

"I'd pay extra if you'll take us."

Bucky smiled. "Hot dang! I'm gonna make more toting you around than I would have if work was running."

"What do you do for a living?"

"I wash down the floors at my uncle's chicken coops. It's a nasty job, but at least I have a full suit and a mask. New regulations since all the bird flu problems."

Tres asked, "Don't you have to keep the coops running? I mean, the chickens don't power off."

Bucky laughed. "Chickens power off... sometimes I wish they would. No, the buildings I clean are at the end of a cycle. We just sent the whole lot to slaughter ten days ago. Without power I couldn't run the pumps to clean the place out. What you do?"

Mace said, "Bartender."

"Now that's a job I couldn't handle. I'd be drinking all the profits."

"Wouldn't be hard to do. Although, I will say that since I've been on the other side of the counter I drink a lot less. Kind of loses its flavor, if you know what I mean."

They pulled into the local gun shop. "Sign says open. Not sure what he'll sell you, since you're from out of town."

Mace hopped out of the truck and made his way through the front door with Tres right behind. One man sitting in a chair looked at him suspiciously while another stood behind a counter.

"What can we do you for?"

Mace replied, "Wouldn't happen to have any sulfur, would you?"

"I do. How much you need?"

"How much you got?"

"Comes in five pound buckets."

Mace reiterated: "How much you got?"

The man thought for a moment. "I got probably forty, no, fifty buckets. Black powder season's coming up and it's popular around these parts."

Mace said, "I'll take as many as you're willing to sell me."

The man's eyes lit up. "I'm willing to sell it all if you've got cash."

"How much?"

The man leaned back his head in thought. "Mmm. Two thousand?"

Mace pulled a stack of bills from his jacket pocket, laying it on the counter. "I just happen to have it on me."

The man smiled as he looked over at the other man in the chair. "I may just close for the rest of the week! Anything else I can sell you?"

Tres said, "Fuse cord?"

The man again smiled. "Got a roll of sixty feet. You fellas planning on blowing something up?"

Mace shook his head. "No, just a fireworks celebration. I like making my own shells. I was going to wait a while, but with power out, got nothing but time on my hands. Thought I'd get an early start on New Year's planning."

The man gave a half smile. "Must be one heckuva celebration."

"By the looks of it, not even sure if it will happen this year."

"You're telling me. This is just crazy. I think it's the Russians or the Chinese."

Tres replied, "Nope. They are out of power too. The whole world's out."

The man tilted his head back. "You don't say. How do you know this?"

"Ham radio, but even that's out now. We're expecting to see some Army or National Guard movements any day now. Your people did well to block off your town."

"It's been good for business, I'll tell you that. Sold half my stockpile of ammo in the last three days."

Mace paid the man for the cord. "If I need anything else, I'll be back to do business with you."

The man said, "Bucky, just pull the truck around back. We'll help you load it."

Once across the river, the materials were transferred to the Jeep, loading it down to its maximum. As they pulled back onto the asphalt, the front end tilted into the air for a short hop. The ride back was slow as the front wheels squirreled around on the roadway due to the weight in the back. When they arrived back, the cargo was carried into the cave.

Johnny and Jane were sent back to Ronceverte in the SUV for any food supplies that could be obtained. Mace took his time on watch duty by the roadway. Soon after he had taken a seat, Jasper came slowly waddling up through the woods.

"What you coming all the way up here for?"

"I love to talk about the cave, but that Tres just asks one question after another. He wants the short version to every question. Keeps cutting off my stories."

Mace laughed. "He's a good kid. Just an enthusiast. The Civil War is one of his passions."

"Yeah, well, I didn't fight in it. I wasn't there. I just have the stories that were passed down to me, and he's not interested in stories."

"Well, you're welcome to sit up here as long as you want."

Jasper nodded. "I know that. I own it."

"You've got that dry sense of humor like Johnny."

Jasper turned to face him. "Johnny? That overstuffed windbag? Always the joke cracker. I'm starting to wonder if I made a bad deal."

Mace was quiet for a moment.

Jasper took a deep breath. "Seriously, though, I am glad you people showed up. I love my sister and her kids, and their kids, but I would be going nuts sitting over there with nothing to do. Would have more fun just sitting out here looking at cows."

Mace crossed his arms. "I'm glad this worked out the way it did too."

Jasper crossed his arms. "You know, I was thinkin'... if we blocked the road just down around the curve here, and just before 52 up here, we wouldn't have to worry about any cars. People traveling through could still go around on 52. We just need the neighbors through this stretch aboard. Put up a sign that says, 'bridge out - use 52.' That would give us almost a mile stretch of our own territory."

"How many people would that be?"

Jasper thought. "Maybe twenty-five homes?"

"Not bad. We could let them in and out whenever they wanted, and get them to help with policing those points."

"That's possible. I know just about every one of them. Only two or three moved in the last few years that haven't stopped by."

A car came up the road. Mace helped Jasper around behind the small building they sat beside.

"You recognize that car?"

"Not certain. Looked like the Jensens. I might could have seen better if someone wasn't jerking on my arm."

Mace laughed. "You are ornery, aren't you?"

"I'm really an old softy. But I'm guessing you already knew that."

"Secret's safe with me."

Johnny and Jane returned an hour later with an SUV loaded with food. Shortly thereafter, a truck arrived carrying two large gas grills and a three hundred gallon propane tank. Attachments were connected to the tank allowing the refill of the smaller grill tanks. The grills were pulled down the walkway into the Chapel Room of the cave, along with a large portion of the supplies.

Mace met them at the gift shop, looking at the entrance to the cave. "Any way we can build a wall across that opening? Maybe a walkway behind it that we can defend from if needed?"

Johnny took a deep breath. "Big opening. We'll need a lot of wood."

Mace glanced toward Ronceverte. "Building supply over there has stacks of lumber. Bet we could get a truckload brought out here. How are we doing with cash?"

Johnny thought for a moment. "I'm guessing we've burned through maybe eight thousand. We brought forty. And don't mention it to anyone, but we have twenty ounces of gold hidden on the RV. I figure the cash is probably only good for a month. The gold maybe a couple months after that. At some point we will want to set ourselves up to barter for whatever we need. I'm wishing I had paid more attention to those prepper magazines."

"You had forty grand in cash laying around?"

Johnny chuckled. "In a safe, but yeah. Was getting time to trade in the SUV for a newer model. I like taking cash so I can wave it in the sales-manager's face when negotiating. Guess it was an opportune time for the world to go nuts."

In the days that immediately followed, two truckloads of wood were delivered to the drive in front of the gift shop. Power tools were purchased and the generator of the RV used to power them. As Johnny and Tres worked at closing off the front of the cave, Jane joined Mace for another run into town.

The following afternoon, a five hundred gallon diesel tank was delivered to the property and filled. The twenty-some-odd neighbors were contacted and the roadway in front of Organ Cave was blocked off. A small building at the corner of 219 and 63 was converted to a storage and drop-off point. Any new materials or supplies would be delivered to that location, before being moved to the cave area or the other homes.

Within ten days of their arrival, the community organized around Organ Cave was bustling with activity. The ladies of the surrounding homes took turns cooking meals as the men continued to work on security and growing food.

Jasper sat in a rocker on the gift shop porch as Mace walked up the steps. "You fellas sure are organized."

"Not like we have a choice. I'm starting to get worried about the size of our group though. The outlying neighbors are wanting in. I don't know that we can support everyone."

"I've been thinking about that. What you might want to do is to organize the surrounding neighbors into their own co-op groups. Let them work on their own security and food issues. To you, they would just be trading partners."

Mace frowned. "Wish it was that easy. You're talking setting up mini governments, and that's not something we had ever planned on taking on."

Jasper crossed his arms. "I don't know... the way I see it, you either get these people on your side or they might be the ones that become hostile. Let them govern themselves. You just trade with them and maybe work out security pacts.

"You could organize this whole valley if you wanted. They're most all good folks. You said you've talked to the sheriff in Union, and the people guarding the bridge into Ronceverte. That just leaves Caldwell, and this valley is mostly locked up tight. Go make deals with those three to not let suspicious people through and we can all be one big happy family."

Mace laughed. "Says the man whose grand-nephew punched him in the eye."

"Not saying you won't have problems—you will. They'll just be on a much smaller scale. A black eye doesn't compare to a bullet in the back."

Mace looked across the property at Vanessa as she walked up to the roadway where Tres continued to stand guard. He wondered if they had done the right thing. Bringing outside people into a situation that seemed to be quickly ballooning out of control had not been in his plans.

He thought of the young girl Tonya and how much better a more sparsely populated Montana sounded than the worry that was becoming West Virginia. Survival here would not be limited to the undertakings of their small group. It would take the cooperation of the valley and the small towns surrounding it. His feelings of woe were broken as Derwood trotted up and sat in front of him. The simplicity of a dog's life had a sudden appeal.

Chapter 22

Repeated trips to Ronceverte and Caldwell had both towns agreeing to a cooperative security pact with the Organ Cave valley. The sheriff at Union was less than willing to combine and coordinate efforts. A trip was arranged with Mace and Johnny making the short trek. They met in the sheriff's office.

Johnny said, "All we're asking is you don't let anyone suspicious through to our side. Sheriff Dillings and Chief Capp have already agreed. Travel on 219 will be restricted to the locals. That means a secure area for your people as well."

The Union sheriff, Dak Lumber, wasn't interested. "The last I checked this was still a free country. I can prevent outsiders from staying in my town, but I have no jurisdiction to keep them from passing through."

Mace shook his head. "Actually you do, Sheriff. Our government is incapacitated at the moment. That leaves the security of your town and its surroundings up to you. We aren't asking for you to turn away all traffic, just that which doesn't belong here. If someone is passing through, they can just as easily go around. The other main roads are open."

The sheriff scowled. "And what happens when the next set of towns and the next block off all traffic? What happens when you can't go around?"

Johnny said, "That's when you have full security. Your kids can go out to play. Your businesses can reopen. Heck, you could even reopen your schools. You could coordinate all up and down this valley to make sure your food supply stays adequate.

The sheriff huffed. "Peh!"

"If you just close off your town, you'll find yourself short on food and other materials. Look, you make a deal with Sweet Springs and you only have to worry about the road coming north. You make a deal with the authorities down in Peterstown and you can have this whole valley secure. We're talking about protecting us all, Sheriff."

The meeting ended with the sheriff asking the two to kindly leave.

Johnny talked as he drove. "What a stubborn mule. We've been two solid weeks without power and communications. What does he not understand about it not coming back on?"

"He's got a dozen generators running in his town. As far as he's concerned, power is back on."

"People like that are just frustrating. You wonder how they managed to get put in those positions."

"I think that's been a problem since the dawn of man. We often disagree. Half the time our only reason *to* disagree is because we can."

Mace held up his hand as they approached the bridge at Second Creek. "Hold up. Maybe we just talk to the neighbors here and block the bridge. Travelers could always cut back over at Pickaway."

Johnny got out at the bridge and looked down in the creek. "That could work. We'd need somebody here around the clock. Maybe even draw from the locals here."

Mace took a deep breath. "I hate to say Jasper was right, but local coordination looks like the way to go. At least at this stage anyway."

As they returned to the cave, Don was landing in the helicopter. "Airport at Roanoke is a goner. Completely overrun by hoodlums. And there must be two dozen fires burning in that city. I flew over the guard armory at Bedford. They're still sitting tight. More vehicles have arrived, but they aren't putting them to use. Although, they do have 460 blocked in both directions. They're turning cars back. I don't think power is coming back on anytime soon."

Johnny said, "We've almost got this valley buttoned up. Tres is out with Vanessa getting statuses from the different co-ops on food. We have eight groups policing themselves, guarding their own roads."

Mace gestured toward the helicopter as Tonya and Cam walked around it. "Those two seem to be getting along well."

Don replied, "I've tried to encourage them to get with the other teenagers in our co-op here. We have four others, but they seem content staying to themselves."

Johnny asked, "She do OK in the helicopter?"

"She was a little uneasy at first. Doesn't seem to have an issue with motion sickness."

Mace said, "There's an airport in Blacksburg. Have you scouted it out?"

"Not in the past week. You up for a ride over there?"

"Johnny and Jane can hold down the fort here. We have a trade for a couple cows coming up tomorrow. Other than that, things are quiet right now."

Mace turned around to face Jasper. "You ever been up in a helicopter?"

"Can't say I ever have. Or ever wanted to."

Mace laughed. "Well, come keep us company. You won't even have to get out of your seat."

"I can handle that."

Forty minutes later they were circling the airport.

Don said, "I don't like the looks of that. See those burned out hulls down there? Last week those aircraft were intact."

Mace looked through a pair of binoculars. "The fuel truck is parked by that hangar. Don't see anyone around it. Take us in lower."

Don frowned. "Just don't want people shooting at us."

"You're a good pilot. I'm sure you can get us out of here if we need it. Take me down where I can get a look inside that hangar."

Don worked the throttle. They soon hovered at a hundred feet above the opposite side of the runway.

Mace said. "I see two people standing in the hangar. Nothing looks out of whack. Take us over. Drop me on the runway, I can jog the rest."

Don replied, "It's your skin."

Jasper asked, "Pass those binocs back here. I'll keep an eye out for you."

"That building over there, it's the fire department. You get into trouble, you try to make the field behind it. I'll pick you up there."

Mace hopped out onto the runway. Don lifted off, heading to what he believed to be a safe distance. After a short jog, he came to a stop in front of the open hangar doors.

Mace yelled at the two men inside, "You guys selling any fuel?"

One of the men replied back. "Who's asking?"

Mace yelled, "Just passing through. We have cash."

A third man emerged from an interior door. "You got anything to trade?"

Mace walked forward. "Possibly. What do you need?"

The man laughed. "Booze. Every liquor store in town has been drained. We've got almost ten thousand students milling around with nothing to do but drink. Has left the rest of us dry."

Mace stopped just in front of the three men. "I thought the university was a lot bigger than that."

"It is. Most of them lit out in their cars trying to get to wherever home is. The rest decided to stay and party, only they're finding out the party is over. Gas stations in town have been drained. Some have tried to steal ours."

"I guess their cars would run pretty good on that 100LL. How much do you have?"

The man in back said, "Enough. What you need?"

Mace scratched his head. "Tell you what, you top us off now for cash and we'll be back for more. And I promise to bring you liquor. No charge."

The man with the shotgun said, "You do understand that promises from people we don't know are meaningless, right? We can't trust every yahoo that comes through here. This is a valuable commodity. What is that, a Robinson you got out there? What's to keep us from just taking it from you?"

Mace replied, "The owner, who isn't out there, is a marksman for one. Used to be a sniper in the military. You do us wrong and he'll come back through those woods and pick you off one by one. You can hold us hostage if you like, but I'm just a messenger. That chopper is worth way more to him than we are. He has another fifty ex-military types working for him as well. So not someone you want to cross."

The three men talked quietly among themselves. "Tell you what. We can part with twenty gallons today. That's at twenty-five dollars a gallon."

"That's half the fuel we'll have used getting here and back today. Although given the circumstances, that seems fair. And I'll do my best to get you that booze."

Mace turned and signaled the hovering helicopter with a broad wave. Shortly after, it settled on the tarmac outside the hangar.

Mace stuck his head inside the door. "I got us twenty gallons for now. They said they would sell us more if we bring back liquor."

Jasper crossed his arms. "You sold me out, didn't you?"

Mace laughed. "No, I wasn't even thinking of yours. I was thinking we might be able to barter for some with the town folks."

Jasper shook his head. "You do realize you are smack in the middle of still country back there, don't you? We can make our own booze. I just don't want you trading out my good whiskey for gas."

Don said, "We do have a brewer living with us. A still might not be a bad idea anyway."

The fuel bill was settled, the chopper was filled, and they were soon back in the air.

Mace said, "Take us over Roanoke. I want to see what it looks like. And Mr. Collins, let me see the binoculars again."

Jasper protested. "No, I got 'em. I'm using them."

Don chuckled.

"Just give them to me. Once I've assessed the situation I'll give them back."

Jasper handed the binoculars forward. "Here, might as well be gouging out the old man's eyes. I can't see anything from this high up."

Mace laughed as he took the glasses. "You act like you're on a sightseeing tour or something. Next time I'll just leave you in your rocker where you belong."

Don said, "You two plan on keeping this up all the way back?"

Jasper huffed, "What's it to you, flyboy? Donald... who names their kid Donald?"

Mace turned. "You know he has the button for the ejection seat up there, right?"

Jasper replied, "Turn your lyin' ass around. I ain't so dumb as to think there's an ejection seat in a helicopter. Now if you'd of said a trap door, I might have been worried."

Fires raged on the ground in Roanoke. A hard bang could be heard coming from one of the skids.

Don said, "That was a bullet. Someone down there's taking potshots at us. Time to go."

Mace nodded. "Could you take us over to Peterstown and then up 219? Just want to get a look at what's to the south of us."

Don replied, "I'll swing down to I-77. It was backed up last time I was over that way. Was a long line coming south from Charleston. Not sure where they thought they were going."

The flight over Peterstown was peaceful. A roadblock could be seen at each of the major roads coming into town. Five minutes later they hovered three thousand feet above the I-77/Highway 460 interchange. Smoke billowed up from below.

Mace gazed through the binoculars. "I'd say they have a major problem down there. That has to be fifty vehicles parked around that semi. A group has the driver out on the ground."

Jasper pressed: "Can I please see the binoculars?"

Mace held up his hand. "Hold on. They're picking him up. Crap! They just executed the guy. And they're pulling packages from the back of the trailer. This is the sort of rolling gang I've been afraid of. They're pulling people out of northbound cars and—"

Mace pulled down the binoculars. "Let's get back to the cave. I think we need to reevaluate our defenses."

The binoculars were handed back to an eager Jasper. "They are taking over that whole interchange, 460 and I-77."

Jasper lowered the binoculars in silence.

Mace glanced back. "Saw something you never wanted to see, didn't you?"

Jasper sighed. "Where's our government in all this? That's just complete lawlessness."

The ride back to the cave was quiet.

Tres and Vanessa had returned from their run to the different co-ops. Food stocks in the valley were adequate, but in need of beefing up with the coming winter.

Mace pulled Tres aside. "What would you say if I asked you to build a still?"

"You mean as in an alcohol distiller?"

Johnny's ears perked up. "Wait, what?"

Mace nodded. "We have some new friends at the airport in Blacksburg that are willing to trade us avgas if we bring them liquor. I figured with you being a brewer that would be right up your alley. And aside from it's obvious uses, it might be something of value to trade. I'd rather not be trading food for other goods. And we aren't trading guns or ammo."

Tres grinned. "I'll get started on a design immediately."

Mace asked, "What are you so happy about?"

"I've been working up a processor for the saltpeter. The troughs back there in the cave the Confederates used are crude. I should be able to get decent quality out of a setup I've been putting together with Vanessa's help. You know, she's actually a very smart girl. She gets how a valve works and how a press functions. Most people just get confused or annoyed when you talk to them about things like that."

"Sounds to me like she might be getting a bit sweet on you."

Tres looked nervous. "You think?"

Mace laughed. "Relax. Just keep doing what you are doing. If she decides she likes you it will be because she likes *you* and not someone you think she might like."

Mace turned around to Johnny and Jane. "We just saw a gang of about fifty vehicles down on I-77. They raided a semi and then a half dozen or so cars that were passing by. Something like that is exactly why we need to secure the roads in and out of here."

Jane asked, "Are they coming this way?"

Mace shook his head. "Can't tell. They had the interchange there locked down tight. My guess is they will move on when the well of people coming their way runs dry."

Jane put her arm around her husband's shoulder. "Anything we can do to deter them from coming up 219? Maybe we could warn the sheriff at Union."

Johnny huffed. "I can tell you what he would do. He would offer them a speed pass through his town if they would just keep going."

"Nonetheless, we should warn them that they might be coming."

Mace said, "Johnny, come with me. We're going back to Union. And, Don, wait a bit and go back and check on that interchange. If they *are* coming this way, set down on the road just north of Union and let us know."

"Will do."

They arrived in the town of Union a short time later.

The sheriff grumbled as the two men approached. "What is it now?"

Mace said, "We just came to give you a warning. There's a large contingent of vehicles down at the I-77 interchange. They are robbing, looting, and murdering everyone who comes near them."

"That's almost thirty miles from here. Why should we be concerned?"

Johnny threw up his hands. "We're just trying to give you a heads up. If that horde comes this way, they could destroy your entire town!"

Mace lowered one of Johnny's arms. "Look, Sheriff, consider this—if they do come this way, what will it hurt you to be prepared? Maybe a couple extra people at the roadblock, and a scout down the highway a bit? Organizing your people for a quick response if they show up? Those might not be bad things to have in place anyway."

The sheriff sat with a placid look on his face. "Are you done?"

"I guess we are. Johnny, we tried. Let's go home."

The sheriff could be heard yelling at one of his deputies as the two men walked away. "I told you I had nothing to discuss with those idiots! Next time they come barging in here, turn them back on their way north. Use force if you have to."

Johnny shook his head as they walked back to the SUV. "That guy almost makes me want to invite that gang up here. If a group that size leaves the interstate, they'd burn this whole valley."

Mace replied as they pulled away. "At least we don't have Don waiting in the roadway. That's a good sign."

The helicopter was landing as Mace and Johnny arrived back at the cave. Johnny pulled the SUV up beside the chopper.

"Come on. We'll give you a ride over to the RV."

Don climbed in the back seat. "Looked like they were setting up camp at the interchange for the night. Should be getting dark before long. I can make a run back down there in the morning."

The remainder of the evening was quiet.

Chapter 23

Jane rang a bell they had hung just outside the RV. Mace helped Jasper down from his usual perch on the gift shop porch. Food portions were handed down from the RV steps. Derwood and Molly circled their feet waiting for dropped morsels.

Jane said, "I don't know who forgot it or if there was none to be had, but this pot of coffee is our last. Those of you who depend on it to get you going in the morning best start thinking of alternatives."

Mace passed on his usual cup.

Johnny asked, "You feeling OK?"

"Fine. I just have an uneasy feeling about those marauders. I'd like to know they were moving south still."

Don said, "We can take the bird up as soon as you think we're ready."

Jane passed down a plate of food as she listened. "I might give it another hour or so. If that group is like what you'd expect, they partied late and are sleeping in. Besides, if they're coming this way, we'll have time to prepare. Besides Union, there are a half dozen other small towns they would be rolling through."

Mace said, "How about this—Jasper, I know you'll protest, but I want to borrow a case of your whiskey until we get the still up and running. We're heading back to Blacksburg to get as much avgas as they will sell us, while we have the ability to do so."

Jasper shook his head. "Nope. Make your still, go into town and get some. That's my whiskey and it's not for sharing or trading. I told you that yesterday."

Johnny laughed. "After we eat, we'll run over to Ronceverte and see if we can scrounge some up."

Don said, "I could fly you over if it would be faster."

Mace replied, "No, we need to preserve that fuel. We'll take the SUV and the Jeep. If we can also get some gas cans we can fill those with spare fuel. I wish we had another three hundred gallon tank to fill."

Jane said, "That tank we got for the diesel was the last one they had. We were lucky to get it. And lucky they would deliver."

When breakfast was finished, Johnny and Mace made a run to town, returning an hour later with two cases of vodka and eight plastic gas containers. The helicopter was warmed up and a run to check on the marauders, and to get fuel from Blacksburg, was begun. The flight over the I-77 interchange showed the horde still in place. A new set of unlucky travelers had fallen into their blockade and were paying the price.

Mace looked down through the binoculars. "I almost wish I could do a halo drop right into the middle of those savages."

Don shook his head. "You might take out eight or ten, but I would have to believe that would be the limit. That's the sort of gang where you want to see the National Guard doing an assault on them."

Mace replied, "Yeah, well, I think we've already seen what their strategy is. Sit and wait. Meanwhile, people are dying."

"I'm with you. Only we don't know what orders the Guard has or doesn't have. Could be they're deployed elsewhere by now, or have orders to sit tight. Either way, we have no way of knowing."

With the marauders still in place, a run was made to Blacksburg. A case of vodka, and cash, was exchanged for a topped-off tank, plus an additional thirty gallons. On the flight back to the cave, Mace took notice of a small plane flipped nose over in a field.

Mace pointed. "Down there. See the plane?"

Don nodded, and slowed to a hover.

Mace looked through the binoculars. "Looks intact. Wasn't a hard landing."

"And it has an intact fuel tank. Might even be full. That plane won't fly again, but we might be able to salvage that fuel."

Mace looked over the area surrounding the plane. "I don't see anyone around her. But I can't see into that clump of trees."

"Let's drop this fuel and bring back a dozen empty cans. We have the empties at the cave. I'd hate to see someone scavenge that high octane fuel to waste on their truck."

A half hour later, Don and Mace circled the field above the downed single-engine plane, landing the helicopter fifty feet from the wreck. Mace jumped out to investigate while Don kept the engine running and blades turning. After a quick look, Mace waved back the all-clear.

Don shut down and climbed out of the helicopter, pulling four cans from the back seat. A gun was put to his head.

"You move or scream and you're a dead man."

Don slowly raised his hands. "We're just salvaging. Thought it was abandoned."

Don turned around slowly. The man backed up several paces.

"What do you want from us?"

The man stood in silence, not having thought out his demands. Don began to smile.

The man asked, "What are you grinning about?"

"You. You're that science guy from TV. My kid loves watching you. What is it... Dr. Jeff?"

Mace poked half his body around the cab of the 'copter with his AR-15 raised. "You move and you're dead."

The man slowly lowered his pistol.

"Drop it. Don, pick it up."

The man complied.

Don said, "You recognize who it is?"

"Can't say I do."

"It's the network news science guy, Dr. Jeff Mousekowitz."

The doctor sighed. "Moskowitz. Jeff Moskowitz."

Mace said, "Well, Doc, you picked the wrong people to rob."

"Rob? Who's robbing who here? That's my plane!"

"This is rich. He's got us on that one. Anyone else here with you?"

Jeff shook his head. "No. Was trying to get back to my home in Florida. Was up in Pittsburgh when the power went out."

Mace glanced back at the plane. "I'm guessing that wasn't your plane back there, and you aren't a pilot."

Jeff took a deep breath. "I bought it. Sort of. Didn't ask who the sellers were."

Don asked, "You have flown before, right?"

"I read the manual. The guy who sold it told me how to fly."

"Yeah, well, looks like he left out a few important details."

Jeff crossed his arms. "I had it right up until the end. It was getting dark, I had to land. Was hoping to make Roanoke for the night."

Don half smiled. "Well, this field did you a favor then. Roanoke is overrun. The airport is under the control of who knows who. Buildings are burning all over that city."

Jeff winced. "Same in Pittsburgh. I was lucky to get out of there. Wanted to drive but the roads were jammed."

They walked back over to the plane.

Mace asked, "How much fuel you have in there?"

Jeff frowned. "You're really taking my fuel?"

"I hate to tell you, but this rig isn't flying again. Prop's bent, and the cowl is pushed back against the engine."

Jeff looked over the damage with a scowl. "Half a tank."

Mace said, "Tell you what, we'll work out a fair trade. We'll take the gas, and you're welcome to come back to our compound until you can find alternate transportation. If you stay more than a day though, you'll have to work and contribute."

Jeff tilted his head to the side. "What kind of compound do you have?"

Don replied, "A secure one. At least for now. We're working to gather supplies for the long haul."

Jeff glanced back at the helicopter. You have that, you must be doing well for yourselves."

Don cut a hose leading from the wing tanks to the engine. Gas poured out into the first of the cans he had carried over. When the last drops of the tank had been emptied, the three men climbed aboard the helicopter.

As they lifted off, Jeff said, "You do know why this blackout is happening, don't you?"

Mace replied, "We've got nothing but the end result. You have information on what's happening?"

"I do. This isn't some solar event."

Don said, "We gathered that. Tell us what you know."

Jeff cleared his throat. "First... none of this is definite. The last time we had communications running, I managed to talk to several of my scientist friends. It seems this interference was first detected from a single point source, probably only an hour after the Large Hadron Collider experiment detected dark matter."

Mace said, "Wait. You're saying this is a result of that experiment?"

"I'm saying I don't know, just that the first signal was detected right after that experiment. Now, I have a good grasp of physics, and I'm completely baffled as to why that experiment would have any effect at all. But here's where it gets interesting. At last check, the interference was coming from four point sources out in space. Those signals are being broadcast."

Don frowned. "You saying someone is purposefully doing this?"

Jeff took a deep breath. "I'm saying I don't know—but I do know this is not a natural phenomenon. The collider experiment timing might have just been a coincidence... but I find that hard to believe."

Mace asked, "Who would have reason to do this? From what we know, it's worldwide. It's not the Chinese or the Russians, they're without power and comm too."

Jeff shrugged. "We just don't have enough information to say. Although, I will say this, the amount of power it's taking to broadcast signals at that level has to be tremendous. It's not something we could do."

The helicopter landed and the three men carried fuel to their small but growing depot behind the gift shop.

Johnny met them back at the 'copter for the remaining cans. "Pick up a stray?"

Don said, "Recognize him?"

Johnny rubbed his chin in thought before his eyes lit up. "Dr. Jeff?"

"That would be me."

Don added, "His plane was tipped over in a field. He'll be staying with us until he finds transportation to go south. Heading for Florida."

Tres joined the men as the remaining tanks were placed behind the gift shop. "Hold it! What's he doing here? That's the TV guy!"

Jeff half smiled.

Don said, "We picked him up in a field not far from here. His plane had gone down. And he has news about the blackout."

Johnny held up his hands. "Please, tell us what you know."

"The interference signals are being broadcast from at least four points in space. They started immediately after the experiment with the Large Hadron Collider. Don't know who is sending them, but they definitely aren't natural."

Johnny smacked Tres on the back. "There you go, your little green men theory is panning out."

"We don't know enough yet, but I wouldn't rule that out."

Johnny played Johnny, continuing to press to get the most out of the conversation. "So you're saying that it is aliens?"

"Can't say. There are billions and billions of stars in this galaxy alone. There are likely millions of Earth-like planets out there that could contain life. The existence of intelligent alien life has been neither proved nor disproved. All I'm saying is that I don't know—we don't know."

The conversations about the interference, as well as the demise of Pittsburgh, continued for almost an hour.

Jane stood listening with her arms crossed. "Have you eaten?"

"Not since yesterday."

"Well, come on. We can at least put some food in you. Don't the rest of you have work to do?"

Johnny laughed. "That's it, boys. Recess is over."

"Where you from in Florida?"

"Orlando area. I usually broadcast from a studio there."

Jane pointed over at a table after climbing the steps into the RV. "What were you doing in Pittsburgh?"

Jeff sat. "Was doing a piece on steel and its contributions to modern civilization. The history of it is a lot more interesting than the science."

Jeff looked around at the cab of the RV. "Nice rig."

Jane smiled as she set a plate of eggs and leftover hashbrowns down in front of him, "I'm into... was into... competitive shooting. Johnny and I would travel to meets in her."

"I thought about getting something like this. I just didn't want to deal with all that driving. For what I do, flying is convenient. Otherwise I would be on the road all the time."

Jane gestured back toward the others. "Johnny hates flying, and the meets we go to are only about every other month or so. RV was a good choice for us."

Johnny climbed the steps, sitting across for Jeff. "Tell me more about these interference signals."

Jeff shrugged. "Don't know what else I can say."

"OK, how about how they're taking out power? I had a generator at home that worked fine, and the generator on this RV has been going strong for weeks now."

"The big issue is with transmission. The interference is strong enough to overload the transmission lines, leading to transformers that are burning out. I talked to a lineman for power up in Pittsburgh. He said every transformer they swapped out blew almost immediately."

Johnny rubbed his forehead in thought. "We've had a tough time running our equipment in the cave from this generator. Finally put a smaller one by the cave. What do you know about communications? We have fiber optics laid all across this country. How is the interference messing with that? And our landline phones?"

Jeff shrugged. "I can only speculate that the interference is happening at the junctions where that fiber is turned back into electrical signals. I don't know if you've seen it or not, but a lot of our electronics are unable to function as well."

"All this interference," said Johnny, "it has to be bad for our health?"

"In the long term, maybe. Short term, electromagnetics at these levels just don't seem to have an effect on us. But again, we don't have any long term studies to point to as to what effects these fields *could* have on us. I would advise you to stay indoors when possible. The metal shielding on this RV would be an excellent place to stay if not for those big windows."

Jane said, "We have a cave we stay in most nights."

Jeff turned. "A cave would be an excellent choice. EM signals, even as strong as these, shouldn't penetrate the ground more than a few inches or so."

Tres popped his head up into the RV. "Dr. Jeff, I'm putting together a still. Would you be interested in looking it over?"

"I suppose I could. Not sure what I could add, but I'll have a look. Fermentation is a basic process."

As Jeff stood, Johnny grabbed his arm. "The kid is a brewer, he knows what he's doing. Just give him a little praise. He'll appreciate that coming from you."

"You people have supplies, you're building stills, penning animals. You have shelter. I'd say it looks like you have a good start on survival."

"Yeah, well, winter is coming. And there are armed marauders who would love nothing more than to take this place apart."

"Pittsburgh has more than its share of those people, Johnny. Hearing about Roanoke doesn't give one a good feeling about being in any city."

"We left Norfolk for exactly that reason. Norfolk and Roanoke were not high-crime cities. I can't imagine what it must be like in Baltimore, Chicago, or LA."

The doctor stood, thanking Jane for the food.

As Jeff Moskowitz walked off with Tres, Jane sat by her husband. "I think we should keep him. We need smart people, and he seems friendly enough."

"If he contributes, he can stay as long as he likes."

Chapter 24

Two additional runs were made to check on the marauders. Returning from the second run, late in the day, Don reported their numbers had grown by at least thirty vehicles, including two semis. Bonfires burned in the middle of the interstate as the group partied in celebration of their achievements. As night fell, another ten vehicles joined them from the north.

Don joined the others on the gift shop porch. "They have to be closing in on a hundred fifty people. All of them armed. That's like a mini army on wheels. I saw a half dozen cars leave going south on the interstate, and at least one that came our way."

"Too bad we can't drop a keg of black powder on them from the helicopter," said Tres. "Strap a couple of those five gallon gas cans to it and it would make a nice fire-bomb."

Johnny said, "We don't have a keg of black powder."

"True, but give me a few days and I'll have a good start on one. Dr. Jeff gave me a few ideas that should speed the saltpeter refining."

Jane said, "Maybe we *should* think about some sort of preemptive strike. If they roll this way with that many people, we won't be able to stop them."

Mace sat on the steps in thought before entering the conversation. "You know, if we take the fight to them, they might follow us back here. If we do nothing and leave them be, they might move on down the road."

Jane scowled. "Sitting and hoping they just go away... I know that's not what's really running through your head."

"What I want to do and what's best are not always the same thing. We have the people up and down this valley to think of."

"And what about the people on that highway? We let them go and they may just continue to get bigger. You said Blacksburg appeared to be somewhat peaceful. A crew like that could take down that whole town."

Mace leaned back. "What would you suggest?"

Jane shrugged. "You have the military training. Throw something at us and we'll see what sticks."

"Discuss it for a few minutes while I walk around. I need to think."

As Mace walked away in thought, Jeff said, "You know, if you want to build bombs, I could help. Tres was telling me about the group in question. If they're ganged together, you could do serious damage from the air. Not that I'm advocating such."

Johnny looked over at Jane. "I'm wishing we had brought that Winchester with us. We have a model 70 that my uncle left me. I've only fired it twice, but it was dead accurate. With a good scope you can hit your target at a thousand yards. I know the newest rifles can best that, but we had a model 70 at our disposal."

Jane said, "If the National Guard is still gathered up at Bedford, I wonder if we could go and alert them. This is much more their fight than ours. It's what they're supposed to defend against."

Jasper rocked in his chair as Derwood lay by his side.

The old man added his thoughts. "Seems to me a midnight raid might do you good. Hit them while they're liquored up, do your damage and disappear into the night. I bet we could—well, not we but you—I bet you could take in a dozen horses. Hitch 'em a half mile away, sneak up with your suppressors on and cut loose. You could probably take out half of them before they figured out what was going on. Then cut and run before they got organized."

Johnny laughed. "So you're for the frontal assault, so long as you aren't involved."

Jasper shuffled in his chair as if he was going to get up. "Why you... listen up, walrus, you're just lucky that's not beach behind you or I'd be rolling you back into the ocean."

Johnny again laughed. "Only problem with that is you can't take your electric scooter on the beach."

Derwood stood and barked.

Johnny laughed. "What, you taking his side? You little traitor!"

Jane held up her hand. "Enough. Let's stay focused on one fight at a time."

Jane scratched at her cheek. "I do like the horse idea. Gets us in and away from there quietly. Only problem is getting the horses down there. That's thirty miles."

Tres said, "There's enough horse trailers around here to truck them down to below Union. Maybe we only need to ride two or three miles."

Mace returned to the steps. The others mentioned their ideas. Johnny again sniped at Jasper in an attempt to poke the hornet's nest.

Mace said, "How does this sound? We find a vehicle and add a couple steel plates on the back of it. Drive it down and get on the I-77 exit below where they are. At the same time, we outfit a second vehicle, driving it to the exit north of them.

"Two or three of us ride up to their location in the first car from the south while a bunch wait back in ambush. The car takes out the first people that approach it. They turn around and lead any others who will chase them into the ambush. Don flies us all to the northern vehicle and we do the same thing again. It doesn't draw them toward us and we might be able to reduce their numbers by as much as ten or twenty, without seriously risking our lives."

Johnny said, "And what if they already have people sitting at those exits?"

Tres asked, "Why would they do that?"

Johnny shrugged. "Don't know—maybe they send a friendly face forward to steer people in their direction. If we were on that road and came across someone that said they were having a revival up the road where they were giving out free food, we would probably speed on up there to see. Maybe not us here, but most people on the road would."

The discussions lasted late into the night. At first light, Don would take Mace on a scouting mission. The interstate exits would be observed as well as places for a moderately safe ambush. Johnny, Tres, and Dr. Jeff would be given the job of finding vehicles and armoring them up. Dawn arrived with a purpose.

Jasper sat out on his porch rocking in his chair as Mace emerged from his sleeping arrangements in the cave. "You know, you lose a single person from this group, you run the risk of losing the dynamic you've built up here."

"I plan on taking every precaution I can," said Mace.

"I know you will. And I only say that because I've grown to like you people. You get the job done without all the hemmin' and hawin' that you would find in most groups. You'll survive this thing so long as you watch out for each other."

The engine of the helicopter spun to life. Don and Mace were soon on their way to the exit south of I-77, below the growing horde.

As Mace looked through the binoculars, he said, "I think I have a good idea for this exit. If they move this way and come back east, we could set up the ambush at that construction site down there. There's a rise in the middle that would allow us to fire at them the whole way around that road. When done, you set down on the road to pick us up. We could signal you with a flashlight or mirror."

Mace sat back in the chair with a smile. "I'm feeling a lot better about this now. Take us high above their camp and let's check the exit to the north."

As the helicopter flew over the marauder encampment, Mace scanned the intersection through the binoculars.

"They're gone!"

"What?"

Mace nodded. "They've moved on. Nothing down there now but burned-out hulks."

Don turned the helicopter hard back in the direction of the cave. "I can't believe we didn't check the road coming this way this morning."

Mace swept the highway heading back toward Peterstown. Two minutes later they had their answer.

He picked up the flight map before returning to the binoculars. "Rich Creek. Looks like they overran a blockade. They're raiding a food store. And I see a half dozen vehicles outside a pharmacy... gun battle going on at a pizza joint... two houses are spewing smoke. If they roll through that town, they're heading right for us."

Mace jerked around as the helicopter spun slowly. "Wait, turn back the other way!"

Don gently pressed the right pedal.

"There we go. The townspeople have the roadway blocked and a picket line setup. I see two dead attackers, but more trucks are rolling in. Wait. No way! One of them, a flatbed, has a cannon mounted on the bed. They're loading it right now. Can you take us over in this direction? I want a better angle on this."

Don pushed the cyclic to the right until Mace held up his hand. "OK, they're lighting the fuse. Oh wow. Someone has fired that thing before. They just took out the lead car in that barricade, along with two of the townspeople. No. No, don't run! Gah! Huge mistake. Three motorcycles just blasted through the break. This is not good. These marauders really look like they know what they're doing."

"What do you want me to do?"

"Turn around. Let's check Peterstown. Maybe we can warn their blockade."

Except for a fleeing car, the road into Peterstown was empty.

Mace shook his head. "They have a blockade set up on the east side. Set us down in the street on the other side. We have to warn them of what's coming."

As the helicopter swooped in and began its descent, a bullet popped up through the floorboard, while another skimmed off the windshield. Don pushed the cyclic hard forward while applying full throttle. A third bullet struck the driver-side door as they turned away.

"OK, maybe that wasn't our best idea."

"They have to be hearing the gunshots coming from Rich Creek. And that cannon. I'd have taken a shot at us too."

As the helicopter blasted up 219, Mace looked over the map. "They're likely to be pillaging that town for days. If they continue in our direction, there are homes all along this highway. Lindside and Rock Camp are next. And they're small. After that, they're at Union."

Don took a deep breath. "You think it's worth warning the sheriff at Union?"

Before Mace could reply, the engine of the helicopter sputtered. Don pushed buttons, adjusted the throttle and flipped switches. The engine roared back to life.

"I'm worried about it being safe to fly this bird anymore. My gauges have been going haywire all morning. That interference must be growing."

Mace grimaced. "We lose our eyes, we won't know when they're coming."

"We seem to be OK now, but if this gets worse..."

The helicopter began a descent as it approached Union from the southwest. They settled in the roadway a hundred yards from the small armed force that guarded that end of town.

Mace jumped out and jogged toward the defenders, holding up his hands as he approached. "Hey, we need to talk to the sheriff. It's urgent!"

One of the men replied, "He's in the morning town meeting. You can talk to him in about an hour."

Mace walked up to the orange and white barricade positioned in the center of the road. "You confident this is going to stop anyone?"

"Has so far." The sheriff's townie buddy laughed.

Mace tilted his head. "Well, I'll give you a message you can take to the sheriff. You can decide when."

The man scowled. "What's so urgent?"

Mace pointed down the road. "Rich Creek and Peterstown are under assault by a gang of more than a hundred marauders. We're talking heavily armed, non-negotiating, pillagers, rapists and murderers. You know, the hardcore kind you always see on TV. Well, they're burning Peterstown now. I would expect them to be here, right in front of your little barricade, possibly as early as an hour from now."

The townie's scowl turned to one of worry.

"Still want to wait for the town meeting to be over?"

The man turned to his friend. "Robert, go fetch the sheriff. Tell him it's an emergency."

Robert nodded before turning to hop on his bicycle.

Mace said, "Really? A bicycle is your emergency vehicle?"

The townie replied, "Gas is precious. We're trying to conserve. Courthouse is only a half mile."

Fifteen minutes later, the sheriff's cruiser pulled up to a stop.

The sheriff stepped out as a deputy jumped from the other side.

The sheriff displayed an agitated expression. "Tommy, what in the... you. What are you doing here? Don't tell me you're the emergency. I thought I told you to leave us alone."

Mace held back his frustration. "We've just come from Rich Creek and Peterstown. They're under assault by a gang of more than a hundred thugs who are killing everyone and taking everything. I thought you might want to know that they may be headed this way."

The sheriff held out two fingers. "Now hold on, you just said they *may* be headed this way. Are they headed this way or not?"

Mace took a deep breath. "Sheriff, I just told you your neighboring towns are under assault. No, I can't say for certain they are coming here, but if I was you, I would take every precaution in the name of protecting my people. This group of people, they even have a cannon."

The sheriff smirked. "A cannon? What is this, a gang of Confederate soldiers?"

The townie laughed.

Mace shook his head. "Look, Sheriff, if you want, I can take you down there right now to see for yourself what's coming. These people are bad. They will burn this place to the ground after they torture and kill all your people."

The sheriff sighed and his normal scowl returned. "You think I'm going anywhere with you, you're mistaken. We've taken good care of this town. The people are fed, we're organized, we are able to take care of ourselves. And if need be, we have a militia of twenty-five townsfolk who can be here in twenty minutes. And I know that to be true because we've tested our response repeatedly. We have a siren in town that everyone can hear."

Mace planted his forehead in his palm. "We are talking about a hardcore group of at least a hundred people, Sheriff. Probably closer to double that. They will roll right over your militia."

The sheriff crossed his arms. "Well, what makes you an authority on any of this?"

Mace stood straight. "I spent ten years in the Special Forces, Sheriff. I did two tours in the Middle-East. I know what gangs of bad people look like and I know what they're capable of. Our brothers and sisters in Peterstown are finding that out right now. I watched from above as their militia caved and ran when the first cannon round hit a car in their barricade."

The sheriff shook his head. "Why do you care what happens to us so much? We don't trade with you, and we haven't been on the best of terms. Why do you care?"

Mace pointed toward the roadway. "Aside from caring about your people, as I do about everyone, I care because if they roll you over, we're next in line. Now, you asked me what I would do. If I were you, there are three ninety-degree turns in the road just south of here. I would take the far one, completely block the road, and take positions on the high hill to the right.

Your twenty-five might have a decent chance of defending against their Pickett's charge."

The sheriff again smirked. "And how do we defend against that cannon? Wouldn't they just blast us off that hill?"

The townie chuckled.

Mace scratched his neck. "You know what, Sheriff, I tried. I tried to save this town and all its people. I can't do any more for you. You've been warned. Whatever happens here in the next few days is on you. Goodbye, Sheriff."

Mace turned and walked toward the waiting helicopter.

The sheriff scowled as he walked back to his cruiser.

The townie chuckled. "Wait! I think I see Stonewall Jackson himself coming this way!"

The sheriff stopped and turned. "Shut up, Toby. Just watch the road like you've been told."

Chapter 25

Mace gathered everyone on the porch of the gift shop. "We need a new plan. The marauders have turned this way. Rich Creek and Peterstown are under assault. And from the initial looks of it, their meager defenses fell quickly. I just talked to the sheriff at Union. He continues to live in some dream world. So let's throw some options on the table."

Vanessa said, "We could always just pack up and leave. I mean, it might take a day to haul everything back out of here, but we could go somewhere else."

Tres hesitated with a response. "I'd rather stay. This place is perfect and we have so many of our needs taken care of now. We have water, food and fuel. And within a week, thanks to Dr. Jeff, we'll have that keg of gunpowder we were talking about, plus more."

Jasper scowled. "I ain't runnin' from nobody. This is my home. I'm old, and I will fight to keep it. Anybody trying to come and take it will end up on the wrong end of my shotgun when I'm pulling the trigger."

Jasper crossed his arms, giving his best look of defiance.

Jane said, "I think we should still consider ways of slowing them down. There's a lot of road between here and Peterstown. Maybe we set up a few sniper ambushes. Pick off a half dozen and they might turn back."

Mace nodded. "OK, good option. Johnny?"

Johnny rubbed his hands together. "I like the ambush route. Hit 'em and run, hit 'em and run. And the Second Creek bridge, we take that out and they will have to turn around."

Mace looked at Jeff. "Doc, you think you could piece something together that would take out a two-lane concrete bridge?"

Jeff Moskowitz sat silent for several seconds. "Any way I can get a run into town? I might be able to build a fertilizer bomb like they used at the Federal building in Oklahoma so many years ago. Park a truck like that there and it would possibly take out a small bridge."

Mace glanced over at Johnny. "Want to give the doc a ride over to Ronceverte? Might do us good to alert them to what's coming as a courtesy."

Jane said, "While you're there, you might go on a recruiting drive for fighters. This might cost us, but we could pay a grand a head for twenty to twenty-five good fighters. Maybe offer a couple hundred extra to a grand for the best shooters."

Johnny smiled. "Mercs. I like it."

Don said, "The road just south of Second Creek would be an excellent location for an ambush. We block the road just out of sight and hit them when they stop. From there we fall back across Second Creek to the hills there. If they make it through the blockade to the creek, we have another one set up there. If Doc can rig up a truck full of fertilizer, we could blow the bridge from up on the hill. Anyone trying to cross the creek and come up the hills... well, it would be suicide for them."

Mace pointed to the helicopter. "Cam, can you bring us the maps of this area?"

Cam nodded and headed off for the maps.

"Those are topo maps, so we should be able to pick out effective locations. I say we look those over and then head down there to see what we could do in the next twenty-four hours."

Don laid the maps out on the porch. "Right here. We could put a blockade here, and line these hills. Take your best shots and then scamper up and over. Then up here at the bridge, stake out this hillside, do your damage, blow the bridge. If their losses are high enough, they may turn back toward the easy pickings."

Mace nodded. "I could get behind that. Take the 'copter up, scout those hills from above. We'll head down in the cars."

Jasper was left on the porch, waiting for Johnny's and Jeff's return. If successful at finding a sufficient stockpile of fertilizer and a truck, Jeff would begin work on his bomb while Johnny went on a recruiting drive for mercenaries.

The remainder of the group, including Tonya, headed for the narrows just south of Second Creek.

Mace was the first to exit his Jeep. "This is good. We tuck a blockade up around that swerve. They would stop right here. We should have excellent firing lines from both right and left flanks. Anyone caught down here will be in a world of hurt."

Everyone was sent up the hills and told to look for good shooting positions. Having an escape route up and over the hilltops was paramount. The run from the top of the hill back to the bridge was three quarters of a mile, which raised concern.

Mace said, "We park spare vehicles here and drive them to the bridge and leave them—cuts that run time in half. The confusion of the attack and them having to get around our blockade should give us plenty of time to get into position."

Tres nodded as he looked over the terrain. "I think we can do this. If we start out close to the top, the run back won't be so bad."

"When we get back," said Mace, "you and I are heading to the neighbors. We'll be scrounging for anything that moves that we can park in that roadway. Whatever it is, they will probably never get it back, but this stand is for their protection too. If we fail, they fail."

Jane said, "We need to position ample ammo at both locations. And we could have another fallback about a mile back up the road. I noticed a nice crop of granite rocks sticking up on the hillside. If we could block the road there it would give us another ambush point. After that, we have the RV and the cave."

Mace pursed his lips. "OK, I think we have a plan. We need to have this in place in the next twenty-four hours, and we need to run a few practice drills. If Johnny can bring a dozen good shooters from Ronceverte, this has a good chance of working."

Jane shook her head. "A month ago, while standing behind your bar, would you have ever fathomed something like this?"

"My imagination is not that good. Had you told me to sit down and to sketch out what might possibly happen if we lost both power and comm... I wouldn't have come close to this."

Jane laughed. "I know one thing, I would have paid a lot closer attention to those prepper magazines. Could have built a bunker under our garage back in Norfolk and not worried about seeing daylight for a year or two. Things would have settled out by then."

Mace helped Jane down off the hill. "What a huge difference a few weeks makes."

The next several hours were spent going from neighbor to neighbor, explaining the coming horror and gathering every vehicle that could be used as part of a blockade. On the road below Second Creek, a sizable front-loader was used to stack cars two high and two deep going across both lanes of the road.

A narrow opening remained for any traffic that needed to pass through in the short term. Everything too large was given directions on how to go around the blockade while still reaching their destination. Each was told of the marauders.

A second blockade was constructed on the Second Creek bridge.

Jane walked up to the front-loader as Mace stacked the last car. "We have a problem."

Mace turned off the engine. "What?"

Jane pointed down the small roadway that ran alongside the creek. "Right there in front of us. A second bridge over the creek. I looked at the map. You can get around and back on this road about a mile up. Unless we blow them both, they will be able to get around."

Mace frowned. "Well, we have enough spare vehicles. I'll stack some over there. Maybe it will at least slow them down."

Jane sighed. "This means our rocky hill for a third ambush site is useless. They could just bypass it."

Mace restarted the front-loader yelling down to Jane from his high seat. "Well, we'll just have to stop them here then!"

Another car was shoved into the roadway before attention was diverted to the second bridge. Forty minutes later, the blockades were set except for the final blocking cars. The group returned to the cave where Johnny and Dr. Jeff were waiting.

Johnny said, "Best we could scrounge was this van. Doc thinks it'll be adequate. We have every square inch of it packed."

Mace asked, "How about the recruiting?"

Johnny shook his head. "No interest. Most responses were people saying they would get in their car and leave. If someone trashes their house, so what, they can patch it up or live with neighbors, but at least they live."

Jane plopped down on the porch. "We need people. Of the nine we have, Jasper can't run, and Vanessa, Cam, and Tonya aren't trained. That leaves five of us. I just don't see that as enough."

Vanessa stepped up. "I can shoot a rifle. And not a bad shot either."

Two pickups turned into the drive, pulling to a stop in front of the gift shop.

Five teen boys and one girl hopped out. "Heard you were paying cash for shooters. Where do we sign up?"

Mace stood. "How old are you boys, and you?"

The girl said, "I'm fifteen, but I can out shoot any of them."

One of the boys said, "That was one time."

The girl angrily replied, "Yeah, let's set up a target right now and see who wins!"

Jane held up her hand. "Who's the oldest?"

A blond-haired boy stepped forward. "That would be me. Syler Sanks."

Jane asked, "Syler, do your parents know you are here?"

The young man shook his head. "No. But we aren't doing anything against the law, right? This is defending our homes. And we're all legally old enough to shoot without needing permission."

Johnny stepped forward. "These people we're going up against... this isn't a game. If they catch you, they will cut your throat without blinking."

Syler replied, "We understand. Look, we're too young for the townsfolk to put us on the barricades, and too old to just be sitting around the house playing card games. We can shoot, and if that gang we heard about is as big as you say, you need our help."

Jasper said, "I know two of these boys. They can handle themselves well enough. You need their help. Heck, too bad you can't get the whole rifle team from the high school over here. They won state two of the last four years."

Mace stepped off the porch, walking to just in front of the five teens. They stood defiant.

"We need them, and anyone else they can bring. You have other team members willing to take this on?"

Syler smiled. "Yes, sir. I believe we do. At least another four. Should we bring them back here?"

Mace gestured toward the highway. As soon as the sun is up we'll be expecting you at the bridge over Second Creek. You will only need to bring rifles with you, and as much ammo for them as you can carry. We'll be shooting at targets averaging about five hundred feet away. And keep this in mind, you *will* be getting shot at. People will be dying. And some of those people might be by your shots. If you don't think you can pull that trigger, don't come out, you'll just be in the way."

Syler Sanks and the other teens piled back into the two pickups. "We'll see you at the bridge at dawn!"

The trucks pulled up the drive and back onto the roadway.

Jane was shaking her head. "This just seems like a bad idea."

Mace said, "We don't have to like it, but we need the help. These are their homes they're defending. This is their valley. If the marauders make it through, it will be their families being slaughtered. Tough times call for tough measures."

Thumps from the rotor wash on the helicopter could be heard as it circled in and landed in the field. Don Rogers hopped out, jogging over to the gift shop.

Johnny asked, "The marauders, where are they now?"

Don stepped up onto the porch. "Peterstown is burning. There were a handful of vehicles forming up on the road coming this way, but they may just be lining up for the morning. I think the mob has grown. I counted at least seventy vehicles that I believe are with them. And each one has at least two people in it. There are also two passenger buses with at least a dozen people each, and they now have four semis that I can only guess is their supply system. And we can add one tanker truck to the mix."

Tres sighed. "That's probably two hundred people now. Where are they coming from?"

Mace said, "Charleston or further north."

Don half frowned. "One of the buses had Detroit city markings. And it gets worse. They have two school buses and I saw them dragging women and young girls onto one of the buses. I think we all know what's happening there. This is just one big nasty hurricane of evil that is wiping out these small towns. How goes our efforts here?"

Jane replied, "We have a van bomb that we hope is adequate for the bridge, and our attempt at rounding up a militia netted us five teenagers. I'm not feeling overly confident at the moment."

Mace held up his hand. "We don't have to kill them all, just enough to turn them back. If we manage ten shooters in a superior position, I still believe we can accomplish our goal."

As the discussion on the porch continued, Tres went for a walk with Vanessa, Molly followed behind her new best friend. "This could get bad by tomorrow night."

Vanessa took his hand. "We just have to do what we can and hope it's enough."

"I'm not a good shooter. I don't know if I can hit anything. Will probably just be wasting bullets."

Vanessa stopped. "It's OK to be nervous. I'm terrified. I mean, I have the confidence to handle a gun, but you've been all over every part of this venture, building structures, making gunpowder, and a dozen other things. And you helped to free Tonya. When you get out there, if you have to pull the trigger, you will do your best because it's what you always do."

Jane called out, "Vanessa, can you give me a hand with dinner?"

"Sure Mrs. T. Be right there!"

Vanessa smiled at Tres before kissing him on the cheek. She whirled around and walked toward the RV.

Tres said to himself, "So you're going off to war tomorrow and all you get is a peck on the cheek? Nice going, Tres, way to show her you're a man."

As the sun began to set on the horizon, one final run was made in the helicopter. Tres, Mace, and Cam joined Don for the ride.

Once high above Peterstown, Mace looked down through the binoculars. "I think you're right. I have twenty to twenty-five cars and trucks lining up on the highway coming our direction. Looks like they are settling in for the evening, but ready to move on."

Mace scanned the ground. "I see the two buses and the semis. The buses are in a small lot and the semis parked on the roadway in front of it."

Tres said, "Wish we could do something for them."

Mace replied as he changed his view from vehicle to vehicle. "Well, maybe we can. Don, take us over Rich Creek."

"What is it you see?"

Mace lowered the binoculars. "I know this sounds crazy, but I don't think they're watching the road where they came from at all. I don't see any evidence of anyone moving about in Rich Creek. And there aren't any cars on the road. What I'm about to suggest, I'll be looking for you three to talk me out of."

Mace again peered through the binoculars. "Those buses. I see one person standing guard. The road south of there is clear. If Tres and I can get in there, we could drive those buses away before anyone knew what was going on. The rest of them are going house to house with their pillaging. Tres, you ever drive a bus?"

Tres shook his head. "No, but it can't be that hard. The ones we had back in school were all automatics. Just give yourself plenty of room to turn."

Mace again lowered the binoculars. "Doesn't sound like you're talking me out of anything."

"How do we get down there?"

Mace looked at Don. "Think you could drop us in Rich Creek? Maybe come low up the river and dump us on the shore? It would be up to us to find transportation from there. It's only a mile from the river. We could drive up to that cemetery, park the car and leave it running, and cut through those trees and then those buildings. If we use the suppressors, we might not even be heard."

Tres asked, "Let's say we do manage to get those buses out. Where do we go with them?"

Mace pointed, "We dump them there, in Pearisburg. They'll be on their own, but at least we got them out of there."

Don said, We probably only have an hour of daylight left. If you really want to do this, you have to start now."

Mace picked up his pack, pulling out the suppressor. Tres looked on nervously.

Mace said, "Didn't bring your bag, huh?"

Tres replied, "Sorry. Didn't think I would be needing it."

Mace pulled two additional magazines from his pack. "Take these, and don't pull that trigger unless you absolutely have to. When we go in, let me clear out anyone standing around. You get on one of those buses and get it ready to go."

Tres nodded. "I can do that."

The 'copter made a wide arc, going south before circling around to the river. Five minutes of low-level flying had the men landing on the shore at the edge of town. Other than the crackling of burning buildings, everything was quiet. A car was located and commandeered, the dead driver pushed out onto the street.

A short ride later the car was parked on the drive leading to the town cemetery. Mace and Tres hustled through the woods, emerging behind a building across the road from the buses. The silhouettes of least a dozen lowered heads could be seen on each bus.

Mace grabbed Tres by the forearm. "OK, when we move, remember to breathe. I see three men in that lot. One smoking in front of the store, and two standing beside one of the buses, talking."

Tres nodded. "I see."

Mace continued with a low voice, "I'll take out these two first. The other I'll have to hit from around the bus. You wait on this side until I give you the all clear. What's our password?"

Tres replied, "Cowboy?"

Mace smiled. "Just do as I said and we'll be rolling out of here before they know what happened."

Tres grabbed Mace's shoulder. "What if we can't find the keys?"

Mace shook his head. "Then we've done all we can for them. Just tell them to be quiet and run toward Rich Creek. And to stay away from the main road."

Tres took a deep breath. "I can't believe we are about to do this."

Mace grabbed his shoulder at the base of the neck and squeezed. "You'll do fine. You always do."

With that, the raid to free the women of Peterstown was underway. After crossing the roadway, Mace approached the men at the bus from behind. Tres followed close on his heels.

Two silenced pops could be heard before the women on the closest bus erupted in horrified chatter. The third man tossed his cigarette to the ground, raised his gun, and took one step off of the sidewalk. A third round dropped the man where he stood.

Tres boarded a bus. "Hush. I need you all to be quiet. We're getting you out of here."

Tres wiped his hand around the dash and the keyhole. "Keys? Anyone know where the keys are?"

A girl in the front seat pointed toward the dead man on the ground. "He had them."

Tres stood and took a step down the open door. The silhouette of a man confronted him.

Three rounds emptied into the floor of the bus before Mace took control.

Mace yelled over the busload of screaming girls. "Here's the key. Go!"

The engines of the two buses turned over several times before coming to life. Tres pulled the shifter handle to D before stepping on the gas and stalling the bus. Mace waved frantically from the other. The engine again turned over and powered to life. The buses, with all occupants holding their breath, pulled out onto the roadway.

As they turned onto Highway 460 going east, Don swooped down in front of them, showing that their way out was clear. Once in Pearisburg, the buses were parked and the women told to disperse. No other explanation was given other than to run and to seek shelter as far from the buses as they could. Don landed on the parking lot beside them. Seconds later, the four men were on their way home.

A quick pass was done high over Peterstown. Several cars and trucks were parked around where the buses had been. Most of the marauders continued their pillaging, while others worked to form a line, readying for the following day's assaults.

Chapter 26

The defenders were up before dawn. Ammunition was gathered and taken to the prospective ambush sites. Seven teens from the local high school were waiting for instruction. Mace took them up the hill overlooking the highway, settling them into their firing positions and giving direction for their retreats.

The final vehicles were stacked in place, closing off Highway 219 coming north from Union. The occasional car was diverted and given directions as to how to go around. Arguments took place, but were quickly quelled with the show of guns.

Up on the ridge overlooking the highway, Jane walked the line making sure everyone had adequate ammo. Instructions were repeated time and again. No firing until Mace, Jane or Johnny opened up first. After that it would be fire-at-will until the call for a retreat. All were anxious and nervous.

Dr. Jeff moved the loaded van onto the bridge, positioning it where it was most likely to cause structural damage. With everything in place, the group of defenders settled in for the wait.

Don landed the helicopter behind the first barricade, Mace came down to meet him. "They're on the move. Fires are already starting up in Lindside. I expect they'll be hitting Rock Camp in about a half hour. And Union maybe an hour after that. The barricade at Union has two men manning it. They'll be dead before that town siren sounds."

Mace said, "OK. Give me one last ride down to Union. Maybe at least some of the people can head out toward Sweet Springs. Besides, we have to let them know the road through here is blocked."

A short ride had Mace jogging toward the northern barricade going into Union.

The two men guarding the road waved him to a stop. "What's your business?"

Mace said, "You need to be sounding that town siren. You have at least two hundred very bad people coming up 219. They'll be here in under two hours."

The man said, "If they've got no business here we'll wave them through."

Mace shook his head. "Not going to happen. They burned and pillaged Peterstown all day yesterday. Lindside is burning as we speak. Rock Camp is next and then they'll be here. They'll kill everyone whether you resist or not!"

The man became nervous.

Mace continued, "Look, this is your last and only warning. Tell your sheriff they are definitely coming. And tell him 219 going north is blocked. If anyone wants to run they will have to go out toward Sweet Springs."

The man nodded. "Sweet Springs?"

Mace sighed. "Yes! This highway is blocked! Now go tell your sheriff he only has about an hour! Two hundred murderous thugs are coming to Union!"

The man turned nervously and began to walk as the other stood with his mouth open.

"Run!" Mace yelled.

Once back in the 'copter, Mace shook his head. "They're dead. That whole town... wasted."

Don said, "We did what we could. Time to go and protect our own."

As they landed, Mace looked over at his friend. "I'll keep an eye on Cam. You can set down on the road north of the creek barricade. No sense in you wasting fuel while we wait. If an hour passes, go for another recon round and bring me back any news."

Mace hopped out and began the short hike up the hillside. Don lifted off, setting the helicopter down on the road north of the creek as instructed.

A heavily-breathing Mace reached the top where the others waited. "Lindside is burning. Camp Creek will be feeling it any minute. Union in about an hour. We gave the sheriff one last warning. What happens there now is all on him."

Jane and Cam walked the line, handing out water and giving statuses to the nervous teens.

Johnny placed his hand on Mace's shoulder. "You did what you could. And hey, you have already gone above and beyond. Two busloads of women have you to thank for their lives. If anyone listens in that town, you will be responsible for them getting out of there and living."

"A part of me wishes I was down there in that town. That's the combat I was trained for and have experience with. This hiding in ambush is not my strong suit."

Johnny nodded. "It's not any of our strong suits, but it's where we are. On a positive note, this will probably all be settled before this day is over."

Mace laughed. "Don't think that's really looking on the bright side of things."

"No. I guess it's not. 'Hunker down' as our defensive coach at Georgia used to say."

Mace replied, "That's where you played, Georgia?"

Johnny nodded. "Seems a lifetime ago."

Mace shook his head. "Seems working that bar was a lifetime ago as well."

"In a way, it was. I can't see how things will ever get back to that. Even if power came back on now, too much has transpired for a quick return to what was normal."

Mace checked over his weapon. "Meh. Normal wasn't all it was cracked up to be. If I went back to that bar next week I'd probably just fall right back into my rut."

An hour passed before the first call came across the hill. "Cars! Here they come!"

Mace took aim through his sight, following the lead car. "What? No... no, no, no!"

Johnny said, "What is it?"

Mace stood. "It's the stupid townspeople! I told them the road was blocked!"

Mace began a run down the hill. "Hold all fire!"

As he slid the last half dozen yards, coming to stand beside the road, the first of the Union cars stopped at the barricade, backing up in a long line.

The sheriff came riding up alongside the others, standing in the back of a pickup. "What is the holdup!"

Mace flagged him down. "You idiots! I told your people the road was blocked!"

The sheriff's pickup stopped beside Mace. "Now look here! You unblock whatever it is you got going there!"

Mace rubbed the sides of his head in disbelief. "The road is blocked! There is no unblocking it! I told your people to tell you to head to Sweet Springs!"

The sheriff stood with his hands on his hips. "Listen up, cowboy, under the authority given to me by the city of Union, West Virginia, I order you to unblock this road and to let us through! These people don't want to go to Sweet Springs. We voted and we are heading to Ronceverte. Now move that blockade!"

A portly man in a suit waddled up to the truck. "What's the problem here, Sheriff?"

The sheriff pointed at Mace. "This man is the problem, Mayor. He's got the road blocked."

The mayor looked at Mace. "Sir, I'm Mayor Ronald Bacon. Could you kindly unblock the road and allow us through, we don't have much time."

Mace shook his head. "Not happening, Mayor. We have the bridge there at the creek set to blow as well. We're stopping those marauders here. I told your sheriff they were coming two days ago. I warned him not two hours ago that this road would be blocked and to go out toward Sweet Springs."

The mayor turned around. "Is that true?"

The sheriff replied, "We voted, Mayor, the people picked Ronceverte!"

The mayor shook his head. "Never hire your cousin just because your wife says to. All right, people! Listen up! We are turning this caravan around and heading to Sweet Springs! And let's be snappy about it. We don't have much time!"

As the cars began to turn, another pickup sped along the gravel on the side of the road, skidding to a stop. "Sheriff! They're hitting the town! Got two explosions on the south side! They blew right through the barricade!"

A nervous mayor turned around. "Mister, I'm begging you to open up that road. We've got nowhere else to run."

Jane and Johnny slid down the hillside behind Mace. "What's going on?"

Mace grabbed the mayor. "Listen to me carefully, Mayor. I'm only telling you this once. You people are going to have to abandon your cars and run. That blockade is not coming down. You hear me? You are walking to Ronceverte. There is no other way!"

The mayor replied, "You can't be serious. Some of these people are elderly!"

Mace took a deep breath. "Mayor, you have one chance to save your people. Tell your sheriff that I'm in charge and you will all do exactly as I say. You probably have a half hour before the people in back here start taking bullets to the head. If you want to save them, you have to make a decision now!"

The mayor squirmed and fidgeted before spitting out the words, "Sheriff, this man is in charge! You direct everyone to follow his exact orders!"

The sheriff protested. "What? You can't be serious. Ronald, this man is just a hooligan! He has no authority!"

Johnny stepped up beside them, bumping the much smaller sheriff. "You made the right call, Mayor."

Mace yelled, "OK, I want every car to pull up as close to that barricade as you can. Bumper to bumper. Park in the ditches! You will be getting out and walking past it. Take only what you can carry for the next twenty miles. And offer whatever assistance you can to get everyone through as fast as possible! Now move out!"

Mace directed Tres: "Get up there. Have them park those cars all the way across. Even into the ditch on each side. And I want all keys taken with them. All keys. And pack them all up as tight as you can. Cam, you lead the teens in getting the people out of their cars and moving. Instructions are to park up as far as they can, drop everything and take their keys. Got it?"

Cam nodded. "Got it."

Mace waved. "Go get 'em."

Cam turned. "You heard the man! Let's get these people past that blockade!"

Jane asked, "What you have in mind for us?"

Mace took a deep breath. We're going as far back as we can and going up on that hill. Slowing down the first to get here is the only chance those people in the back have."

Mace slung his pack over his shoulder as he broke into a jog. Seconds later, the horn of a truck sounded behind him.

Jane and Johnny stood in the back with the sheriff. "Get in! No sense in running!"

Johnny threw out a hand, taking hold of Mace and pulling him up as the truck rolled by. The line of cars stretched back almost a mile.

Mace looked at the worried sheriff. "How you feel about your decisions now, Sheriff?" The sheriff scowled. "Not what I had planned. This road should be open."

Mace nodded. "On a normal day it would be, but today's not normal. And guess what, Sheriff, you're going to stick with Johnny, Jane, and me until we get the last one of your people past that barricade."

The sheriff stuck by his decision. "I acted rationally. We're a democracy. You don't own this road! If anyone dies here today, it's on your head! You'll be standing in front of a jury begging for leniency!"

As they approached the last fifty cars, the cracks of gunfire could be heard and muzzle flashes seen. The windshield of the pickup was peppered with lead and the stunned driver swerved into a ditch and slammed to a stop against a rock. The four passengers in the back flew out onto the grassy side of the road. The sheriff rolled to a stop, ending up in a sitting position. The top of his skull split apart as two slugs impacted at the same time.

Mace flipped off his safety and began shooting from his prone position. Johnny rolled over behind the dead sheriff, taking aim and squeezing the trigger. Jane followed, lying behind the sheriff's legs. The five marauders in the first two vehicles saw an early exit as their windshields became riddled with bullet holes. A third vehicle skidded and steered onto the roadside, striking three townsfolk as they ran, before stomping on the throttle and coming toward the overturned pickup. The driver took head shots from two separate rifles before slumping over, flipping the car into the ditch.

Mace was first up, grabbing Jane by the arm. "Come on! We have to get up on that hill!"

As the three climbed, two trucks with half a dozen men between them sped past on the other side of the road. Hapless townsfolk were gunned down as they attempted to flee their cars.

At fifty feet up the hillside, Mace took position behind a tree. "Keep going! Get as high as you can and work your way back!"

Jane yelled down as she continued to climb. "We aren't leaving you!"

Mace took careful aim, making a kill shot on the driver of the lead truck, sending it into the back of a nearby sedan. The second truck slammed into the back of the first before coming to a stop. The marauders began to pepper the hillside with lead. One by one, Mace took careful aim, taking out the remaining five.

As he turned to scamper further up the hill, three sedans skidded to a stop and eight figures jumped out. Again the hillside turned into a field of popping rocks, trees, and dirt as countless bullets impacted.

Johnny and Jane countered, taking out all eight shooters in ten seconds, six going to Jane. A flood of marauder vehicles then followed.

Mace yelled, "We can't help these people now! Let's get back to the blockade!"

A full run along the ridge took ten minutes. Two dozen attackers were climbing over the stacked cars, shooting into the crowd of townsfolk as they ran. As Mace, Johnny and Jane reached even with the blockade, Cam came up the backside of the hill behind them.

Mace directed, "Spread out across here and take out anyone shooting at the people first!"

The hillside erupted as a half dozen teens fired their rifles. Six marauders standing on the backs of cars fell at once. Six more climbed up to take their place. Another volley saw the same result. Seconds later, gunfire was directed at the defenders' position. One of the teens was the first to be hit, taking a hot slug to the calf.

Mace yelled, "Hold the line until those people make the bridge! Forty seconds!"

The first fatality of the defenders was Syler Sanks. His body rolled forward, tumbling down the steep hill before coming to rest partially upright against a tree. The body drew a hail of bullets, offering the group an opening to move.

Mace yelled, "Townies are on the bridge! Fall back to the vehicles! Move it!"

The group scampered over the crest of the hill and down the northeastern face. Johnny carried the injured teen. They got into the vehicles they had positioned and spewed grass and dirt as they charged across the open space toward the bridge. Marauders stood on the blockade, firing across the field at the vehicles. After skidding to a stop, the four adults and seven teens scrambled across the bridge and began their climb up the next hill.

Dr. Jeff was waiting for them. "The van is ready to go. See that set of silver tubes across the back? Each one is filled with gunpowder. Hit any one of those and you set off those propane tanks beside them. I soaked half that stack of fertilizer with diesel. Everyone will want to cover their ears, even from up here. In fact, I would move everyone just over the hilltop but the shooter."

Jane stepped up. "I'll take the shot. From this distance it's a no-brainer for me."

Mace glanced over at Johnny, who was nodding his head. "OK. If you can wait until some of them get close, maybe we can take out a few extra."

Tres pointed. "They have a front-loader of their own! That barricade will be down in a few minutes!"

Mace patted Jane on the shoulder. "Squeeze the trigger, cover your ears, and keep your head down. This will be far bigger than anything you have ever experienced. I've been within a hundred yards of a few intense explosions. They can be disorienting, even from this distance. Give us a yell just before you pull that trigger."

Jane staked out her prone shooting position. "Got it. Get over that ridge. The first of them are coming across that field!"

Mace scrambled up, taking position on top of the crest. "All of you listen up. When you hear her yell, roll back and cover your ears quickly. Until then, it's open season on anyone crossing that field!"

The teens spread out on the crest. One rifle after another echoed down the hill. The occasional marauder fell.

As the far barricade came down, the front-loader crossed the field with a half dozen cars passing it.

As the industrial machine reached the bridge barricade, Jane yelled out, "Four!"

Two seconds later, a tremendous explosion rocked the ground. The valley echoed back and forth as a grand fireball rose up from the bridge. Parts of the van pinged and plinked on the hilltop around them. Fifteen marauders lay silent and flat on the field below. Another dozen behind them were crouched or crawling, moving slowly. The front-loader was in flames.

Mace looked down at the bridge. The explosion had cleared the other vehicles, but the base of the bridge remained intact.

As the smoke cleared, Mace stood. "Get up! Move it! The bridge didn't blow! Go! Go! Go!"

Jane scrambled the last thirty feet up the hill, shaking her head from the concussion wave that had just passed her by. "I can't hear a thing! Ears are just ringing!"

Johnny took her arm and pulled her along.

Mace yelled, "Get down to the vehicles and go!"

Tres yelled back as they hopped and jumped down the back face of the hill toward the roadway below. "Vehicles are gone! Looks like the townspeople took them!"

Mace replied, "Skew to the left! We need to stay away from that road!"

The rotor wash from the helicopter thumped overhead as Don swooped in just above. As Mace looked up, Don pointed at the field in front of them.

Mace yelled, "To the field! Move it!"

The dozen defenders scrambled out of the woods as Don set the chopper down in front of them. Mace pulled open the door. You teens first! Can you carry them all?"

"I can! I'll have to come back for the rest of you!"

"Drop them at the Ronceverte bridge. They can fill in the townspeople there. You can catch us going in this direction!"

Seconds later the overstuffed chopper lifted off. The strain of the engine could be heard as it lifted higher, disappearing over the next hilltop.

Mace looked at the others. "Who needs ammo?"

Tres replied, "I lost my bag at the other hill. I have half a magazine left."

Jane checked. "Four mags."

Johnny added. "Two."

Cam shrugged. "I'm out."

Dr. Jeff: "Don't have a rifle, just this pistol."

Mace said, "I have three mags."

Mace waved everyone on as he began to jog across the field. "We've got three miles to get back to the cave. If Don can't make it back to us, we're running the whole way. Jane, give one of those magazines to Cam. Tres, here, take this one. And the two of you preserve that ammo. This is all we have until we get back. Jeff, you stick with me!"

Nods were returned as the group hustled across the open field. A brief view of the roadway below showed a long line of Union townsfolk slowly moving along. Mace cringed at the thought of what they were about to endure. The marauders were coming.

Mace mumbled to himself as he ran. "Hope the buzzards are already pecking at your eyes, Sheriff. You just killed all those people."

Chapter 27

The helicopter landed in the next field, extracting the final defenders before heading back to the cave. Everyone averted their eyes from the slaughter that was happening on the roadway below. Tears were held back as the anger welled up inside them.

After landing at the cave, a decision was made to evacuate. Jasper held his ground and his shotgun as he rocked back and forth on the gift shop porch, refusing to budge from his beloved property. Don lifted off in the helicopter with Cam, Vanessa, Tonya, Jeff, and the two dogs.

The RV was backed around and the trailer hooked up. As the rig came up the drive toward the roadway, the first of three trucks skidded to a stop. Dozens of high caliber bullets began to spider the bullet resistant glass of the heavily armored vehicle.

Jane yelled. "Hang on! Gonna have to push 'em!"

As the RV plowed into the first truck and the high torque hybrid drive engaged, the pickup began sliding backwards. As it pressed up against the second truck the RV powertrain showed its mettle. The third truck was collected and pushed with the first two.

Jane was grinning. "Come on, you big buffalo! Push those swine off the road!"

A fourth marauder vehicle, a sedan, skated across the grass on the road's edge, plowing into the left front wheel of the RV. Jane was thrown to the side striking her head against the glass. A small drip of blood ran down from her forehead as she pushed herself back into the captain's chair.

The forty-five foot, heavily armored monster came to a sudden stop, the traction of the back wheels unable to overcome the now locked up left-front and the skid of the trucks it tried to push.

Jane yelled, "Crap! Just lost the drive!"

Mace popped open the front portal and began to spray the men outside. The door was opened, Johnny jumped out, finishing off the last two. The hum of approaching engines could be heard from down the road.

Jane yelled, "Watch out! Taking us back!"

The big rig began to slowly back down the drive, dragging the left front wheel across the asphalt. "It's no good! We have to leave her!"

Mace, Jane, Johnny and Tres sprinted back down the drive and across to the gift shop. Jasper was collected from his chair by Johnny and carried the last fifty yards to the cave entrance in protest. As the five entered, a makeshift door was closed.

Mace said, "Tres, you and Johnny bring up ammo. We have four portals to shoot through. We have lots of rounds, but we need to make them count. Jane, get Jasper to sit down and shut up. Then get back up here on this wall. You pop everything that moves out there. That will give us time to plan out a longer defense."

Mace yelled back to Johnny: "How sturdy is this wall?"

Johnny nodded. "It'll hold. Two sheets of three-quarter plywood on the outside, six inches of packed dirt in the middle and another three quarter inch on the inside. Nothing they're shooting is coming through. Unless..."

Mace asked, "Unless what?"

Johnny shook his head as he set down a box loaded with prefilled magazines. "Unless they bring that cannon."

Mace let out a long breath. "OK, Jane, you see them positioning that cannon, anyone who is around it has to be taken out. I'm betting there are only a handful who know how to operate that thing. You take them down and that problem solves itself."

Jasper came waddling up the ramp. "Look, I'm sorry. I just got spooked. Tell me what I can do and I'll do it."

Mace said, "Can you prepare food?"

Jasper scowled but nodded. "I can."

Mace replied, "Then scrape something up for us. We're gonna need our strength, and we may not have another chance to eat anything. Oh, and by the way. If they come through this entrance, you're in charge of leading us out of here."

Jasper replied, "Out there?"

Mace laughed. "No, you numbskull! Back through the caves!"

Johnny set down a box of magazines and began to howl with laughter.

Jasper again scowled. "Oh shut up, you overgrown moose!"

Jane took aim. "One down! They're moving in on us!"

Mace looked out through a portal. "We have a clear shot at that diesel and propane tank. If we have to, we'll take them out. Don't want them using our fuel against us."

Jane continued to pick away at the marauders as they moved down toward the gift shop. After the first half dozen deaths, the attackers quit coming.

Jane said, "Been quiet out for ten minutes."

Johnny replied, "Listen, I don't hear any engines running out there."

Tres agreed, "Haven't been running for the last five."

Mace shook his head. They're still out there. A group like that will want revenge. They'll camp out here for a month if it takes that long to get it."

Tres said, "We've got food in here for three. And water. And hand-crank lanterns if we need light. If they want to camp out there for a month, let 'em."

Mace frowned. "They won't just be camping, they'll do whatever it takes to get in here."

A voice could be heard from above the cave mouth. "You in there! Come out peacefully and we'll let you go!"

Johnny laughed. "They must think we're dumber than Jasper."

Jasper came back. "I heard that!"

Johnny turned and grinned. Jane punched his arm with a scowl.

Mace yelled out. "We aren't coming out, so you might as well go ahead and leave."

The voice replied, "I've taken a few minutes to analyze your attempted ambushes. Impressive. We could use people like you. All transgressions will be forgiven."

"Don't think that's gonna happen, Paco."

The voice hesitated before asking, "Is that meant as a slur against my ethnicity?"

Johnny flinched. "What kind of an idiot is this guy?"

He yelled out: "Doesn't much matter what color you are on the outside, a turd is the same color all the way through!"

The voice replied, "I see. Then you have made my decision for me."

Mace shook his head. "Not trying to piss him off, are you?"

Liquid began to splash down from above the cave mouth.

Jane stepped back. "Gasoline!"

A heavy thump and a roar told of its ignition. Flames flickered through the gun portals.

The voice called down. "What kind of fighter builds a fortress out of wood? Didn't you study history?"

Johnny pointed at Tres. "Hit the pump!"

Water jetted from two nozzles positioned on each upper corner of the manufactured wall. The flames were soon dowsed, the gasoline rinsed from the face of the wood, burning out on the ground.

Johnny yelled out with a grin. "Fighters with a sprinkler system, asshole!"

Jane yelled at Johnny, "Enough, we aren't in a comedy faceoff here!"

The voice again called down. "Inventive. But not effective for what's coming. And please be patient with me, I have other callings at the moment!"

The remainder of the afternoon was quiet. The occasional body could be seen sprinting one way or another in the distance. The attackers remained, pinning them in the cave.

The long afternoon turned into a sleepless night, followed by another long and uneventful day. On the third day, activity picked up. Engines could be heard approaching, along with the big diesels and their air brakes. The full force of the marauders had arrived.

The cave top was quiet for fifteen minutes as the others rested back in the main room. Jane swiveled from side to side. "They're not in line of sight. I'm getting a bit nervous up here."

Johnny stepped forward. "Here, put on these goggles. That'll give you 3X at high resolution, and some eye protection."

Jane said, "I'm not as worried about my eyes as I am this wall crushing in on me from a cannon round."

Jane spun to the right, looking left. "Wait... I see movement to the left over behind the gift shop. And... it's the cannon. Four, no, five men moving it. OK, I have the guy directing them ID'd. And the loader. Come on, someone else show me something."

The wall was silent for several seconds before five short bursts left Jane's gun. "Hold it, one's still moving. And... done."

Mace said, "Did they load it?"

"They did. Charge only though. Cannonball is sitting on the ground next to the guy that was holding it."

Mace glanced out the portal. "Think you can get a shot down that barrel?"

Jane grinned. "I was just thinking the same thing. Give me a second to see if anyone else comes up to it."

Ten seconds of silence passed before two short bursts ignited the cannon charge. A thunderous boom echoed back and forth within the cave.

Jane laughed. "OK, I know that was somebody dying there, but I have to admit, that was kind of fun."

Johnny said, "Who's working the comedy show now?"

Jane replied, "Shut it."

Jasper chuckled.

"I can hit anyone coming in contact with that cannon from this spot. They move it two feet to the left, not so much. Crap. They just parked a big truck in front of it."

"I would suggest the rest of you get back away from this wall. If they hit it, it's gonna be a mess in here."

Johnny said, "Baby, you don't have to do this."

Jane winced. "Oh but I do. If I can catch them before they light that fuse, they can't shoot that thing."

The others moved down the ramp.

Mace said, "If you don't have a shot, get your ass back here."

Jane replied, "I got this. Hang on."

The engine of the truck came to life. As it slowly rolled back the cannon became exposed and Jane got her chance. A quick burst from her AR-15 saw the trigger man flop over before the fuse was lit.

Jane grinned. "Turkey shoot. Who's next?"

Several minutes passed before a long branch, lit with fire on the end, came into view.

Jane frowned as she took several shots at it. "Not fair!"

The cannon fuse was lit.

Jane dove onto the ground as she yelled, "Incoming!"

Seconds later, the cannon round impacted the cave mouth beside the door, blowing it half way from its hinges.

Tres held his ears. "Where on Earth did they find live cannonballs?"

Johnny sprinted up the gangway, rolling his wife over. "Jane?"

Jane scowled. "Ears are ringing, can't hear a thing!"

Johnny picked her up, running down the gangway as Mace ran up to the portal. "They're loading it. Don't have a clean shot. Time to fall back. Jasper! You're up!"

Jasper stood. "Bring what you can and follow me."

The group moved back in the cave, stopping to take up position where they had a final view of the door. Three additional cannon blasts took out three quarters of the makeshift wall. Daylight streamed into the mouth of the previously darkened cave.

Voices could be heard from outside.

The leader's voice sounded. "Trapped like rats! Still not too late to join us! As I said, all will be forgiven! We could use your talents!"

Mace leaned out from around his corner position, pumping three slugs into the first silhouette that appeared in the entrance. "We'll take you down one at a time if we need to!"

The voice came back. "Wasting your time. We pick up a dozen new members with every town we visit. There are leaders like me, there are followers like these people around me, and then there are victims like you. And you *will* be a victim, it's only a matter of time."

Mace yelled back: "And what makes you so qualified to be a leader?"

The voice replied, "Not really sure. Just a natural ability, I guess. Before all this I wrote crime fiction. It was fun having characters who tortured, maimed and killed whenever they liked, taking whatever they wanted, but I have to say, doing it in real life is far more entertaining. I almost wonder why I didn't do this before."

Mace responded: "Should have your brain carved out and fed to the pigs. In fact, when I take you down, I think that's exactly what I will do!"

The man could be heard yelling, "Bring those generators and fans around. Set them over here."

Johnny said, "If he's talking regular fans, that can only mean one thing—he's planning on pushing air into this cave. Jasper, tell me there is another way out."

Jasper replied, "There are several, but I haven't been all the way back to them. I mostly stayed on this end of the cave. Never was much of a climber, and those exits include some climbs, or so I've been told."

Mace shook his head. "If there are other exits, they'll be able to force air through here. Could be an attempt to smoke us out."

Jasper half frowned. "This is a big complex. We could find pockets to stay in that wouldn't be affected for days."

Jane added, "If they force us away from the entrance, who's to say they don't move their smoke fires further in, keep pushing us back."

Jane yelled back, "Light your fires, asshole! We aren't scared!"

The voice laughed. "Fires? Oh goodness no. Why waste time on fires when your chemist enjoys making arsenic pentafluoride! You can filter smoke for a time with a wet cloth. This, however, this is pervasive! You will be my first experimental rats! What a wondrous villain I would have made for one of my books!"

Mace turned to Jasper. "You have to get us out of here."

Jasper shrugged. "I can take you to what I know, but that isn't out. I'm sorry, Mr. Hardy. I—"

Automatic gunfire and yelling could be heard from the cave entrance.

As Mace leaned out to look, Jane asked, "What is it? What's going on?"

Screams of rage echoed, along with explosions. Thousands of gunshots sounded for most of ten minutes.

As the din began to die down, Mace stood. "I'm going to check. Keep an eye on that entrance. You see anybody coming after me, take them out."

Johnny and Jane each positioned themselves for clean shots at the cave entrance. Mace sprinted down and across the floor before hopping back up on the gangway going out. He slowed as he reached the top.

After several minutes, curiosity got the best of Jane. "I'm going up there."

Johnny and Jane dropped to a crawl as they came up behind a prone Mace. "What's going on?"

"Someone is attacking the marauders. I can't see who. A couple dozen of them just ran up that hill."

Seconds later, the first of dozens of green camo uniforms emerged from the woods by the roadway.

A Marine captain stood in the drive. "I want every one of those scumbags rounded up! Time they saw justice! Bowers! Take your men around through that field. Cut 'em off before they get to those woods!"

Three Humvees and two dozen uniformed men scrambled down across the small creek and up into the field.

Mace looked over to Johnny and Jane with a smile. "Looks like the good guys finally made it!"

He stood with his gun raised over his head, walking slowly out on the ramp.

The captain pointed. "We have a live one over here! Bring him to me!"

Seconds later, a disarmed Mace Hardy was standing in front of the Marine captain. "Can't say I ever wanted to be rescued by a Marine, but thank you, Captain. There are four more of us they had trapped in that cave, including the owner."

The captain turned to the man next to him. "Lieutenant, go clear out that cave!"

Mace said, "One second, Captain. I don't want anyone shot by mistake."

Mace yelled out, "Johnny, Jane! Come out with your guns up over your heads! Everyone!"

The others emerged from the destruction surrounding the cave entrance with their weapons in the air.

An ornery Jasper had his shotgun aiming at the ground.

The lieutenant barked an order. "You! Get that weapon held high!"

Jasper replied, "You want it held high, you come do it yourself! I ain't got the arm strength to do that anymore!"

The captain shook his head. "Now that sounds like a local."

Mace replied, "He's the owner."

A barrage of gunfire, lasting several minutes, erupted from a home up on the hill behind the cave. The last of the marauders would not be taken alive.

When the final gunshot cracked, Johnny said, "Good riddance. That filth wasn't worth keeping alive to just lock up."

After validating the group's stories and gathering up the dead and the few that were captured, the military units that had come to their rescue packed up to leave.

Mace asked, "Is this the start of the government trying to reestablish order?"

The captain replied with a frown: "We still haven't received orders. We sent two teams of couriers out to our commanding base. They never returned. If they want to give us orders they will come out and do so."

Mace caught a glimpse of the patch on one of the men's arms. "Wait, that a Virginia National Guardsman?"

The captain nodded. "As are most of these men. We came over from Bedford."

Mace said, "This is West Virginia. I would've thought you'd stop at the border. Glad you didn't, by the way."

The captain pointed up at the sky. "Your friend up there alerted us to this gang and what they were doing. I decided it was time to act."

Jane said, "Glad you killed that ass that was running this show —please tell me you did so."

The captain shook his head. "He was definitely crazy. We have four of his men. The rest fought to the death. His body is over there in front of the cannon."

Jane scowled. "Excuse me while I go spit on his dead face."

The captain held up his hand. "You won't find a face. He knelt in front of the cannon. Took his head clean off."

Jane walked toward the body. "Then I'll spit down his neck!"

The captain turned and watched as the five-foot-four-inch woman stomped on and kicked the body repeatedly.

The captain chuckled. "Doesn't hold a grudge, does she?"

Johnny had a stunned look on his face. "Never did before. Sweetest woman you could ever know."

The captain sighed. "Well, folks, would love to hang out, but your friend told me thugs were running Roanoke. I suppose it's time we reasserted control."

Mace asked, "Any word as to whether or not power will be coming back?"

The captain shook his head. "You know as much as we do. For whatever reason, there have been no orders coming out of D.C. or from the governor. It's like they're all hiding out from something. You know those EM waves aren't coming from here, right? And they aren't natural."

Johnny said, "What's that supposed to mean?"

The captain shrugged. "Draw your own conclusions."

Mace grabbed the captain's hand. "Thank you for your help, sir. If you ever find yourself in need of a place to shelter, try coming back here. You'll be most welcome."

The Guardsmen and their Marine captain emptied the back of a semi before loading it with the bodies of the dead. The captain gave a furtive nod as his transport pulled away, with the other vehicles following.

Johnny said, "What you make of his comment about the interference?"

"If it's not natural and not from us it has to be from someone. Maybe we're not as alone in this universe as we thought we were. Tres' little green men might be out there."

Johnny laughed. "Thought he said gray."

Tres replied, "You said gray. I said they may not be little."

Don landed the helicopter. Vanessa ran to meet Tres. Dr. Jeff walked over with the others, stopping on the porch of the gift shop where they stood. Jasper Collins rocked in his chair with his shotgun as Derwood and Molly settled at his feet.

Don said, "I can't believe they made it."

Johnny replied, "They were just about to gas us in there. Those Guardsmen couldn't have arrived at a better time. Thanks for risking the bird to save us. I know they could have taken it from you."

"Bird's not important. This group is important. I'm just glad the captain was a reasonable man. I think he's been itching for an excuse to take action. The gang I described to him finally set that pot that had been simmering for the last few weeks boiling over. Hopefully, this is the start of order being restored."

Mace shook his head. "Order for us maybe. The rest of the world will be hitting starvation soon. Things could easily get just as nasty as we saw here, only the murderers and thugs could be normal families just trying to survive."

"Always the ray of sunshine," said Johnny.

Jane crossed her arms. "Looks like they were trying to fix the RV. Bum wheel's off of her."

Johnny hopped down from the porch, walking over for a look. "Axle looks OK. Frame is bent. We find a welder and Tres could probably fix her up."

Jane walked around and up into the cabin. "Uh, reeks of the unwashed in here. I bet wacko was looking to turn this into his parade bus for his crazy tour. Gonna take a month for me to fumigate this place."

Over the week that followed, the valley around Organ Cave returned to one of normal peace and tranquility, but a pall of sadness hung over her. Thirty homes around the cave complex had been burned to the ground, their residents chased away or killed. Three quarters of the town of Union had been executed on the roadway. The valley had been severely wounded. And time would not bring back those who were gone.

The wall of the cave was rebuilt, supplies were stored, and trade with the local towns and co-ops reestablished. The wheel of the RV was fixed and the rig once again parked in its usual spot. A half dozen horses from a neighboring, burned-out farm now grazed the small pasture by the horse pen. The group was slowly getting back to their new normal.

Mace stood by Don in the field, halfway to the helicopter.

Don said, "Just making the standard run down to I-77, over through Blacksburg, and up by Roanoke. I can't stand not knowing if another one of those gangs are running around. Should be back in about forty-five minutes."

Mace replied, "I think we all want to know. After this, we really have to watch our fuel. Having that bird doesn't do us any good if we can't fill it up."

Once Don lifted off, Mace walked over to the porch where Jane was taking a rest from her morning chores. She stared at the cannon that now sat in the grass in front of the gift shop.

Mace asked, "What's picking at your brain this morning?"

"Am I the only one who thinks the wacko didn't blow his head off with that cannon? I mean, no doubt he was insane, but he didn't seem insane in that way."

"I had the same thought. My last trip to Caldwell, I asked around to see if anyone had come through there on that day. One van. It had a black man with a beard driving it, a big white man with a round bald head in the passenger seat, and a red-haired woman covered in tattoos, with a little red-haired boy in back. Barricade guard said they looked nervous, but no more so than any other car they ever stopped. They let them through. We have no way of knowing whether that was our guy or not."

"Hate to think he just skated away. I just don't understand how people can be that messed up."

"You put people in a desperate situation and you'll find a lot of us have at least a little of that in us. Not to justify what he did in any way, but maybe it just comes as part of being human. None of us are wired exactly the same. Leaves room for lots of errors."

Johnny walked up.

Jasper said, "Speaking of errors..."

Johnny looked at Jane and Mace as they both chuckled. "What? What'd I do?"

Laughs persisted until Mace stood. "Come on, we have a lot to accomplish today if we want to keep this camp running. Hope you brought your boots. We have two dozen cattle we need to bring down the road to this pasture over here—owners were killed. We'll share the beef with anyone in the valley who needs it. It's getting time for us to focus on the long term."

Johnny shook his head as he followed Mace off the porch. "End of the world and I end up a cowpoke. Go figure."

Mace stopped to look up at the sky. "Strange how something you can't even see can so wreck the world. We're a lot softer than we thought we were."

"Who's softer?"

"People. We totally weren't prepared."

Johnny looked up. "You think we'll ever know what really happened?"

Mace shook his head. "Who knows. We'll survive, if we can survive each other. But those who grow up after this... they're gonna have a hard life. We've only just had a taste of it."

Johnny chuckled. "You just keep pumping out the rainbows don't you."

~~~~~

What's Next!

(Preview)
HADRON
(Vol. 2)
Axiom

This Human is asking for your help! In return for that help I have a free science fiction eBook short story, "THE SQUAD", waiting for anyone who joins my email list. Also, find out when the next exciting release is available by joining the email list at comments@arsenex.com. If you enjoyed this book, please leave a review on the site where it was purchased. Visit the author's website at www.arsenex.com for links to this series and other works.

The following preview of the next book in the series is provided for your reading pleasure. I hope you enjoy!

Stephen

Chapter 2.1

Power and communications had been down for seven weeks. Streams of cars had filled the highways, only to be abandoned when the fuel ran out, their occupants leaving in search of food. Hungry hordes attacked peaceful homes and encampments. Hundreds of passersby had been turned away from the cave as the group struggled to maintain their own security and sanity.

The field of cattle had been poached and slaughtered during the night. The carcasses dragged away. Two of the horses had been eaten, forcing Mace and the others to begin chasing away the hungry during the day. Patrols of the property were a constant after dark. The group was forced to bringing the remaining animals inside the cave each day as the sun set. The weather continued to get colder.

Jane stood beside Johnny as they took their turn at guarding the rebuilt cave entrance. "Hon, I don't know how much more of this I can take. Those two children out there with their mother today... my heart was breaking turning them away. I feel like there's no humanity left inside me. We have enough that we could at least share with some."

Johnny frowned. "We may not have enough to last us to spring as it is. And I hate to say it, but they'll just be like stray cats. You feed them once and they'll keep coming back. Winter is here now. We can't make any more food than what we have. This all sickens me too, but we don't know if we have enough to keep ourselves alive. The rest of the world will have to find their own way."

Mace and Tres walked up the gangway. "Next shift is here. Go get yourselves some rest."

Jane fought back the tears. "I'm having a hard time with all this."

Mace nodded in sympathy. "We all are. When I was up at Caldwell this morning, they had their third attack on the barricade this week. And a dozen other instances of people sneaking into town to steal. We're at that bad stage now where it's down to ultimate survival for everyone. We can try to keep ourselves alive in here through the winter; we can't keep everyone out there alive."

Jane sighed. "Driving them off just seems wrong."

Mace leaned against the cave wall. "Seems that way to all of us. We could let these stragglers set up camp out there and organize and gather firewood to keep themselves warm, but they aren't in need of shelter. There are plenty of abandoned houses around. We don't have enough to feed them.

"If we share what little we have, we run out. We're left starving and desperate just like they are. I hate to say it, but without power and communications, this planet can't support the people it has on it. When this is all settled, I doubt we have a quarter of the population we have had."

Tres said, "Dr. Jeff thinks when spring comes, if we organize and coordinate with the other people around us, we might be able to grow enough produce to feed everyone here in the valley for the next winter. He said the resources would probably be strained as we figured out what we were doing. And that we wouldn't likely be able to support anyone coming in from outside. He thinks we can do it, even though most of us in the valley aren't farmers."

Johnny said, "I thought you studied agriculture."

"I did. I've had some time to think on it, and I've realized that I'm probably not as educated on the subject as I thought I was. You know, it's easy to say you could do something you haven't done before, but actually doing it can be far different from what you envisioned. I learned that with trying to get us a garden ready to plant come spring. It's a lot more work than I thought, if you want a real shot at success."

Johnny held Jane as they walked down the gangway into the main room.

Mace looked out through the portal. "Will drop well below freezing tonight."

"I can already feel it," said Tres. "Wish we could build a fire up here next to the door."

"Would just draw people in. Maybe you could run a piping system up here with water we heat in the back."

Tres sat on a makeshift chair. "Wish I could get home to see if my family is OK."

Mace looked over at him. "I feel the same way about my mom. Only, no way I can make it out to California. You, at least, might be able to make it home, if you decided to go."

"I could scrounge up a vehicle, and probably the gas to get me there, but I can't get myself to take that trip alone. I'm too scared of what I might find when I get there. And how fair would it be to the others here if I was to try to bring back four more people without the means to support them?"

Mace glanced out the portal at the moonlit landscape. "In a world gone mad, you have to wonder if survival is even worth striving for. All those things we've taken for granted for so long, the phones, cars, TVs, beer, toilet paper... those will all just be distant fond memories before long."

Tres said, "The beer problem we can solve. The still is giving us a couple gallons a day. We could ramp that up to as much as we want given the supplies we have in here. I could build us a brewery if we wanted beer. We have the bags of grain and the other ingredients we need back there in storage. You just say the word, and Dr. Jeff and I will build you a brewery."

"You two just keep working on that alcohol and tell me when you think it's 100 percent safe."

"It's drinkable right now, but if we're wanting to use it for trade, we need to add some flavoring to it to make it palatable."

Mace asked, "How long would it take you to make fifty gallons if you thought it had sufficient taste?"

Tres squinted. "Mmm. With that setup, most of a week. Let me scale it up and we could pump that out in a day."

Mace looked back out through the portal. "Do what you need to make it a commodity we can trade, and then scale it up. The sooner you have it ready, the better we can supply ourselves for this winter. We're rationing to ourselves right now. Things will get worse before they get better. Alcohol... we can trade for what we need."

Mace stood firm. "Get up, we've got company. Somebody's moving up toward the helicopter. Wish we had somewhere to tuck that thing away."

Tres scampered down the gangway, alerting the others. "People outside. Don't know how many."

Don, Johnny, Jane, and Jeff joined Mace and Tres. The door to the wall was quietly opened and the six armed defenders slipped out into the night.

Two men stood near the helicopter with a hose and a can as Mace sprinted up behind them. "Freeze! Hands where I can see 'em!"

The men complied. "Just looking for fuel, mister."

Mace gestured toward the road. "The fuel on this property is taken, you'll need to move along."

The men nodded before turning to leave.

Mace waved his weapon. "Hey, you, come back here. You're gonna want that hose."

The man slowly reached down for his means of siphoning.

Mace again gestured toward the roadway. "Now go. And don't come back this way... and good luck to you."

The men hurried away into the moonlit shadows.

Jane said, "You always handle that so well."

Mace took a breath. "Just glad I haven't had to pull the trigger yet."

The guns were lowered.

Jane turned. "Everyone back inside. Johnny and I are gonna walk the perimeter with Mace."

Jane pointed toward the roadway. "Might as well make sure they've left."

As they began to walk, Jane said, "What's our long term goal here, fellas?"

Johnny replied, "What do you mean?"

"We have to have more on our minds than just surviving this winter. I'm talking about reestablishing a community, or joining one. I'm in agreement that we stick it out here for the near term, but what about next winter?"

"You saying you don't like living in a cave?"

"Do we want to do something like move into Ronceverte or Caldwell? Somewhere where we can share the responsibilities with a larger group? Maybe have a co-op of farmers, a town baker or blacksmith, or a gunsmith even—you know, something sustainable?"

Mace replied, "I think that's something to certainly consider."

"I say this because I think we need hope. We need something to look forward to. I don't care if that means starting our own community or joining one. I just think it's something we'll want to do. And we need to find Mace a woman so he stops flirting with me."

Johnny flexed his arms. "You been hitting on my wife?"

Mace laughed. "Every chance I get. Just trying to stay in practice."

"Should have taken up with Vanessa when I said. Now she's taken with that skinny little brew-master kid."

Jane asked, "You liked Vanessa?"

Mace shook his head with a smile. "No. That was just Johnny poking fun at me when this all started. I like Vanessa, just not in that way."

"Well, we at least need to get you to town more often. There has to be a lady out there for you somewhere."

"Now wait a minute, how'd this conversation turn from 'What will we do as a group long term?' to 'How do we hook Mace up?' You two need to be focused on our survival for the next six months."

Jane replied, "I just know how much I rely on Johnny for sharing how I feel and for comfort. I want you to have the same."

"Wait, you suggesting the three of us should be a couple?"

Jane sighed. "No, stop being an idiot. Just saying we need to find you that special girl who will give you purpose, keep your thoughts occupied when you have nothing else you have to do. Look how happy Tres and Vanessa are. I want that for you. And when I'm finished here, we'll work on Dr. Jeff and Don."

Johnny nodded. "Matchmaking at the cave. A compelling story about romance and love."

Jane shook her head. "The two we need to keep an eye on are Cam and Tonya. I mean, I'm glad they have each other to keep company, but teens don't always think through their actions. Especially when they're two bodies just trying to keep each other warm in that cave at night."

Johnny replied, "Neither do adults."

Johnny reached out, grabbing Mace by the shoulder and pulling him close. "Keep me warm, Mace. I promise I'll keep my hands to myself."

Mace replied with a clenched mouth. "Get your hands off me... you dirty ape!"

Jane shook her head. "Well, at least you two keep it somewhat entertaining. Not sure where I'd be without you."

Mace laughed. "Don't forget Jasper. He's a big part of this comedy team."

Johnny scowled. "That old coot. We need to carry him and that rocker out to the field, shove a broom handle through his shirtsleeves to keep his arms up, and leave him out there to scare off the crows. That way he can constantly disparage them instead of me."

Jane smiled. "You like that old man, don't you?"

Johnny faked wiping a tear. "More than I like life."

The three walked up the ramp and into the cave. The door was closed and latched. The remainder of the night saw no outside activity.

Another week passed before the first winter storm dropped two inches of white powder on the valley. A snowball fight ensued. Johnny took the opportunity to drill Jasper in the back of the head as he sat in his rocker with a blanket over his lap.

Jasper turned around, waving his shotgun in the air. "Johnny Tretcher! Don't make me come out there and beat you with this!"

Johnny laughed, taking a face-full of snow from Vanessa. Tres had scampered behind him to hide from her wrath. The event went on for fifteen minutes until a group of huffing and puffing survivors took a seat on the porch around Jasper.

Mace said, "I love a good snow."

Don replied, "Want to go for a ride down the valley? It's been a couple weeks since we did a check. Was going to make a run to Blacksburg with a few gallons of that shine Tres and Jeff have been brewing."

Mace shook his head. "Thanks. Have too much to do here this morning. I'll give you a hand with the gas cans, though."

Mace followed Don around behind the gift shop, retrieving the empty cans for refilling. Cam was given direction to bring two gallon jugs of the moonshine out to the 'copter. Tonya eagerly followed him.

Mace said, "OK, you have four cans in there. You think they're still open for business in Blacksburg?"

"I sure hope so. Otherwise we're gonna have to get the good doctor to brew us up some fuel this bird can handle."

Cam ran up. "Two gallons. Dad, can Tonya and I come with?"

Don nodded. "Sure. I could use the company since Mr. Hardy turned me down."

The teens raced around to the other side, with Cam opening the door and helping Tonya up and in. Johnny, Jane, Vanessa and Tres walked back into the warmth of the cave.

Don hopped up in the pilot seat. "Be back in an hour, maybe?"

Mace nodded as he closed the door. "Just keep an eye out for trouble."

Mace walked back to the gift shop porch as the helicopter blades spun up to speed. With a change in the blade pitch, the 'copter lifted up toward the east, moving slightly forward before banking hard toward the southwest. As it climbed up over the treetops and looped around, ultra-bright flashes crisscrossed the sky.

Mace covered his eyes as Jasper flinched. The chopper, in a hard bank at the time, went silent, rolled over, and plummeted toward the ground. No time was left for an autorotate maneuver.

As Mace unshielded his eyes, the helicopter, carrying three of his extended family, crossed over a gravel road and slammed into an abandoned trailer-home.

Mace jumped from the porch at a full run. Seconds later, as he climbed the hill toward the trailer, the wreckage erupted in flame. An explosion, followed by another, told of the fuel and the two gallons of alcohol igniting. Mace came to a stop fifty feet from the entangled burning melange of rusted trailer sheet metal and helicopter. With the high flames, there would be no survivors.

Jane, Johnny, Tres, Vanessa, and Jeff joined him as the fire at the crash site raged. Black smoke rose up toward a blue sky filled with thin puffy clouds. Johnny pulled Jane in close.

The six of them stood in horror-filled silence for several minutes as Jasper watched quietly from the edge of his rocker.

Mace turned to the others with a look of deep sorrow. "Nothing we can do here."

Tres wrapped his arm around a sobbing Vanessa, turning her slowly away. Jane refused to move as Johnny attempted to comfort her.

Jeff shook his head slowly as he pursed his lips, walking beside Mace on the way back to the gift shop porch. "What happened? We lost the lights in the cave and heard the crash."

Mace shook his head. "He was still banking and climbing when the engine just went dead. It dove before he could do anything. Strange, though. Doesn't make sense."

Jeff stopped as they stepped up onto the porch. "What doesn't make sense?"

Mace pointed up. "There were some kind of bright flashes, high up in the atmosphere. I mean super bright. They were spread out all over, but in a grid. Happened the moment before his engine failed. Only saw them through the corner of my eye, extremely bright. Not even sure what I was looking at."

Jasper said, "I saw it, too. Still seeing spots."

Smoke began to billow out from under the hood of the SUV. The battery suddenly exploded, denting the hood and setting the engine compartment on fire.

"Hold on," Jeff said.

He jumped off the porch, opened the door to the RV and climbed the steps. He turned the key in the ignition and flipped several switches. A worried-looking Jeff jumped down from the RV and raced back into the cave, returning seconds later with a key to the Jeep. The key turned, but nothing happened.

He hopped out of the Jeep and raced back into the cave, emerging less than a minute later at a slow walk.

Mace said, "What is it?"

Jeff stopped and took a deep breath. "I believe what you witnessed were EMP blasts. All of our electronics are shot. Which I don't understand."

Johnny winced. "EMP?"

Jeff cleared his throat. "Yes, an electromagnetic pulse, or a series of them in this case."

Johnny replied, "I know what EMP is, Doc. Who would do this?"

Jeff shook his head. "I couldn't say, but they just rendered every vehicle we have useless. That helicopter was commercial. It wouldn't have had shielding to protect against an EMP blast, let alone a series of them, if that's what that was. That plastic body would have left a lot of those electronics exposed.

Probably the only thing moving or flying now is military. And what I don't get is the SUV and the Jeep. Those are under metal hoods. That EMP would have to have been extreme to affect them both, plus the RV, although with the RV I can see it, because we have those spare power lines running from the generator into the cave."

Johnny replied, "The generator hurts, but we need those vehicles."

Jeff frowned. "Well, the generator also ran our water pump and the filtration system on that RV. We probably have fifty gallons of potable water right now, and then we're out. We'll have to boil."

"So all vehicles are out?"

"Hard to say. We really don't know what we're dealing with here. In a normal high-altitude EMP, most of your vehicles would probably be unaffected. Those that were running might be a bit more susceptible, but most would be fine. What happened doesn't make sense, because multiple EMPs are not additive, and studies suggest not effective. Once you ionize the air with one blast, it takes time before you can do it again."

Jeff shook his head again. "This has to be something different. Similar, but different. And much, much stronger."

Mace looked over at the burning wreckage. "Ten seconds sooner and they would never have left the ground."

Johnny reiterated his question. "Again, who would do this?"

Jeff shrugged. "Some misguided politician? The Russians or the Chinese? Our chance of finding that out is probably zero. Could be somebody fired a nuclear missile that MIRV'd. What I do know is that if our vehicles are out, probably every vehicle within five hundred miles of those blasts is now inoperable. We can say goodbye to powered transportation, at least anything with electronic ignition."

Mace said, "Maybe now we know why the government has kept our military in place. Fear of an invasion."

Johnny turned to Tres. "Power out worldwide from a mysterious electromagnetic interference, massive EMP blasts... and planes crashing because of no crew aboard. Your alien theory is starting to sound plausible. But we haven't seen anything that would tell us something conclusive."

Tres shook his head. "What do we do now without transportation?"

Mace glanced toward the roadway. "I did see several old vehicles in this valley. We might see if we can get one or more of them running. And we still have two horses."

Johnny held up a finger. "Hold on."

A quick jog to the RV trailer had the door open. Seconds later an engine could be heard turning over. Johnny emerged from the trailer after the fourth attempt at starting the four-wheeler ended in failure.

As he walked back toward the porch he threw up his hands. "That's a solid metal trailer. Should have been more than adequate protection. If that was EMP, it was far stronger than even a nuke would generate."

Jeff nodded. "That's precisely what I was saying. This is something different, something much more powerful. And not something I believe we are capable of."

Tres called out from the end of the porch. "Guys! Over here! Uh, I don't know what I just saw, but it was big."

Tres pointed toward the top of a snowcapped ridge, as Johnny, Jane, Mace, and Jeff walked up beside him. "Not sure what that was. Long and gray. Only saw it for a moment before it went into the clouds and behind that ridge."

Johnny asked, "A plane?"

Tres shook his head. "I don't think so. Couldn't be a blimp either. Was too big and not round like a blimp, or shaped like a plane."

Johnny pressed. "Well, what was it?"

Tres slowly shrugged. "I... I don't know. But I did see something... definitely a craft or vessel. And it wasn't one of ours."

Tres took a deep breath. "I don't think it was from here."

"Russian or Chinese?" asked Johnny.

Tres frowned. "No, I mean not from this planet."

~~~~~

Once again, this Human is asking for your help! If you enjoyed the book, please leave a review on the site where it was purchased or downloaded. And by all means, please tell your friends! Any help with spreading the word is highly appreciated!

Also, I have a free science fiction eBook short story, titled "THE SQUAD", waiting for anyone who joins my email list! By joining, also find out when the next exciting release is available. Join at comments@arsenex.com. Visit the author's website at www.arsenex.com for links to this series and other works!

Take care and have a great day!

Stephen

Printed in Great Britain
by Amazon